THE FALL OF OUR SECRETS

Tracy Gardner Beno

e•LITBOOKS

THE FALL OF OUR SECRETS

Published in the United States by E-Lit Books

www.e-litbooks.com

Cover Art and Design by Martin Blanco

For information on the subsidiary rights, please contact the publisher at info@el-litbooks.com

ISBN: 978-0-9894011-7-3

978-0-9894011-8-0

For my dad, the reason I am strong.

For my husband, my soul mate and forever friend.

For my kids, the greatest adventure I could ever imagine.

CHAPTER ONE

The first thing Laura thought of when Nicole came back into her life that warm afternoon in Dallas was the roof of her father's station wagon. Nicole stretched out in her pink and black bikini, trying to tan her long freckled legs, Laura on the blanket beside her, nose in a book. It was the only place in their two yards the sun wasn't obstructed by trees, houses, or Nicole's annoying little brother James. It was also the best place in the world for planning the future and their freedom, conjuring the beautiful life awaiting them. Laura realized even then that she couldn't really mimic the desperate, determined drive Nicole had to get away. She didn't mind the small town, the quiet community, her cookie cutter family life. Nicole's life was a different story. Anything would be better than living in that house. The walls were thin and sound carried, even in the winter.

Laura stared at the tall redhead standing next to her, seeing her fifteen year old best friend, and feeling like she was looking at a ghost. Nicole shifted her purse to the other arm and pressed the ground floor button as the elevator doors closed, returning her attention to the sequined pink cell phone in her hand. A name badge hung face-down from Nicole's lapel.

"Nicole?" Laura's voice was quiet and tentative in the nearly empty elevator.

Nicole's eyes met Laura's with curiosity in the raised brows. "Yes?"

Laura cleared her throat, "Sorry, um … Nicole Murdock?"

A barely perceptible shift appeared in the woman's eyes, a veil, curiosity turned to caution. "Do I know you?" Her Texan accent was crisp and all business.

"Nicole, it's me. Laura. Laura Miller? You know, from Michigan?"

It took a moment, but Nicole began to smile, and Laura could almost see the walls come down as she relaxed; the woman's ingrained defenses dissipated and her entire face lit up, rendering her even more beautiful. "Laura, my goodness! How? What are you--" She interrupted herself, grasping Laura's arms and then pulling her in for a hug, laughing. "What in the world are you doing here?"

Now was Laura's turn to laugh, "I could ask you the same thing! Texas? And … how long has it been?" She thought about it, searching Nicole's face for clues to the lost years stretching between them.

Nicole tucked a stray red curl behind her ear. "Seventeen years. My goodness," she said again, keeping one manicured hand on Laura's arm. She found the elevator wall behind her and leaned against it, staring through Laura for a moment into the past.

Laura remembered. Seventeen years. Seventeen years since her best friend had fled her hometown in the middle of the night, no explanation, all of the furniture left in the house, all of the neighbors left speculating.

The elevator doors slid open and a handful of people shuffled in. The plaque on the wall behind them read 'North Dallas Business Park, Floor Two.' The two women stood side by side, silently descending one more floor and finding themselves standing in the lobby of the office building.

Nicole, sufficiently recovered, spoke first. "Never in a million years, Laura … you are the last person I'd ever expect to pop up here."

Laura met her friend's eyes. "Nicole, all this time, I thought … I don't know. How are you? You look fantastic, are you … I mean, are you okay?" She knew she was tripping over her own words, but she wasn't even sure what to ask. Long after that night, Laura had come to reconcile the idea that she would never see her best friend again, never learn what happened to her.

Nicole returned Laura's gaze unflinchingly. "I'm just fine," she said, to Laura as much as to herself. She tossed her hair with mock drama. "You know me, Invincible Nicki," she joked, bringing back a rush of memories: leaping off Laura's bed at six or seven years old, wearing only ballet leotards and capes made of bath towels. They'd created super-hero alter egos as kids, Laura remembered, unable to recall her own moniker.

"The Lovely Laura," Nicole told her, as if reading her thoughts. Laura smiled to herself, realizing now that they'd each chosen names to endow themselves with the qualities they'd wished more than anything to possess.

"Listen," Nicole said, "Do you have time for coffee? I am not letting you go without catching up. And you have to tell me what you're doing in Texas." They walked out into the warm sun and Nicole turned to face Laura, her face painted with curiosity, wondering what in the world her friend was doing in the building that housed her husband's law firm.

"I'm here for a conference, we're on break. I work for the County Sheriff's Department back home as an Evidence Tech." Laura glanced at her watch, worried she might be running behind. But how could she leave Nicole now? She'd always assumed she'd never see her childhood friend again, and here she was. The last image frozen in Laura's mind was not Nicole in her bikini. It was Nicole in her green pajamas, sitting with skinny arms wrapped around skinny legs on her porch.

"Something bad is happening."

She'd told Laura that the night she disappeared. Laura's throat closed now as it had then, a hot, hard lump that made it hurt to swallow. When she'd pressed her friend, Nicole had shaken her head and glanced furtively back at the living room window where her house was eerily silent. No Danny laughing, no James blasting music too loud.

Laura scooted closer to Nicole on the porch and took the girl's hand. "Tell me what I can do," feeling so helpless, wishing she was grown, not a damn fifteen year old with no power, no voice.

Nicole faced Laura, eyes huge, peering for too long into her friend's. She finally took a long, deep breath, exhaling it in a forceful, hitching sigh as her eyes left Laura's. She shook her head. "I don't know," she whispered.

Laura recalled being gripped with fear then, bony fingers squeezing her shoulders and making her cold all over. Nicole always knew what to do. Laura hugged her, and hugged her more tightly, the fear worming its way into her heart as she felt Nicole's hand come up limply and pat her half-heartedly on the back. It was like she was already gone, Laura thought. Nicole had known something was coming. She'd tried to tell Laura.

Laura blinked now in the bright sunlight, unable to see this beautiful woman before her without seeing the broken girl she'd been.

She placed a hand on Nicole's forearm. "I can't lose you again," she said quietly, "but I have to hurry and get back. Please, could we meet later somewhere?" She felt as if the woman might stroll down the sidewalk and vanish once again, leaving Laura wondering if she'd imagined the whole thing.

Nicole's hand covered Laura's on her arm. "Of course." She fished around in her purse and came up with a pen and slip of paper. "I will meet you whenever you're free, call me," she jotted down her number as she spoke. "I can't believe my luck, running into you, Laura," her green eyes glistened with tears. "I've missed you so much, you have no idea," she said quietly, handing her the paper.

Laura swallowed around that lump in her throat and simply hugged Nicole tightly. She stepped back and searched her friend's unmasked, vulnerable expression, looking for something that would tell her Nicole really had come out of whatever happened that night without terrible scars. She found no reassurance there.

Laura bought a coffee from the café on the main floor and headed back up to her conference. Now she wondered what Nicole was doing here in this building. The badge she wore bore the logo for Dallas Children's Hospital, which was right down the street. She had so much to ask her old friend.

Three hours later, in a cab to the restaurant where she and Nicole had agreed to meet, Laura finally let her mind wander. This was her first time away from home since college. She felt as if she'd lost a hundred pounds, and knew it had nothing to do with the number on her bathroom scale this morning. She'd been worried Charlie would have a problem with her leaving, and she was always nervous about flying. Charlie had been fine yesterday when she left, happy to spend the next few days with his grandparents, and the flight was smooth and uneventful. And now, she'd run down to the lobby to grab a coffee and run smack into her best girlfriend from childhood. What a day. She drew in a deep breath, a black cloud of tension she hadn't even known was there floating away into the warm breeze as she stepped into the restaurant.

She spotted Nicole at a table toward the back, waving. Her long red hair cascaded down her back over the stylish black ensemble. Laura's hands smoothed her own beige suit from the JC Penney's clearance rack and self-consciously fluffed her short, newly highlighted blond hair as she wove her way to the table. She wished she'd skipped the cookie table at the conference. The suit was pinching at her waist.

Nicole met her halfway with a big hug. "I still can't believe I found you, Laura!"

Laura could hardly believe it either. She and Nicole had become best friends at the age of three, when Nicole's family moved in next door. They were inseparable throughout their years together in school in the small town, the two always seated near each other due to the alphabetized seating charts the teachers seemed to love. She looked at Nicole now and shook her head, smiling. "Look at you. You look like you just stepped off the pages of Vogue. You haven't aged at all!"

Nicole motioned her over to the table to sit. "Oh, yes I have. I just hide it well sometimes, that's all."

Laura gratefully ordered a beer when the waitress appeared, then sat back and smiled at her friend. "All right, Nicole, you have to tell me how you've been. I missed you so much after you … left. Do you live right here in Dallas? Are you married? What do you do at the hospital? Why were you in my conference building? Did you--"

Nicole held up her hands, chuckling. "Stop! Too many questions! All right, here goes. We're not in Dallas, but just outside the city in Westlake. Been here for a while, my father moved us to San Angelo when I was 19 and I must have liked Texas, 'cause I'm still here. I do the scheduling for the volunteer department at the hospital … guess it's the closest I ever got to becoming a nurse like I planned. And I was having lunch with my husband when I ran into you today, he works in that building. We've been married two years. You'd really like him, Laura, he's so...." Her voice trailed off, eyebrows furrowing while she searched for adjectives to describe her new husband. "He's nothing like Daddy," she finally said, and left it at that. "But now what about you?"

Laura caught the reference to Nicole's father but let it go for the time being. Though they'd been so close so many years ago, she didn't feel right asking the big questions just yet. Nicole would open up when she was ready. "We'll get to me. Now finish! Tell me about your husband. How did you meet, what's his name, what does he do, come on, details woman!"

"His name is Harry. We met four years ago, through a ... mutual friend," she said after a pause. "He's an attorney; he has a private practice, and he does pro bono work for the public defender's office, so he's pretty busy, but he's a really great guy. He's the man you and I daydreamed about years ago, trying to conjure up the perfect husband. He kind of swept me off my feet, and saved my life doing it."

"Wow," Laura breathed. "Nic, I feel so good that you've got this life now, you seem happy. Content." She hesitated a moment. "What do you mean he saved your life?"

"Oh, it's a long story...." She waved her hand in the air dismissively and the late afternoon sun glinted off the enormous diamond adorning her ring finger.

"I love long stories," Laura said, recalling the easy volley of their long-ago friendship. "You know, I haven't seen you in forever. I never thought I'd see you again, to be honest. I wish I had more time," she added as an afterthought.

"When do you leave?"

"Tomorrow morning, 10 am flight."

"Oh honey, that's horrible. That doesn't give us any time! What are your plans tonight?"

Laura laughed. "Big plans. I have an important appointment with my fluffy bathrobe and some overpriced pay-per-view chick-flick."

"Laura," said her wonderful old best friend, "you are going to see this town tonight, that's all there is to it."

The women barely registered the various plates that were placed in front of them and then cleared away, falling back into their easy companionship as if no time had passed. Nicole excused herself to "make a few phone calls, be back in a jiffy darlin'," and Laura leaned back and stretched her legs under the table, feeling better than she had in a long time.

Nicole was just as she remembered, but was somehow very different too. Aside the added polish, Laura thought it was something to do with her walk, the way she carried herself. She never had that confidence years ago in Michigan. But then again, she'd lived in a constant state of anxiety and fear. She fished her own cell phone from her purse and made a call to check in and reassure herself that everything was fine at home, finishing up just as Nicole arrived back at the table. "Okay, let's go," she said, taking Laura's arm, and just like that, they were in a cab to the hotel.

"Change into something fun, whatever you feel like," Nicole said, flouncing down onto the double bed that was about as soft as concrete.

Laura ducked into the bathroom to quickly wash her face and apply fresh deodorant, bustling back into the room wearing her robe. She began shuffling through the few items she'd hung up. Stepping behind the closet door, she pulled on the nicest thing she'd brought: a white eyelet camisole followed by a navy blue blazer and matching skirt. She found Nicole grimacing and shaking her head. "All right, come on you, I have an idea."

When they stepped out of the hotel, Laura stopped short in front of a shiny black limousine, a spiffy chauffer holding the door open, obviously waiting for someone. She felt a little like Alice when Nicole took her hand and led her into the limo. She stared at her, half expecting her to turn into a white rabbit.

"What are we doing?"

"We're going out on the town," Nicole smiled.

Laura continued to stare at her. "And what are we doing in a limo? Who are you?" she joked, shaking her head at the one person in her life who'd always been a source of worry and concern for Laura. She'd spent her childhood being afraid for Nicole, and another seventeen years afraid to imagine what horrible thing might have happened to her after she disappeared.

Nicole was quiet for a moment, then, almost apologetically, began, "Well, I have money now. I won't say I worked hard and saved to get it, but it was part of the package with Harry, and boy did I ever go through hell before finding my Prince Charming. Harry's family is old money; he looks at it as sort of an incidental. We are going to use it to have fun tonight, so no arguments!" She paused. "Does it make you feel weird?" She grinned sheepishly at Laura, waiting for her reaction.

Laura threw her head back and laughed. She laughed until tears welled up and rolled down her cheeks, and her shoulders shook, and her stomach ached, and still she couldn't stop laughing. She finally gained control, getting it down to a few snorts and hiccups. "This has been the strangest day. Do you know, for years and years Nicole, I really thought you were dead."

CHAPTER TWO

The limo was suddenly very quiet. Nicole shifted around in the big car and sat next to Laura, pulling her into a tight embrace. "I'm so sorry." All the defiance had gone out of her. "I really am sorry."

She swiped at the tears on Laura's cheeks as well as her own, tears of sadness for the friendship that had died abruptly when they were fifteen, for reasons she'd never been able to explain.

Laura shook her head. "You were just gone one morning. I didn't even know you were moving, you were just gone, and that was it. I got one letter from you, Nicole, and you never wrote again. How could you do that? What happened?"

"I don't know. None of us knew. Daddy woke us up in the middle of the night. The car was packed. He wouldn't even let me take the time to leave a note for you or pack my favorite things...." Nicole leaned back in her seat and met Laura's gaze. She felt as if all of the air had been sucked out of the small space. "I didn't want to do this now," she said softly, almost to herself. "I've missed you, and we don't have any time, and I just wish it would all go away so I wouldn't have to think about it."

Laura squeezed Nicole's hand. "Listen, you don't have to tell me. Not now. It's not important."

Nicole's pale green eyes stared ahead at nothing, a chilling, haunted look to them. The silence stretched on uncomfortably until Laura finally spoke again. As she did, Nicole's head jerked a bit toward her, startled out of the past and back into the safety of the present, her hand enveloped by Laura's two.

"Nic, I grew up with you. I know it's been a long time, but part of me feels as if I just saw you yesterday on your back porch. Whatever it is that has you looking like that, let it go. I don't need to know."

Nicole thought of that terrible night so long ago. As was always the case when she allowed herself to remember, her mind tried to shut down. A black screen seemed to slide across the landscape of her memories, normally so comforting, protecting her from the pain. Nicole could almost hear the deep scraping sound of the heavy black shield as it walled off the unwelcome images flashing in her head. This was the impenetrable door to her vault, the thing that kept her from being crushed and reduced to nothing under the weight of all the things in her life she couldn't undo.

She closed her eyes and took a deep shaky breath, stunned by how close to the surface all of these things lurked. She wanted to be home with

Harry right now. She wanted to have a baby, the baby they'd tried for since the wedding. She wanted to be an orphan, no history, no secrets. She wanted to pretend that this was all there was, the now. But more than any of that, she wanted to be free of her past. Nicole had known for a long time that she couldn't outrun it. That only left facing it.

She stared with new intensity at Laura, scrutinizing her almost as if seeing her for the first time. Laura squeezed her hand, naked worry in her features.

"I can't let it go. I have so many questions. There are so many things I wish I had answers to. It's like there's a hole right in the middle of my childhood, where my first life stopped and then after a long time my next life started." Nicole paused.

"I'll tell you what I do know," she said finally. "You knew me better than anyone, and even now I'm sure I can trust you." She shut her eyes and drew in another deep breath, storing up resolve for the long dive down, and began.

He is shaking her shoulder, scattering the dreams from her. Her eyes find the bedside clock. 3:16 am. That can't be right. Must be morning. I'm late for school, she thinks.

'Get up. Nicole Marie, get up now. We have to go.' His voice is serious and not at all slurred, no stench of whiskey on his breath, which is what makes her wake up fast.

This isn't right. Not normal. What's he doing? She sits up and swings her feet over the edge of the bed, noting the darkness out the window, the moon high in the sky. 'What, what's wrong?' She hears the confusion in her own voice. Her mother rushes past her doorway with an armload of clothing. Now she can hear Daniel crying in the next room. She'd stayed with him at bedtime tonight until he fell into a fitful sleep after his traumatic afternoon. He always sleeps through the night, now she wonders if maybe he did hit his head too hard earlier. What is going on?

'Get your journals, a few changes of clothes, and get out to the car. You have ten minutes,' her father tells her matter-of-factly.

She shakes her head to clear the jumble of questions running through it. 'Daddy, what are we doing?'

'Just do it!' he barks, his tone now much more characteristic of the father she knows.

She doesn't argue, just begins gathering clothing into her pink flowered suitcase. She moves to the desk and takes out a piece of paper, but his hand is on her wrist before she reaches the pen.

'No notes. No time. Let's go.'

Now she argues, 'I have to, please! Laura will--'

'Laura will be fine. Finish up. And don't forget your journals, all of them,' he orders.

Nicole glances at her bedroom window, through it across the driveway to Laura's bedroom window. Nicole's heart races, now finally catching up with the doom that has been in her house all afternoon, all her life. She rushes to the window, panicked, grabbing her flashlight. The SOS signals she and Laura devised give way to urgent, rapid blinks of light aimed at her friend's window. She must see Laura, tell her she is leaving. She cannot go without seeing her. She doesn't know where her father is taking them, but Nicole feels like she is about to walk off a cliff. Laura's bedroom window remains dark. She wishes she was dead.

Now it is 8:22 am by the dashboard clock, and rush hour traffic is picking up. Daniel is on one side of her asleep, nine year old James on the other side reading a comic book. Her parents are up front not speaking, in fact not having said a word to each other since the car started rolling. The car is packed to the brim with their things, and the car carrier on top as well. She knows something bad has happened, it must be very bad, and she's already put her fifteen-year-old imagination to work conjuring up worst-case scenarios; but how can she ask?

And now it is weeks later, feels like years later. She is in the second or third high school in as many months, and she has a brand spanking new last name to go with the new school. It is the day of the letter. She is in the bedroom she now shares with her two younger brothers when she hears his heavy feet stomp into the apartment and the door slam.

He has her by the front of her blouse, the material all bunched in his big hands, and she realizes her feet aren't touching the floor. She feels hysteria lurking just behind a thin curtain, waiting to break loose, and bites her lip, knowing she better not laugh. I've only seen this on Tom and Jerry, she thinks, didn't know you could actually pick someone up by the collar. Nicole swallows a burst of laughter that sounds crazy now bouncing around in her head. She concentrates and tries to ignore her father's bright red face, the beads of sweat running down his temple, the thick sweet stench of whiskey reeking from his pores, and Daniel crouched in the corner crying already. She sees James' pale serious face in the doorway, his arms hanging limply at his sides, frozen. He takes an uncertain step toward them and she wills him to stop. She pulls her eyes from him and back to her father's angry bloodshot ones. She must concentrate, what is he saying?

'Goddamn stupid cunt, I can't believe what you did, when did you write to her, tell me, how long ago goddammit!'

James is suddenly pulling at their father's arm, yelling at him to let go, to stop. John Murdock swats at him as if at a fly and her brother smacks into the wall, his head whip-lashing back just after the impact, a look of surprised pain in his expression. She remembers Daniel's face from the last bad time, remembers his eyes rolling back into his head, his body limp. Keep your eyes open, James, she thinks. Look at me. Stay here with me, don't leave me.

'Daddy,' she tries, now feeling the full force of the correct emotion envelop her: fear.

'You wrote to that Miller girl! Do you know what you've done? You've given them a trail! Look!' He waves a crumpled letter in her face; she spots Laura's flowery handwriting. 'LOOK!' He is struggling now, she sees he can't get any other words out, she can read the fight for control in his eyes. Her heart feels like it might burst from her chest and she holds her breath. In an instant he has thrown her to the floor and she feels the barrel of his gun on her forehead.

She closes her eyes and forgets to breathe, and feels with dismay the warm flow of urine soak her faded Levi's. She hears a tiny voice tell her, don't worry about it, least of your problems now. She finds the will to open her eyes after an eternity, looks up at him, this man who had once loved her so many years ago, who'd given her airplane rides and taken her to ballet, this man for whom she now feels nothing but bitter hate. 'Daddy,' she whispers.

The gun resonates next to her ear; there is a deafening roar, and then absolute silence. She focuses on Daniel in the corner, his mouth open, face scrunched up. Looks like he's crying, but no sound. She is deaf. Her father is gone.

The car was silent. Nicole leaned back and kept her eyes closed. She couldn't stop the streaming hot tears running down her face. She took a deep breath, then another. Control. Get control, stop this, she thought. She couldn't stop. She felt lighter, better, but oh so sad. All she wanted in this world was a child of her own. How could her father have treated his children this way? What if she became a parent and turned into him? Her chest constricted and she felt panic clawing at the edges of her sanity.

Laura's hand squeezed hers and it grounded her. She knew her friend would sit beside her for as long as it took.

Laura whispered, "It's okay. Just breathe, Nicole. I'm right here with you."

Nicole had no idea how much time passed. Finally the tears stopped, and she bowed her head, pulling a tissue from her clutch and drying her cheeks.

"We had to move again then. That afternoon. New apartment, city, school, name. That's why I never wrote to you again," she finished, unable to meet Laura's eyes.

The limo had stopped obediently at Neiman Marcus department store and was idling; the driver had discreetly stepped outside for a smoke. Laura sat watching the gray tendrils from the cigarette curl up into the air past the shiny black visor of his cap. She gently turned Nicole's face toward her own. She wouldn't lift her eyes to Laura's.

"Nicole, I'm so sorry. I didn't know. Please look at me."

Nicole spoke softly, "I know now what I should have done. I know I should have reached out for help. Maybe I could have written and told you what had really happened; your parents would've found a way to help. I should have gone to the police somehow. But he had all of us so terrified." She locked eyes with her. "It took six months for me to regain partial hearing in my left ear. But Daniel … I wanted to kill him for how he ruined Daniel. I dreamed about murdering him in his sleep. But I was too damn scared. I wanted to get out so badly, but I couldn't just leave the boys there. It took him another four years to leave us."

Nicole paused here and looked at Laura. Trust, she reminded herself. Her friend would not judge her for the actions of her father. "He took off after killing a man at a store in Texas. We never saw him again." Nicole rushed on. "He shot an innocent man right in front of Danny and our mother. I don't know why he even wanted us around in the first place. He was like two people. He was so deluded, I think he actually thought he could have the nice normal all-American-family. It was like he completely ignored the damage he caused every time his anger got out of control. I actually wish I could find him and make him see what he did to us. He's haunting me and he's not even dead yet—at least as far as I know." She sat back and took a deep breath, exhaling forcefully. She was exhausted. In more than three years of therapy, Nicole had never gone back to that night. She'd skirted around it, focused on the Texas years after her dad was gone … but never that night.

Laura sat motionless, still absorbing all of the details. "What about James and Danny? Where are they now?"

Nicole sighed heavily. "James has his share of problems. He's young, still, and stupid, like I was--" her gaze darted to Laura for a second before she continued. "I don't know where he is. I haven't seen him in months, not since just after Christmas last year. He needs to grow up, pull his life together. He's created a lot of his own problems, but then they get ahold of him and take over," she finished cryptically.

Laura paused before finally asking about Danny, about what Nicole had meant when she'd said her father had "ruined" him.

Nicole gazed out the window of the limo into the night, the headlights of other cars whizzing by them in a blur. "Danny is sick," she said, thinking, boy is that the understatement of the year. "He's in a private group home right now. He's been there nearly a year, since just after his twentieth birthday. It's a good place for him. He's doing better there, he's even gone back to school. He's…." she hesitated, choosing her words carefully. "He's been in psychiatric care for a while now. These past few years, since his mid-teens, have been really rough; it's been a terrible struggle for him. We're hoping he'll stabilize on the right medications and maybe eventually be able to get his own place, hold a job."

"I don't know what to say, Nicole," Laura shook her head.

"You know, he's a smart kid. They tested his IQ in high school and he was way above normal, genius level. If he can stay on his meds, he might do okay. I just don't know how it's going to go. We've got the best guy in the state working with him." Nicole thought of her baby brother, recalled an image of him that was probably like what Laura remembered. White blond hair, chubby toddler legs, bright blue eyes. Round laughing cheeks as Nicole tickled him. He'd laugh so hard she had to stop and let him catch his breath. She hadn't seen him laugh in ages.

"Nic … " Laura began hesitantly. Nicole looked at her expectantly. "I know what your father was like, there were always problems, and he and your mom ... I remember the fights. I remember the police getting called out to your house. But then things always seemed to sort of go back to normal. Something must have happened for him to make you guys leave like that. I'm sorry, I just ... never mind, it's none of my business."

"No," Nicole disagreed, "It's fine. It is your business, Laura. You were the only true friend I ever had, the only one who knew me. You knew how he could get. Part of me hates my mother for putting up with it all those years. And the other part of me knows she did the best she could.

I think she thought she was protecting us. It's hard to tell. Or maybe she was just too weak to do anything about it, stand up to him." She stopped, shaking her head. "Why couldn't my family have been normal like yours?"

Laura didn't argue that her parents weren't perfect, either. By comparison they certainly looked that way when you were standing in Nicole's shoes. Instead, she voiced a thought that drifted to her from so many years ago. "I think you're right about your mom's intentions. I know you love her. But she had her own part in what happened to you growing up. I remember hearing them fighting across the driveway late at night. I was always scared of your father, but there were so many times I wished your mom would do something. I wished over and over that she'd take you guys and just get out." She shrugged. "She was a victim, too, I suppose, like you."

Nicole nodded. "Daniel's doctor calls it enabling. He says that she probably imagined she could change our dad, and when she saw she couldn't, she still wouldn't leave because she felt that he needed her to take care of him, help him." She toyed with the diamond studded bracelet on her left wrist. "I do love her, and I feel bad for her. But sometimes I--" her voice broke off, uncertain.

She shrugged dismissively. "I know it doesn't make any sense, but sometimes I catch myself with these little rushes of anger toward her, sometimes it's hard to see her as the victim. I actually have a recurring dream where it's both of them." She shook her head.

"How do you mean? The abuse?"

"No, it's ... after we left Michigan, and especially once Daddy was gone for good, Mother was never the same. She always seemed like a copy of herself, there, but not there. She just withdrew, and got so secretive."

Laura was quiet for a moment. "She probably carries around a lot of guilt for what you three went through."

Nicole nodded. "I'm sure she does. That's probably all it is."

CHAPTER THREE

Laura's mind reeled, trying to make sense of all she'd just heard from her friend. She recalled checking the local papers for weeks afterward, looking for clues, something that would catch her eye to help make some sense of the disappearance. Now, she didn't have the heart to press. Nicole seemed too deflated already.

She felt sick when she replayed Nicole's words in her head. As kids, James was always buzzing around them like a mosquito, vying for their attention. She still didn't fully understand what Nicole meant about him being controlled by his own mistakes, she'd been purposely vague. And it was impossible for Laura to think of Danny as anything other than the sweet little toddler who always begged her for the red popsicles.

Laura's intrepid friend always did possess a reserve of strength that was surprising. Nicole sat up straighter suddenly, threw her head back and ruffled through her long red curls. "You know what? I am done talking about this right now. I just can't--I'm done. It hurts too much, worrying about the boys, wondering about my father. He is not my life, he's a bad memory. He can't hurt me or my family anymore, and I have given him enough of my time tonight." She turned and looked at Laura. "Okay?" she asked, and Laura saw the pain still raw in her eyes, and the intense need to close the door on it for now.

"Whatever you say. Just promise me something."

"Anything."

"Promise me you will use some of your riches and come visit me in Michigan. Please. I can't lose you again. You were the best friend I ever had, Nicole."

"I absolutely promise. I do," she smiled, and her expression had already softened, relaxed enough so that she was again that same ageless, beautiful woman Laura had discovered earlier today. "Now let's go."

"Where?"

"Why, to buy you a real dress, of course," she laughed. "You look like a soccer mom in that thing!"

Laura opened her mouth to reply, and then oddly enough thought better of it. They'd already been through enough catharsis tonight. She could wait. Nicole needed to do something light-hearted and fun. Laura could feel that as sure as she could feel her own excitement over going to shop at a department store as fancy as Neiman Marcus for the first time ever. She tipped her head back as they went through the entrance, taking in the striking two-story wall of glass doors and windows that made up the entire front of the store. Nicole glanced sideways at her and smiled.

Laura watched in wonder as sales clerks and even the store manager greeted Nicole on their way to the evening gown section. "Good evening, Mrs. Peterson," said one. "Help you find anything, Mrs. Peterson?" said another. While Laura was in the fitting room trying on heaps of glittery, silky things, Mrs. Peterson was seated on a plush white sofa enjoying some apparently high-end sparkling water. Laura checked her reflection in the multiple mirrors around the dressing room and saw gaiety in her expression. She truly felt as if she'd gone through the looking glass. She'd never have guessed this is what she'd be doing tonight, hundreds of miles from home, with her long lost childhood friend, in a strange city and state she'd never seen.

She tried on one dress after another, mildly embarrassed when she had to ask the sales lady for the next size up after the first two wouldn't zip. She should have just owned up to her actual size to begin with. Somehow, she thought, these dresses fit her body better than the closet full of clothing she had at home. Now, in the mirror, instead of seeing her too round tummy and her too wide hips, she took in a pretty, feminine silhouette that for once she couldn't criticize. She twirled around for Nicole, loving the feel of the rich, fluid fabric and the deep crimson tone of the curve skimming Zac Posen gown.

"Wow! That's the one Sugar, look at you! And to think you were going to wear that frumpy outfit to the hottest nightclub in the south. Look at the body you were hiding!"

Laura laughed self-consciously. "Are you sure it isn't too much?"

"I told you not to look at the tag," Nicole scolded her.

"Uh … that's not what I meant," she smiled sheepishly. "I mean, I don't know if I can wear this. My butt's too big for this dress, and look at the cleavage," she exclaimed, peering down at the neckline. "It's so not me!"

"Just quit bragging, some of us are not fortunate enough to be so well-endowed." Nicole glanced pointedly down at her own slender chest. "Your butt and boobs are great, you should show off your curves more anyway. You need to do something wild and crazy, have a little fun!"

"Okay, okay," Laura chuckled. "If you're sure that it's not too much? I mean the price now," she said, reaching around in back to look for the tag.

Nicole dove at her and grabbed her hand. "Grab your clothes and let's go find some shoes, the town's waiting for us!"

In the time it had taken Laura to try on over a dozen gowns, Nicole had slipped into a short, shimmering black dress and found new 4-inch heels to match. Laura took one look at the already statuesque redhead, then down the impossibly long legs ending in black pumps with gold detailing, and shook her head, smiling. What she wouldn't give for Nicole's confidence--and body!

They breezed through checkout with Nicole flashing her American Express Platinum, despite Laura's protests and attempts to pull out her own Visa card. The sales woman at the cosmetic counter on their way out of the store gave them a nod and a genuine smile, calling, "You girls have fun!"

Laura shook her head at her friend once they were seated again in the long black limousine. “I just can’t get over it, you look the same, seem like the same old Nic, but you’re so different now,” she said. “I know you haven’t had it easy, but you seem happy.”

“I am now. I wasn’t for a long time,” she answered seriously. “I made some mistakes, some bad choices … you wouldn’t have known me a few years ago. Harry really helped me turn my life around.” She paused to pour Laura a glass of champagne from the well-stocked mini-bar (“I don’t drink,” she told Laura flatly). “It’s funny how sometimes we end up hurting ourselves in an effort to hurt someone else. I can see that now.” She glanced out the window beyond Laura’s shoulder.

“Well, we’ve all made mistakes, haven’t we? Nobody’s perfect. But some mistakes can wind up being exactly what you need to become the person you’re supposed to be.” She knew they were speaking in riddles, but it seemed right. They’d been out of each other’s lives for so long, neither of them wanted to use up all of their time together now on confessions and painful details of the past. Laura knew there would be time for that. “Where are we going, anyway?”

“It’s called the Snake Pit. It’s a good place to start, but we won’t stay long. I want to show you a couple of the great night spots.”

Laura smiled to herself. It had been years since she’d been in any type of bar or night-club, and she was pretty sure she had never been to the kind of place Nicole was taking her.

Laura found over the course of the evening that Nicole still retained her quick wit and easy out-going attitude, turning strangers into acquaintances and acquaintances into friends within minutes. Nicole learned that Laura was ever the introvert, quiet, reserved, and always observing, almost as if taking mental snapshots of each stage of the evening, each new location or introduction. That changed once she'd had her fourth or fifth glass of champagne in half as many hours. Gradually Nicole found the other Laura, the one she remembered from Michigan and their years of friendship, the eager, optimistic, goofy Laura that normally took months of sincere friendship, or, it seemed, five drinks, to find.

"Oh, I love this song! Come on, dance with me!" Laura pulled Nicole onto the dance floor, her hips already moving to the rhythm of the heavy bass.

When the number ended they collapsed onto a soft suede couch at the edge of the crowd. "Honey, you can still shake it like you used to!" Nicole tossed her hair and fanned her neck as she complimented her friend.

"I haven't danced in … I don't even know how long," she spoke loudly, straining to be heard over the music. "I must make quite a sight! I'm having such a great time. It's been forever since I did something like this. If Charlie could see me now!"

Nicole's left eyebrow went up with interest. "Oh really? And who is this Charlie? I told you all about Harry and my life here. You've neglected to tell me a single thing about your life back home. Is there an interested gentleman, perhaps? A hot catch?"

Laura's laughter came out in snorts before she could stop it. "Charlie is my son, you dirty-minded hussy!"

Nicole leaned in closer. “Charlie is what? I thought you just said son. Do you have children, Laura?”

“Just Charlie,” she smiled, feeling warmth and pride wash over her once she was able to share her best treasure, the best part of her life, with her old friend.

Nicole stood abruptly and, taking her hand, said, “I cannot hear you. Let’s get out of here.” She led them in and out of clusters of sweaty, dancing club-goers to the fresh cool air on the pavement. Nicole turned to face her, grasping her upper arms in both hands. “Laura, you have a son? You had a baby? When? How old is he? You--you are a mom,” she announced in wonder.

Laura shrugged self-consciously with a little smile. “I know. I had him when I was young. Charlie just turned fourteen last month.”

Nicole was speechless for a moment, shaking her head and smiling back at Laura. “Well.” She continued to shake her head. “I just … congratulations, honey. You must be a wonderful mom,” she said softly.

“He’s a great kid. I got lucky. And I had a lot of help from my parents. It was hard at first,” they’d begun walking, arm in arm, past the many shops and restaurants in the north end of Dallas. “I was young.”

“No kiddin’ you were young,” Nicole said, screwing up her face in concentration. “You must’ve been only eighteen or so? Were you still in school? God, all these years when I’ve thought of you up north, somehow I just always figured it all went according to plan for you.” She shut her mouth and snapped her head to look at her friend. “I mean--”

"I know what you mean. I figured it would go that way too. You knew the plan: go away to Northwestern after high school, get my four years in, then on to law school. Maybe I'd meet a nice handsome doctor or lawyer along the way, we'd get married after I joined a successful practice, have 2.5 children and a white picket fence…." she finished a little wistfully.

"So…." Nicole encouraged.

Laura told her how she'd instead met a nice handsome guitarist her second month away at college. She'd been a naive, chubby virgin, and he told her everything she needed to hear. She shouldn't have been surprised when the pregnancy test was positive, but it had thrown her plan into a tailspin. The entire time she was pregnant, she'd never once even thought about what life would be like after the baby was born. Laura reasoned she was probably in denial enough to think she'd go right back to classes, finish up and continue with the plan. She rolled her eyes at her own youthful ignorance.

"What did you do? Did you move back home to Orsonville?"

"I had to after he was born. I was so obstinate, determined that I didn't need anyone's help, but I was delusional," she laughed.

"Oh my," Nicole said, shaking her head. "Of course you were. You were a kid! What about his father?"

"He wanted to help at first. But I think he got a little overwhelmed. His band took priority over fatherhood at the time. He definitely was too young. He got back in touch with me when Charlie was four or five, and now he's very minimally involved. He sends a card with money for his birthday and Christmas, and Charlie emails back and forth with him now and then. I think that's all his father's capable of where Charlie's concerned."

"Wow," Nicole breathed, letting it all sink in. Then, gasping a bit as the thought occurred to her, "My God, what did your parents say?"

"Oh, you know. Imagine telling Mr. and Mrs. Roman Catholic themselves that their daughter is pregnant out of wedlock. But I have to hand it to them: they really came through for me when it counted. They're a big part of Charlie's life."

Nicole squeezed Laura in an impulsive hug. "I can't even imagine what you've been through. I wish I could have helped you. I bet you're a great mom."

Laura shrugged. "I guess that depends on the day. He's a great kid," she said, smiling.

Nicole's cheeks were red, and this time not from all the dancing. "You're amazing, Laura. I'm sorry I didn't pull all of that out of you earlier tonight. I've missed you so much. After my father made us leave, I think I kind of forced myself to let go of things. I was sure I'd never see you again. I'm so happy I was wrong. I'm so glad you found me today." She was shaking her head, marveling at Laura. "You have a son. I should shut up and listen more."

Laura laughed. "I knew I'd tell you about him, just wanted the right moment. Besides, we have been a little busy, what with all the catching up, dancing and boozing, you know."

"Well, now I really need to come back to Michigan, I absolutely have to meet your son." She whipped her sequined pink cell phone out of her tiny sequined purse and began browsing through her calendar. "How about in two or three weeks?"

Laura's face lit up with a huge grin. "Perfect! You call me with your flight info and I'll be there to pick you up. You're staying with me."

CHAPTER FOUR

After much protest and some arguing, Nicole finally directed the limo driver to drop Laura off back at her hotel. It was past 2 in the morning, and Laura lamented that she felt so energized and wound up she didn't know how she'd sleep, but knew she had to try. She'd be heading to the airport soon.

"I don't see why you can't just come back to the house and spend the night, it'd be just like we're twelve again," Nicole whined.

"All my stuff is here, it's easier to stay. But I appreciate the offer. Next time, okay?" The car had stopped in front of her hotel and she leaned in and gave Nicole a tight squeeze. "Call me next week about your flight to Detroit, all right?"

"I will, I promise. I'm so glad to have you back."

Laura had been safely delivered to her hotel and thirty minutes later, the car pulled onto the long winding drive that led to Nicole's house.

She watched the enormous home approach through new eyes, taking in the stunning architectural design: the large centerpiece peak that was intersected the entire circumference with stained glass, the imposing double front door with beveled glass and brass highlights. Against the backdrop of the past she'd come face to face with tonight, it struck her how absurd it was that she should live in a house like this. Never in her wildest dreams would she have imagined herself here. She thought of her little bungalow next to Laura's in Orsonville. Her mother was always outside trying to seed the patchy grass. Nicole remembered the shutter that banged outside her window in the wind until a thunderstorm took it away one night. She hadn't worried about money as a kid, all of her friends lived in houses like hers. Seeing where Harry lived for the first time had been an immediate dose of perspective.

The amazing thing, the grand prize inside the envelope, was that Harry was the real deal. He truly was everything she'd told Laura. It had taken Nicole a very long time to trust his love for her. She'd had trouble understanding why or how he could feel so strongly for her, especially given the condition in which he found her. She understood it a little better now, after two years of weekly counseling appointments that she never missed. But somewhere beneath all of those sensible, healthy, confident feelings was still the mistreated little girl, the 'you'll never amount to anything, you're stupid and useless just like your mother' little girl, who'd heard such things so frequently and from such a young age that they were embedded in her consciousness. Harry had saved her life on many levels.

She found him in his study, bent over a spread of official looking papers. She stopped in the doorway for a moment, as he hadn't heard her come in. The muscle in his jaw was working and his eyebrows were furrowed in concentration, making those two tiny parallel lines between them. She noticed with some surprise that his wavy brown hair was thinning on top; she could actually glimpse a hint of scalp through it. Though nearly fifty-four, he still possessed the firm build that she imagined he'd had in his twenties. She loved the square set of his wide shoulders, his angular cheekbones and kind smile, and she even loved the scant bald spot that was beginning to show. She took a step into the study and he looked up. "Hi Baby," she smiled.

"You're home! I didn't hear you come in." He sat back in his chair and removed his glasses, rubbing his eyes with one hand. "How's your old friend?"

Nicole crossed the room and nudged his rolling leather chair back a bit to sit in his lap. She wrapped her arms around him and nuzzled his neck, breathing in the scent of him. "Mmmm. I missed you," she murmured.

He chuckled deeply. "Well, you should go for a girl's night out more often. Did you have a good time?" he asked, kissing her collarbone.

"Wonderful," she said, and kissed him fully on the lips. Her warm tongue sought his and she felt her pulse quicken as his hands went to her breasts, and the kiss deepened, grew in urgency. She straddled him, and his hands were under dress and she raised her arms obligingly while he stripped it off her. An electric tingling coursed like lightening from the top of her head, through her breasts, belly and to her very core, sending off warm-up ripples as she pressed herself into him. She arched her back, her head rolling toward her shoulder while his tongue danced down the length of her neck. He'd always been able to do this to her, take her from lukewarm to hot in seconds. She realized that her attraction to him was deeply entangled in how well he treated her, how much he'd changed her life. In that moment, though, her hands running over his taut, muscled arms, her desire for him felt overpowering and basic, carnal.

"Baby, I love you," she whispered, biting the skin on his neck as a moan escaped her throat. Her hands pulled at his worn, soft t-shirt until he helped her get it over his head. She instantly bent to his tan, muscled chest and the line of fine fur that led the way from his navel to the place she loved, kissing and licking her way down.

Her flaming red hair spilled over his thighs and he groaned, letting his head fall back as he closed his eyes and lost himself in sensation. He finally coaxed her back up, his hands on her waist as he lifted her with ease, then settled her against him and she slid down, feeling the warm, hard fullness of him and how well their bodies fit together. He buried his face in her neck as he rocked her, arms tightening around her while she felt the fireworks begin and intensify.

When it was over, she melted into him and rested her head on his chest, trailing one finger lazily in swirling circles over his heart. She sighed, deeply contented. Harry brushed a curl off her face and let his arm fall back around her.

Tilting her head to him, she met his eyes and smiled. "I'm so lucky I found you," she told him, and this time the surge of happiness she felt was only faintly tinged with a familiar foreboding. It seemed every time in her life she was happy, something always came along to squash it. But not with Harry, she thought. This is different. This is all mine.

Nicole set the alarm to rise before Harry the next morning, as was her habit. She moved efficiently around the kitchen preparing an omelet, hash browns and biscuits. Harry snuck silently up behind her and slid his arms around her waist just as she flipped the omelet onto the plate. Her hand jerked and the cheese oozed from one side as the omelet landed half on the counter. She spun around, laughing. "You scared me!"

"Why? Worried some dirty old man might be wandering around your house, Mrs. Peterson?" His eyes twinkled.

"If you're the dirty old man, I'll lock the doors and hide your car keys right now," she smiled, kissing him before breaking loose to set breakfast on the table.

He poured himself a steaming cup of black coffee. "I'm glad you had a good time with your friend last night. Laura, right?"

"I still can't believe I ran into her. She was there through everything with my family, my father, 'till we moved away. It's so strange to think about all that back then. We had such fun, but, my," she shook her head at Harry, "what we were dealing with at the time. She was like a sister to me."

"I remember you telling me about her. She lived next door, right?"

She blinked at him for a short beat before replying. "You sure do pay attention. Yes, her parents still live there, I guess. And she's still close by, same town. She had a son, Harry." She tried to smile and it felt grotesque on her lips, the sting of hot tears burning her eyes. She looked down at her plate, suddenly concentrating on picking at her omelet. She didn't want to start their day like this. And she didn't want to feel this jealousy toward Laura. She'd fought that her entire childhood.

He reached across the table and took her hand, acutely aware of how this news must have affected her. "You know it'll happen for us, Sweetheart."

She took a slow breath and nodded, meeting his eyes. "She didn't have it easy, either. She was so young … she slept with the first boy who showed any interest, and that's all it took. She's raised her son alone, I think, with some help from her parents. She's so much stronger than I remember her, but still the same in so many ways. I want you to meet her."

"I'd like to. Will she be back in town?"

"Well, actually, if you could spare me, I'd like to go home and visit her."

Harry didn't miss the use of the phrase "go home." He was quiet for a moment, studying his wife.

"You've got that business trip soon anyway, that might be a good time."

"Are you sure you're ready to go back there?"

She nodded. "It'll be fine. It's not like there's anyone I know up north now anyway. I want to go. I want to meet her son. I can't believe I've been without her for all these years, Harry. I need her back in my life. She knows me better than anyone."

He nodded in return. "You're right. She sounds like a good friend. And I would like to meet her, if she decides to come back to Texas again."

"I made her promise. I don't know when yet, but we'll talk about it when I go."

"Call Matt today and set it up. Let him know when you want to fly out. He'll get you a suite somewhere close, and have him arrange a car at the airport for you."

She shook her head. "I'll stay with Laura. She already invited me. And she said she'd pick me up at the airport when my flight comes in, so I won't need a car either."

He frowned at her. "Nicole, it's been a long time since you were back there. Have you thought about how you'll handle everything? Wouldn't you be more comfortable in your own hotel? Just in case…."

"What?"

He shrugged. "What if you need some time on your own? You don't know how it's going to feel seeing your old house again, the old neighborhood--"

She stopped him with her hand on his arm across the table. "Baby, I appreciate you worrying about me. But it'll be fine, I promise. Laura and I were like sisters growing up. If I'm going to Michigan, I need to be with her." She rubbed his arm. "If I don't feel comfortable, I will get a room, I swear. Okay?"

He stood and set his empty plate in the sink, bending to kiss her on his way to the foyer. "Okay. You're a big girl. I know you'll be fine."

She wrapped her arms around his waist and kissed his stomach through the fine fabric of his Italian suit. "I love you," she told him, smiling up at him.

Harry's car hadn't been gone two minutes when Nicole heard an urgent knocking at the garden door. James was standing on the stoop, shifting his weight from one foot to the other. He gave her a quick grin when he saw her approach.

She held the door open for him, pulling her brother into a hug when he stepped inside. "Where have you been?" she demanded, standing back from him to search his face.

He avoided her gaze, peering through the parlor into the kitchen. "Oh, here and there. What are you cooking? Smells good."

She led the way into the kitchen, scooting a chair out from the table on her way to the stove. "Sit down, I'll make you breakfast. Coffee?"

She appraised her brother's thin form covertly from the stove. His elbows rested on the table and she couldn't help but notice the long sleeves on this already hot morning. His feet beat a steady rhythm on the ceramic tile and she watched his bony knees jitter up and down. Dark circles were under his blue eyes and a yellowish cast colored his skin. A good week or two's beard growth crept over his once handsome jaw and chin. "How are you doing, Honey?"

"Good, fine," was all he'd offer at the moment. He gulped down the coffee she'd poured him and rose to refill the cup. As he passed her she caught a whiff of the stale cigarette smoke and strong body odor she'd noticed when he came in. But no scent of liquor, she thought, grasping at morsels of hope.

She set the eggs in front of him with hash brown potatoes cooked with onion and green pepper, like their mother used to make. The two sat in silence, she in her tan silk bathrobe, diamond studs in her ears, fluffy kitten-heeled bedroom slippers on her feet, he in worn and faded jeans and dirty sneakers, his limp, neglected dark brown hair falling in his eyes. She felt a stab of pain in her chest as her eyes journeyed over his angular shoulders, jutting collarbones, the hollows in his cheeks. After a while she instead gazed out into the lilac bushes that lined this end of her garden. A Hummingbird flitted cautiously around her potted geraniums, stopping for nectar before quickly darting away, only to return seconds later, as if afraid of what might happen if it stayed in one spot too long.

James finally sat back and pushed his empty plate away, resting a hand on his non-existent belly. "Thanks Nic. Just what I needed." His left hand was curled around his coffee cup. He peered out at the flowers, then looked around the kitchen, and after an eternity, met his sister's eyes.

She smiled warmly at him and took another sip of her own coffee. "I missed you, little brother."

"I know. I'm sorry I didn't call." He rubbed the back of his neck, then dropped his hand back to his jittery knee and pressed it until it was nearly still.

"Where are you staying now?"

"I was at a friend's for a while. I can't go back there." He watched her expression and braced himself.

Instead of leaping to assumptions, she asked, "How are you feeling, James?"

"Lousy. Goddamn terrible, if you wanna know." He abruptly fell silent. She didn't push him. Then, "I'm trying to clean up. I'm really trying this time."

"How long's it been?"

"Three days. But that's a lot for me. I'll do it. I have to. I just can't go back there; I can't be around all that shit."

"Good. Good for you. Don't go back. Do you have any place to go, hon?" She wanted to believe in him, but she'd been trained by experience not to.

"No." He cleared his throat. "But that's not why I came here. I don't want a hand out. I just knew you'd be worried."

"I have been. You haven't called in six months this time, Jamie. I always worry about you," she reached across the table and squeezed his sinewy forearm. Nicole knew her brother's problems were something even money couldn't fix; she'd tried that route. All she could hope was that he'd let her help him.

He looked at her and was still for a rare moment. He smiled at her, and Nicole saw her twelve year old brother: silly, tentative, all action and hesitant words, always trying to show the world he was fine. Still the same. "Well, I'll get better. I mean, it's rough, sometimes it's bad, but—

breakfast helped. Maybe I can even keep it down," he joked half-heartedly. "I can do it this time. And I've still got my old car. Nice big back seat to sleep in." There was not a trace of beguilement or any thought of inducing guilt in this, just matter-of-fact reasoning.

Nicole sighed. How many times would this make? She'd lost count. Maybe five? Six? He hadn't stayed with her since the third failed attempt to get clean, when he took half the contents of the guesthouse with him in the middle of the night, presumably to hock and get his fix. She ran her fingers through her hair irritably and squared her elbows on the table, holding his gaze with hers. "You can't sleep in your car, James; you'll get picked up. Go upstairs and take a shower. You can stay in the spare room." She thought for a moment. "Three days. How have they been?"

"Not too bad so far, maybe this time will be easier," he said, lifting his eyebrows hopefully and making the dark circles under his eyes even more pronounced.

She gave him a weak smile. "Maybe," she told him, while silently taking an inventory in her head of what supplies she had on hand. The last time she'd tried to help James detox, they'd started at the Summerland Center, and after two weeks Harry had used his connections to get James released to their care. There was still a seven or eight days' supply of Methadone locked away, and she recalled some strong pain pills--Percocet--being left over after Harry's knee surgery.

Once she got James settled in the bed in her bright, sunshine-yellow spare room and she heard his breathing become slow and even, Nicole crept back down the stairs and down another flight to the walkout basement. Behind a large seascape painting in the rec room she digitally entered the combination to their safe. She placed one Percocet and one tablet of Methadone in a medication cup and closed the safe and painting. Back up in the kitchen, she prepared a tray with clean washcloths, a pitcher of ice water, a glass, and the medication cup. She left the tray on the buffet at the base of the stairway and set about the other half of her task when James came to stay. In less than thirty minutes, she had a basket full of their finer possessions from the living room, family room, parlor, and dining room; to this she added the jewelry box retrieved from her bedroom and took the haul back down to the safe. God she hated this version of herself. She still remembered the pull of her own addiction from nearly four years ago. She would have stolen from the pope to get her fix. She'd just plopped herself down in her favorite overstuffed chair when she heard her brother wake.

A loud thump as his feet hit the floor, then fast footsteps to the bathroom where he collapsed to retch up his breakfast. She appeared in the doorway to see him shuffling unsteadily back to the bed, drenched in sweat with tears rolling down his face. She helped him sit on the side of the bed and supported him as she emptied the medication cup onto his tongue, then coaxed him to take a sip of water. He hung his head and covered his face with shaking hands. "I can't do this again," he whispered.

Nicole hated this, hated it every time. She would give anything, everything, for James never to have gone down this road. She knew she was to blame. She wrapped her arms around him and squeezed her eyes shut, wishing she could protect him, willing strength into him. “You can, Jamie. I know you can. I’ll help you,” she held him and rocked him gently.

“I can’t. It won’t work. I’m not like you,” he cried.

CHAPTER FIVE

Laura watched Detroit Metro Airport come into sight as they began their descent. Finally almost home, she repositioned the tiny airplane pillow behind her head as her thoughts drifted back to Nicole, to the genuine happiness in her voice when she spoke of her husband, and then to the haunted look in her eyes when the topic turned to her father or brothers. Laura still felt a deep sadness and worry when she thought of Daniel as he was now, and Nicole had been so vague about James. The years of living with her ogre of a father, and even the years since, seemed to have trained her well to be guarded and private.

She was jarred from her reflections as the wheels of the plane gently kissed the runway and the hum of the cabin pressure fluctuated, popping her ears. The man sitting next to her, the one she'd ignored the entire flight just because she was so exhausted and anxious to get home, touched her elbow as she stood.

"Let me get that for you," he offered as he reached well above her and plucked her bag from the overhead storage. "Have you been traveling a while?"

Glancing up at the man as he handed her the bag, she was uncharacteristically lost in his sea blue eyes for a full three seconds before she found her voice. "Um … well, it feels like I have."

"You have that look. The look of someone who is glad to finally be home?" He smiled warmly at her.

She nodded, staring into those liquid blue eyes of his. She noticed how thick and wavy his black hair was, not missing the little cowlick at his right temple.

"Exactly," she agreed, telling herself to snap out of it, get a grip. She must be overtired. "Seems like I've been gone forever even though it's only been a few days," she smiled back at him politely.

"I know the feeling. When you miss home, days can seem like years. Were you in Texas for vacation?" he asked her conversationally while they waited for the long cluster of people ahead of them to deplane.

"No, more or less for work," she said, not wanting to bore him with the details of her short trip. "And you? Are you coming home too or catching another flight?"

"Nope, glad to be home myself." He shifted his jacket to the other hand to help the elderly man in front of them get into the aisle.

The line began to move and he stepped aside to allow her to go first, taking her coat for her as she struggled with her carry-on and laptop. They made it off the plane and into the terminal and Laura paused just to the side of the roped posts, setting her things down to get resituated. The man stopped with her and waited while she fitted the laptop into her carry-on bag, then handed her the coat.

"I can't believe it's only October and I need this thing already. It was 90 degrees when I left, I almost didn't pack it."

"That's Michigan for you. Don't like the weather, wait a minute," he said, using a well-worn local truism. "I'm Adam, by the way," he offered his hand.

She took it with her free one, the coat now slung over her arm. "Laura Miller. Thank you for your help, Adam," she said, mentally giving herself a pinch to quit acting like a flirtatious teenager and get going. He just happened to be a helpful, handsome stranger. He'd helped that old man on the plane, too, and anyway, she had Steve waiting for her outside in the car. She gave him her best PTA smile.

"It was nice meeting you."

"Likewise," he returned, and, as they were both headed in the same direction to the baggage claim, he fell into step a few feet apart from her.

They walked for a while in companionable silence while travelers strode purposefully this way and that, each wearing a set, determined look about them as they headed to or from their respective gates, each with an extra ingredient or two thrown in: anticipation; anxiety; excitement; fear. Laura loved imagining the details of their purpose there, creating little snapshots in her head of the reasons behind the emotions.

When the silence had changed from companionable to awkward, she turned as they walked and said, "Are you from this area?"

Clearly glad she'd chosen to speak with him again, his face became animated. "About an hour away, just outside of Lansing. I run a vet clinic there. We have a conference in Texas every fall around this time. There's another one in the spring in Florida, so I get to do Disney World while I'm there."

She checked his expression to see if he was joking. He didn't appear to be. Then she understood, chiding herself for the pang of disappointment she felt. "That's great. Your family must love it."

"Well, I've never invited them. My parents aren't really big on Mickey Mouse or Cinderella, and my brothers and sisters think they're all too old to enjoy it." He glanced sideways at her, a ridiculously sexy half-smile on his face.

She felt pink heat creep into her cheeks and smiled self-consciously. "I'm sorry, I just assumed--"

"That a grown man would never go to Disney World all by himself just for fun?"

"Well, yes!" She stepped onto the down escalator that would take them to baggage claim.

"My brother and his wife live near Orlando. I usually steal his kids and go for a few days." His eyes twinkled at her. "So you were half-right."

"See, you tricked me," she told him, smiling, as they arrived at the conveyer belt for their flight.

"What do your bags look like?"

"Gray and pink flowered," she answered, slightly embarrassed. She'd never bothered to replace the old set her parents had given her for high school graduation. “Listen, you don’t need to do that, I’m fine, really.”

He shrugged and grabbed one of her bags before it could speed by, setting it at her feet, then reached out quickly again and got his own small black suitcase. “Laura,” he said, facing her squarely.

“Yes?”

“I never do this, I really don’t. But would you have a cup of coffee with me? I’m not ready to let you go quite yet.”

A thrilling, lit-sparkler type of feeling shot from her lower belly up to her neck and she hoped it was not evident in her expression. She smiled apologetically at him, noticing now the very faint spattering of freckles that branched out over his nose and cheeks, and of course those blue eyes. She took a deep breath.

“I’m sorry, I can’t. But I’m flattered.” She tore her eyes away toward the luggage carousel, for something to look at other than him.

“How about another time? I’m a nice guy, really. I’m not an axe murderer or anything, I promise.” He raised his eyebrows hopefully as she glanced back up at him, one corner of his mouth curling up.

She had to laugh at that. “Because I’m sure you’d tell me if you *were* an axe murderer, right?” she joked.

He laughed with her. “Okay, you make a good point. But seriously, what do you think? I could call you….”

She looked down and shook her head. “I’m sorry, Adam.”

He turned abruptly and she instantly regretted her response, but he reappeared in seconds with her other bag and set it down.

"Here's my card," he reached into his jacket pocket, pulling out a plain white and black business card. He took her hand and placed it in the palm, closing her fingers around it. "I would really like to see you again, Laura," he gazed at her intently now, "please keep this in case you change your mind."

She couldn't move her hand; it was still enclosed in his larger one. The warmth of his skin seemed to travel through hers, right up her arm, across her collar bone, to her neck and cheeks. There were those tingles again. It was such an innocent thing, their hands touching. Why did she already feel guilty, disloyal to Steve? Because her heart, her body, knew what it wanted, that's why, she answered her own question. I don't even know this man. This is crazy, she silently argued. He reluctantly dropped his hand from hers and caught her gaze. He was standing so close to her, she realized she was forgetting to breathe. It's not crazy, she thought. It's right.

She didn't know what to say to him, so she tucked his card into the back pocket of her jeans, the uninvited thought popping into her head that she was glad she'd worn the flattering pair of faded, curve skimming ones rather than her worn yoga pants she'd considered at first. She bent and picked up her bags, arranging one over her shoulder and taking the other two in her hands, coat now on. "Listen, Adam, I--"

He stopped her with a light touch on her upper arm. "It's all right," he said, "maybe you'll think about it. Maybe you'll change your mind." He glanced toward the street beyond the wall of doors behind her. "Do you have a ride?"

"Yes, I do. And thanks again," she told him, knowing her attraction to him was unmasked in her own dark brown eyes.

He nodded, took his cue and strode away from her and out the doors.

She felt suddenly deflated watching him leave. And almost immediately on the heels of that, she chastised herself again for acting so silly. The man was ridiculously handsome and charming. He could probably have any woman he wanted. At the very least, he'd given her a little ego boost and there was nothing wrong with that.

She carried her bags to the curb, set them down and leaned out to search up and down the pick-up/drop-off area for Steve's car. As she watched people loading and unloading, and no sign of Steve, she felt a little guilty she'd taken so long at baggage claim. She'd probably been standing there talking to that doctor for longer than she thought. She scooted her suitcase closer and perched her butt on the end to wait.

After thirty minutes of breathing exhaust fumes and cigarette smoke, peering anxiously up and down the road for his lemon yellow Mustang, she gave in and fished her cell phone out of her purse to call Steve. He picked up on the fifth ring, "Hello?"

"Steve? Where are you?"

"Whaddya mean? I'm in my office," (by that he meant in his recliner in his bedroom watching any number of football, basketball or hockey games on ESPN). "What's going on?"

"I'm at the airport," she said flatly.

"What? Oh! Shit! That's today, isn't it?"

She closed her eyes. "Yes, that's today."

"Okay, you said two-fifteen, your flight comes in at two-fifteen … shit, it's almost four o'clock! Babe, I'm so sorry! I'm on my way right now!"

She heard the jingle of car keys as he raced around his apartment, the door slam, and his car start with a rumble. Stupid loud customized mufflers, she thought unkindly, before catching herself. Steve was not a details man. So he forgot to pick her up. Losing track of time was just something he tended to do. He was always there for her when she really needed him. They'd been dating for over two years now, and she knew he loved her, though it had crossed her mind more than once to wonder if they'd ever wind up getting married at all, or just go on dating forever.

She'd never have introduced him to Charlie if they weren't serious. He was, in fact, only the second man she'd dated since Charlie's father. She purposely delayed beginning to date at all until Charlie was ten, and even then, established a strict code within herself that she wouldn't burden her son with her social life unless she first ascertained it was going to be a lasting relationship, not just a few dates. Unbeknownst to the two men she'd gone out with, they'd each undergone a checklist of sorts by the second date. The first hadn't made it past that point. Steve had done a little better.

Now, on the phone, she heard Steve apologizing again and interrupted him.

"It's all right, I'll see you in a while," she told him and hung up, still feeling irritated, but now more with herself for excusing him so much.

She allowed herself the luxury of letting the feeling grow and flourish a bit, something she didn't normally do.

He was, if she was honest, the ultimate slacker. They'd met working together in the small factory in town where she'd moonlighted for extra cash occasionally a few years ago. Though she'd always felt he was interested in her, he never acted on it until the day her car broke down and he was the only one leaving at the same time and able to give her a ride home. He'd stopped her getting out of his car with his hand on her arm, and asked her if she'd like to "hang out" sometime. She remembered clearly stifling the urge to ask him what that meant, thinking it sounded like a phrase more apt to come from a teenager than a thirty-three year old man. Now she tried to recapture the emotion that had caused her to accept his proposal to hang out. At the time that she was flattered by his attention, mostly because she didn't receive a lot of male interest these days, but also because he was undeniably good looking.

By the second date, she'd discovered he was also sweet, funny, a good cook and a mama's boy. She'd let the first few outweigh the last, even when she learned on the third date that his living situation was a glorified version of still living at home with his mother: he shared a duplex with her, he upstairs and she downstairs. This, he explained, was out of necessity, to look after his mother, who was in her early seventies, and how could Laura argue with that?

Depending on point of view, he was either the doting son or the still-living-with-mom grown man. Initially, she felt she couldn't criticize him for wanting to take care of his mother. But now, after more than two years of watching the woman happily keep her busy schedule of bridge games, golf games, weekend "senior-trips" with her ladies group, and the occasional volunteer work, always finding the time to do nearly all of Steve's laundry and regularly tidying up his apartment, Laura harbored a secret wish that Steve would sever the apron strings.

Steve seemed to be in no big hurry to think about marriage, but for some reason recently, it was on Laura's mind. Did she want to spend the rest of her life with him? Could she imagine her life without him? He'd been so much a fixture for these past two years, they did almost everything together, how could she even consider a future without him? But then again, what type of future did she envision for herself? Would things change if they did get married?

And then his car appeared in front of her and he was out and around to her side in a flash, grabbing her and pulling her into a bear hug so tight she felt her feet leave the pavement. He set her down and she gazed into his smiling face, unable to resist smiling back at his dimples and obvious happiness to see her. The irritation in her evaporated as he kissed her warmly, stopping to say, "I missed you, Babe."

CHAPTER SIX

It was late that night by the time Harry made it home. He'd phoned around six o'clock to warn her he'd be late and not to hold dinner for him. She hadn't the nerve then to tell him about her brother. The kitchen was spotless, his plate already prepared in the fridge for a quick warm-up when he got home, she'd turned the lights down and lit several soft ivory candles here and there in the foyer and dining room, and even had Vivaldi playing unobtrusively in the background. Her plan was to break it to him gently over the Chicken Cordon Bleu and hope for the best. Things didn't turn out that way.

At quarter to ten, James woke again from his fitful nap, and this time it was bad. He hollered for her until she appeared panting in his doorway, to see that he hadn't made it the bathroom this time and was sitting in his own vomit on the floor. His sunken eyes peered out at her from deep in their red-rimmed sockets, his arms clenched over his chest as he shook uncontrollably, the t-shirt she'd given him clinging to his thin frame with sweat. She crouched next to him and he winced before she even touched him, doubled over in misery.

"You gotta gimme something, Nic, I can't stand it," he begged, meeting her gaze. For a moment, a flash, she saw him clean. Handsome. Funny. Charismatic. The guy everyone wanted to be around. Always living just on the surface. Nicole thought she probably hadn't known James at all in a long time. The heroin was his shield, as it had once been hers. Without it, he couldn't survive in that surface world for long.

She carefully, gently placed her hand on his cheek, holding his gaze. His beard stubble scratched her hand, the boniness of his face making her heart ache. She closed her eyes and touched her lips to his forehead, feeling the trembling calm a little. Oh, little brother.

She stood and turned her tear streaked face away from him and went to the sink, returning with a cool washcloth which she gently used to sponge his sweaty forehead and cheeks. "You're going to be okay, James, I promise," she whispered, terrified that she was wrong.

At that moment, she heard Harry's car door close and, shortly after, his key in the lock as he let himself in. "Nicole?" he called, dropping his keys and briefcase at the buffet.

She hesitated for a beat, then reluctantly answered him. "I'll be right down," she called back, "pour yourself a glass of wine and I'll get your dinner." She couldn't very well tell him not to come up, but she hoped he'd be too pooped to want to trudge all the way up the stairs looking for her when he could just sit tight and have a drink.

Her plan now completely gone awry, she heard him on the stairway and then he was standing in the doorway of their normally cheerful yellow guest room. James hung his head down between his skinny raised knees and grasped two fistfuls of greasy hair. His entire form was pulled into a tight little ball, all lanky arms, legs and hair, as he rocked back and forth.

She rose and went to her husband. “He came this morning. I didn’t want to tell you on the phone,” she offered an apologetic explanation. “I haven’t seen him in so long, I--”

Harry slid a hand around the back of her neck as he bent to kiss her briefly, his expression painted with concern over her level of distress, and shook his head. “Okay. It’s okay.” His eyes moved to James and she saw him take in the mess on the floor before returning his attention to her. “He’s trying to get clean?”

She nodded. “This is his third day. It’s bad, I think. I gave him a Methadone and a Percocet early this afternoon, but he’s so miserable, Harry.”

“I’ll get another dose; it’s been long enough by now.” He started out of the room.

She cast a troubled glance back at her brother, then caught up with Harry in the hallway, her hand on his arm. She dropped her voice to a whisper. “I know this isn’t a good idea, but he had nowhere to go, and I can’t just turn him away.”

She watched her husband, trying to gauge his reaction to the chaos he’d come home to. She’d spent the last few years making a conscious effort to squelch her fear that one day Harry would realize what he'd really signed up for when he'd asked her to marry him. Nicole knew that in some very fundamental ways she and her brothers remained a true product of the environment in which they'd been raised. All of the progress she'd made in her own life dissipated against the backdrop of James shivering in the throes of heroin withdrawal on the bedroom floor.

Harry stared at her wordlessly for a moment, and she waited. "Nicole, he's your brother. Don't ever apologize to me for that. We'll do what we can for him. I know he has good intentions, and I know you love him. We'll try. I'll make some calls in the morning, and we'll go from there."

He leaned down and kissed her temple before heading downstairs, leaving her standing in the hallway. Maybe Harry was her compensation for the childhood she'd endured, she thought. James huddled in her peripheral vision and that ever present anticipatory dread, a heavy stone in her stomach, turned over. What about James?

Nicole got him calmed somewhat and administered the pain medicine Harry brought, cleaned up the vomit and put new sheets on the bed, helped him back in, and even coaxed him into eating some chopped up Popsicle pieces. She left him awake but starting to feel the effects of the pain medicine while she hurried back down to get Harry's very late dinner. She stepped into their bedroom on the way and quickly stripped, washed her hands and face, and threw on her blue satin robe before continuing on downstairs. She stopped short in her rush to the kitchen as she glimpsed him eating dinner at the dining room table out of the corner of her eye.

She chose the chair next to him and he gave her a tired smile. His plate was already mostly cleaned in front of him, his burgundy tie loosened and his glass half empty. “Rough day, huh?”

“Yeah. How was dinner, anyway?”

“Delicious. Really liked the ambience, too,” he smirked, referring to the dim lights and soft music.

She blushed. “You caught me. I just wanted to ease the blow when I told you.”

He frowned in concern. “Are you doing okay with all this?”

“I am, knowing he’s not out sleeping in his car somewhere or back using already.”

“What about a longer inpatient stay this time? Or somewhere different than Summerland?”

“I don’t know … I don’t know what’s going to do it for him. It breaks my heart every time, and every time I tell myself he can kick it. I was lucky I had you to help me.”

He leaned on the table and rubbed her arm. “You did the work, Nicole, not me,” he said quietly.

She nodded. “I don’t know how I was able to do what James has tried seven or eight times to do and just can’t. I can see he’s bottomed out, and that’s right where I was. Even now it hurts to think about the way I was, the things I did … but, Baby, you have to remember, I kept trying to see the light at the end of the tunnel. I was pretty sure there’d be no way you'd have any interest in sticking around after what you saw me go through, but I let myself dream about it anyway. I know that gave me some extra motivation." Nicole had beaten her own heroin addiction exactly three years and eight months ago. What remained in her heart, unspoken, was that there had also been the motivation of despising what she had become so much that, at the time, the only other alternative would have been suicide, not returning to the drug.

His deep voice resonated in the room and filled her with warmth. "I could always see you. The real you. You just had to help me get to you."

She felt chills run up her arm where his hand rested and her eyes welled up. What about James, she thought again. Didn't James deserve the same chance she'd been given? The same chance at a life? She shut her eyes and swallowed, knowing she had tried over and over again to give him that chance. But he had to take it.

She sighed heavily and looked at her husband, her cheering section, savior, best friend and lover all rolled into one. She wished James had someone or something in his life that would make him want to live. She hoped she and Danny were enough.

She pushed her chair back and went to sit in Harry's lap, wondering if he would ever really understand the impact he'd had on her life. She tucked her head into his neck, inhaling the warm remnants of his cologne from this morning. She ran a hand across his firm chest and kissed him, her flesh tingling in an altogether different way as his hand slid inside her robe, making her want more. This. This was the added bonus of having a man like Harry in her life. She would never get enough of him, she thought, unbuttoning his shirt and loving the feel of his skin against hers. He stood and scooped her up with him, heading toward their bedroom.

Her eyes went to the top of the stairway and she prayed James would have a restful night. "Shhh," she whispered to him, "don't wake him."

He murmured against her mouth, "We'll just have to play quietly then, won't we?"

Much later, Nicole crept to the doorway of the cheerfully decorated room where James was snoring softly. She tip toed in and knelt at the side of his bed. She was loath to disturb him, she only wanted to be near him. She'd missed her brother so much. She missed him still. James had never been like Danny. Danny was the thinker. James was all action; good, bad and in between. Never at rest, not even now. Nicole reached out a hand to touch his sweaty hair and it hovered over his head instead. She would not take the chance of waking him, he was so much more peaceful now than earlier this evening. She finally rested her head on folded arms on his bed, and, without meaning to, found herself praying.

Let him come back to me. Help him overcome this, help him find his way back, help him know we're here, we need him, please. He's fought so hard, please, God, she thought, please just give him a chance. The word God, even in Nicole's head, sounded foreign. She had stopped praying when she was a little girl. She knelt in the dark and pushed past the awkwardness of the word and silently sent up her plea for her brother's life.

James stayed three more days. Each day he seemed to improve a little more, with less vomiting, less pain, less agitation. He started to talk about looking for work when he was better, and he even mentioned speaking to Daniel on the phone a few weeks earlier. On his seventh heroin-free day, when Nicole poked her head into his room to check on him before she went to put on the coffee, he was gone. This time, as she walked through the house with a heavy heart, she found nothing missing, nothing out of place. Until Harry left for work and was unable to find his car.

The front door swung back open only an instant after he'd kissed Nicole goodbye, briefcase in one hand, car keys in the other. She hadn't even turned to go back to the breakfast dishes yet. "What did you forget?" The smile faded from her voice as she saw his expression.

"My car is gone."

"No. It's in the garage." It has to be, she thought desperately.

"No, it's not. I parked it in the driveway last night."

She shook her head and came to stare out the front door with him, as if he'd somehow simply overlooked the big black fully-loaded Hummer. "Maybe you just forgot. I'll check the garage," and she flew back toward the kitchen and through the side door entrance to their garage. She opened the door to reveal her little red convertible, Harry's sleek black sedan, and the empty spot where the Hummer usually rested.

She turned to find Harry right behind her, also taking stock of the garage. She read fury in his expression and realized she hadn't seen that look since … since the last time her brother had come to stay, she thought with dismay. Only this was worse. She couldn't believe James would do this to her, to them. "Baby--" She reached out to touch his arm but he was already striding purposefully toward the phone on the kitchen wall. She followed at his heels.

"Don't try to talk me out of it, Nicole," he turned angrily on her. She opened her mouth but before she could speak he cut her off. "I didn't file a police report last time because he's your brother, and it was the first time. But he stole my goddamned car!" He was incredulous.

"I wasn't going to talk you out of it. I wanted to say I'm sorry," she told him quietly.

He rubbed his eyes, the crease in his frown lines very pronounced now. Shaking his head, he paused and looked at her sadly. "I'm sorry. I'm not angry with you. I just can't believe he'd do this to us."

She wrapped her arms around him and hugged him tight. "I never should have trusted him. This is my fault. Call the police. He deserves whatever he gets," she declared, feeling a series of icy pinpricks crawl over her back and shoulders as she said the words. 'Keep him safe,' she heard her own voice whisper in her head, to that estranged god she seemed to call on only during the hard times.

She listened to Harry's end of the conversation as he spoke with the police, watching him anxiously as he set the phone down. "What did they say?"

"They said they're on it. I know how this works. Your brother may be a thief, but he's not stupid. He won't be joy-riding around; he wants it for the money he can get out of it. The police will find it stripped in a few days, or else not at all," he dropped into the kitchen chair, defeated.

"Harry, I'm--"

"Nicole, don't say it. I know you're sorry. This isn't your fault. I agreed to him being here. I knew what the risks were." He was noticeably calmer already, flipping open his wallet to pull out his insurance information. He stood and headed for his study. "I'll call Dennis and get things squared away, then I've got to go in, I have to be in court this afternoon."

She brought him a second cup of coffee while he was still on the phone with the insurance agency. He finished the call as she was on her way out of the room. "Nicole?"

"Yes?"

"I'll take the Lincoln today, if you don't need it."

"No, I'll take my car. I have to get to the hospital in an hour, you know, to train the new volunteers for the children's wing."

"I forgot that was today. Didn't they start last week?"

She smiled at his effort. "Last week was orientation, today we just go over stuff like therapeutic play, special needs cases, that sort of thing."

"I hope they know how fortunate they are to have you. I see how much time is involved in handling the volunteer department."

"It's mutually beneficial, you know. I love the days I'm in the children's wing, it makes me feel good to know I've helped someone even a little. I should've finished getting my nursing degree, I always liked the work."

Harry pulled her to him and kissed her before stooping to grab his briefcase again. "You could go back to school anytime you want. You're making a big difference doing what you're doing, though. I'll see you tonight."

The hospital was a thirty minute drive away, and she had time to unwind and try to put James out of her mind, thinking instead about her trip to Michigan. She planned to go soon, but hadn't thought about it or looked into airfare with her brother here. She felt a little surge of happy anticipation at the thought of the trip, and then a dark cloud of queasiness struggled to squash it when she thought of James, back at that house he'd mentioned, sitting in some dingy corner with a needle sticking out of his arm. She knew there were options, she could go looking for him; she had a fair idea of where to start. But then what? She shook her head to clear it, determined not to dwell too much on the situation. She'd done what she could for him.

Her hospital shift flew by, as it usually did when she was handling the children's section. There were three new volunteers she was training, and each seemed to catch on quickly, the quietest girl among them perfect for the sickest kids, the ones who were forced to stay in their beds and couldn't come participate in the playroom. Nicole praised each volunteer for their good efforts today and watched them head toward the exit, and then turned back down the opposite hallway, passing the neonatal unit on the way to her office.

She allowed herself the luxury of not looking today, thankful there were currently no new volunteers to train for the nursery. The babies just hurt her heart, tiny soft pink bundles of love and tenderness and a wide open future in their little bassinets. She wrapped up the day in her office, tacking next month's completed schedule to the board and locking up.

She took the long route home, pulling into the parking lot at Meadowview House nursing home to see her mother. She looked at the front door until her eyes watered and she remembered to blink, recalling the hole-in-the-wall place she used to have her mom in. It had been the best she could do at the time, which wasn't saying much.

She was 25 when the police found her nightgown-clad mother walking down the median of the expressway, disoriented and barefoot. Nicole was still waitressing then while taking a couple nursing classes at the community college, and she'd come home one night to find an officer sitting in their tiny, dirty living room with her mom. James was out, as usual, and thirteen year old Danny had retreated to his room. The doctors had called it early onset Alzheimer's.

Nicole had dropped out of college and found a second waitressing job to help pay the difference between what Medicaid covered and what the monthly nursing home charges were. It didn't take long to see that her combined income wasn't going to cut it. After approaching James for help and getting nowhere ("fuck her," he'd said, "what's she ever done for us?"), a girlfriend got her an exotic dancing gig at Hot Tamales and she started making more money than she'd ever seen in her life.

Looking back, she wondered if she'd made a mistake petitioning for guardianship of Danny. She was determined to keep their dissipating family together. She'd tried to be everywhere at once: Danny's school events, the baseball practices and games that were so important to him, pushing James to find a job, visiting her mom, all while trying to pay the bills. She'd spun so far out of control over the course of the next few years, she knew she'd failed her baby brothers. She'd never be able to take that off her long list of regrets.

After her own arrest and grueling journey through recovery, she finally told Harry about her mother. He'd already been in touch with James who, miraculously, had picked up the slack while she was incarcerated, and paid the nursing home bills and mortgage. She never asked him where he got the money to do this. The first thing Harry had done once their relationship had changed from attorney-client to romantic was to move her mom to Meadowview House, a private-pay facility, the monthly rent triple what the other place was getting. But you get what you pay for, Nicole thought. At least here, she knew her mother was well taken care of.

I don't have the energy to go in tonight, she thought. Maybe I'll just come back tomorrow or next week. She stepped out of the car anyway. She swished in through the automatic doors, signed her name in the register and headed down two long hallways. Her mother was already in bed for the night at 7:00, covers neatly tucked in under her armpits, the smell of fresh linen, antiseptic and underneath it, old-age and sickness hanging in the air. The private room was tastefully decorated in pale greens and aqua with a nice wallpaper border and soft table lamps rather than the usual institutional fluorescent lighting.

"Hi Mom," she sat in the bedside chair and held her mother's hand, lightly rubbing the tissue paper skin with her thumb.

Her mother turned her head to face her, her eyes blinking slowly. She hadn't been asleep yet, but close to it. She addressed Nicole with polite disinterest. "Yes?" she asked. "Is it time for my pills?"

"Mom, it's not the nurse. It's Nicole," she paused while her mother's gaze dropped and she frowned in concentration. "Your daughter," she added.

Her mother blinked and focused again on Nicole. A minute stretched into two while she waited, smiling patiently and holding her mother's hand. The new medication the doctor had started her on obviously wasn't improving anything as of yet. Finally, a spark of recognition flared in the older woman's face and she said, "Nicole, my Nicki," and squeezed her daughter's hand. "But where's Daniel?" Her eyes moved to the door, searching for her youngest boy.

"He's not here Mom. Just me today," she said, as if Danny came with her to visit all the time.

Irene nodded, seeming to become a little more lucid. "Such a good girl. How's your Harold?" Her voice was quiet and raspy.

"Harry's good, Mom. He sends his love." She moved closer and sat on the bed gingerly, straightening the already smooth sheet at her mother's side. "How do you feel?"

Her mother's eyes clouded over. "What have you done with my Danny? You can't take him from me, I won't let you!" she exclaimed, her tone registering fear and anger.

Nicole stood. Hands in her pockets, she backed away a bit. "Mom, I'm going now. Danny and James are fine. I'll come back another day."

"You tell John that I'll kill him before I let him hurt my son again!" Her mother struggled to sit up, kicking her scrawny legs at the bedding. "We'll be gone soon anyhow," she muttered, more to herself than to Nicole, hands busy knotting and twisting the sheet in her lap. "He'll never find us, you know," she looked back up at Nicole. "You go tell him that, tell him he can't bury everything!"

"I love you Mom," she said, and turned and left the room, not even seeing the nurse zip by on her way down the hall to check into the commotion. She should have known better than to visit at night, when all of her mother's rational thought was used up. Nicole's heart raced and she felt as if her whole body was shaking as she made the long trip through the hallways to get the hell out of there. Her father's face floated in front of her all the way out of the facility, his bulbous, pickled red nose, bloodshot eyes, thick black brows furrowed into his permanently dissatisfied grimace.

This day, from start to finish, was the darkest day she could recall in recent history, at least since before she'd met Harry. She knew--she knew with every furious molecule in her body that she would not be living this day if not for her father. James would not be a thieving heroin addict, because she would not have been a whoring heroin addict who allowed her brother to join her on that road. Her mother wouldn't have lost her mind. Her baby brother wouldn't have lost his; mental illness didn't even run in their family, how did Danny wind up sick if not for the fucked up environment he'd been born into? John Murdock caused this day. If not for him, she could have led Laura's life. Two caring parents. Or hell, even just one. No killing drugs, no side jobs to pay for nursing homes, no group homes for a 20 year old genius. No rape.

Nicole knew as she stepped out into the cool night air, the scent of her mother's dementia still clinging to her skin, that she had to find her father. She'd always wanted answers, but it was more than that. She was stalled, split, living her life in halves.

She felt a hot tear roll down her cheek and it only fueled her anger at the ghost of her father. The entire week since seeing Laura again, something had been nagging at her thoughts and now she saw clearly the solution. Laura worked in the Crime Scene Unit at the County Sheriff's Office. She must have connections. If anyone could help her find John Murdock, Nicole knew this was the way it would happen. In the place it all had started.

Back in the dark comfort of her car, the shaking stopped. She was covered in a cold sweat, chilled now, but flooded with the relief of the decision. She knew she was ready. She would make the call, have Laura put things in motion; she would give her everything she'd collected over the years searching for the monster. She needed to find him. So that she could leave all of this wreckage at his feet, where it belonged. And so that she could walk away. For the first time in years, Nicole found herself hoping the man was still alive.

CHAPTER SEVEN

Laura climbed the front steps to her porch, waving as Steve drove off down her street. She actually felt relieved that he forgot she would be home tonight and had made plans to go with his buddy Ron to a Lion's game. She was looking forward to a nice quiet evening at home with Charlie. She dropped her bags just inside the front door and found him in the living room with her mother. The sight of her mom, colorful vest decorated with embroidered cats, eyeglasses with the little chain attached, holding a video game controller and leaning forward on the couch next to Charlie, seemed both strange and touching to her. Laura bought her house in the same neighborhood as her parents' years ago, and she and Charlie saw them nearly every day. She stood silently and watched them for a moment, their backs both to her.

"Come on, you son of a--" her mom shouted at the screen, apparently upset that her kung-fu fighter was losing.

Charlie laughed and turned to look at his Grandma as she cut off her own sentence just short of the "bitch." He caught Laura out of the corner of his eye and hit the pause button as he jumped up to hug her.

She met him halfway and wrapped her arms around her boy. "Oh, I missed you!" She hugged him tight, and too long, she guessed, because he laughed again as he eased back from her grip.

"Okay, okay, Mom! I missed you too, but geez!"

She stood back and stared at him, positive he looked older in her two day absence. "So how was it? What'd you guys do? How was school?" Charlie had started the eighth grade this fall. It still blew her mind that her kid was in middle school, with high school creeping up too fast.

He headed toward the kitchen, calling over his shoulder, "School's good," as she pulled her mom into a hug as well.

"Thank you so much for staying with him. I never worried," she smiled.

Jane Miller shook her head and shrugged. "Don't thank me, we had fun. And your dad didn't mind either. He loves your satellite dish. He's been over here every evening flipping through the channels."

They followed Charlie into the kitchen, where Jane began pulling things from the refrigerator while he filled Laura in on what she'd missed: too much homework from his too strict math teacher, how his basketball team this season was shaping up, and his Grandma's weakness for late night brownie and ice cream sundaes.

Laura looked at her mother and laughed. “He ratted you out, Mom. Thought you could keep it a secret, huh?”

Her mom shook her head, smiling and smoothing her short, frosted brunette curls before moving to the counter to join Charlie in making what was apparently going to be their dinner: French toast with sliced peaches and whipped cream, bacon and sausage. The kitchen was soon filled with the aroma of frying pork, making Laura’s stomach growl.

“I see you ate well while I was gone,” she kidded her son. It was no secret that Laura’s cooking skills were limited to mostly hot dogs or macaroni and cheese.

“Grandma knows how to make anything,” he told her, “even lasagna.”

The three of them sat around the old Formica table after the food was gone, exchanging chit chat once Laura had filled Charlie and her mom in on her trip, and answered Charlie’s multiple questions about whether she’d gone to the Hard Rock Café (she did), and if she’d gotten him the t-shirt he requested (she had). Laura leaned back in her chair and stretched, stifling a yawn.

“So, you won’t believe who I ran into while I was in Texas,” she told her mom.

Jane raised her eyebrows, mildly interested. Charlie excused himself to go work on his homework and Laura addressed her mother.

“I saw Nicole Murdock.”

Now her mom’s eyes were open wide, staring at her. “Nicole? You saw her? Where? You’re sure it was her?”

She nodded. "I'm sure. She works at Children's Hospital. She's married now and lives just outside Dallas."

"I remember that family so well. Those poor kids. And Irene … such a mouse of a woman. What ever happened to them? They just disappeared one day, years ago, you were sixteen or so, I think."

"We were both fifteen. She says her dad made them run away. He packed them all up and moved them in the middle of the night. And he--" she stopped abruptly. How much of what Nicole had told her was to be kept quiet? Well, she answered internally, who am I protecting anyway? Not Nicole, who wasn't guilty of anything except having a rotten father, and who said herself she'd do anything to see him pay for what he'd done to them.

Jane jarred her gently from her thoughts. "He what, Laura? What did Nicole say?"

"He was just as bad as we always thought, worse, even. He made them all change their names, a couple times, I think, and they moved around a lot. He was running from something that happened here. Nicole doesn't seem to know what, even now. About four years after they left, he shot and killed a man at a convenience store in Texas, and disappeared completely after that. He's never been found." She'd left a lot unsaid, she knew. She met her mom's gaze.

"That man was a monster," Jane said quietly. "I always knew it, I guess. I used to hear him sometimes, carrying on at poor Irene. Even when we called the police, he must've somehow talked his way out of it." She shook her head, remembering, her expression clouded. "I always felt like I should have helped Irene somehow. I prayed over my rosary so many times for that family. What about the boys? And is Irene … well, how is she these days?"

"James and Danny both have their problems. And Irene has been ill. She's in a nursing home." She saw the sadness in her mother's face and searched for the silver lining. "But Nicole is doing great now, Mom. Her husband sounds wonderful, she's got a job she loves and she really seems happy. She'll actually be coming to visit soon."

"Good," her mom nodded, "I'm glad she's doing so well. She certainly deserves it. Make sure to let me know when she's coming, you two and Charlie will have to come over for dinner."

Laura treated Charlie to her laughable video game skills after Jane left. She normally didn't have much time to goof off and play with him, but video games were his passion second only to basketball. Her few days away had refreshed her perspective and reminded her how little time she actually spent doing non-essential activities with her son. She'd always harbored guilt over Charlie's lack of a father, even with her own dad so attentive to him.

She stole glances at her teenage son as they played. His hair was just like her sister Jenny's, a nice chestnut brown and silky straight, falling easily into place no matter what he was doing. He was at least an inch or two taller over the last several months, and his limbs suddenly seemed so long and lanky to her. It struck her how handsome he'd be when he grew up. He'd already gotten a couple phone calls from girls this school year. A positive, outgoing kid, Charlie seemed to take most things in stride, definitely a glass half full person.

She elbowed him gently while making a pathetic effort with the controller to throw a pass. "So tell me about your game yesterday. I really wish I'd been there."

He shook his head at her. "Mom, concentrate!" He nodded at the TV screen. "We won by six points, it was so cool! Everybody was sure the Badgers had it, but our defense was awesome. Coach told Grandpa we're way better this year. Grandma's embarrassing, though."

"Yeah, tell me about it. What did she do?" Laura gave him a sideways smile, certain her mother had been in the bleachers cheering and waving a Gladiators banner.

A week had passed when the phone rang late one night and Laura was thrilled to hear Nicole's voice. She'd wondered if their chance meeting would be just that, or if they really could pick up where they'd left off. Even when she told her mom Nicole was going to visit, she wasn't certain. Her old friend looked the same but she wasn't. As candid as she'd been with Laura just days ago, she wore armor now. Laura had the feeling she'd only scratched the surface of what Nicole's life had been like since she'd known her last.

She hung up the phone happy in the knowledge that some friendships were unbreakable, and now her mind was spinning with the anticipation of delving into the mystery of what had really happened that fateful night so long ago. Nicole asked Laura if she could use her position in the Sheriff's Office to find some closure to the greatest mystery of her life.

She mentally reviewed their conversation from their night out. She'd been an Evidence Technician since she'd finally finished her degree just a few years ago and she found her training and experience were working: she remembered most of the details in spite of the booze and music and everything else going on that night. She could talk to the family, but Nicole's mom wouldn't be much help, Laura thought, almost hearing the click as she switched into work mode. Danny was living in a group home, he'd had some sort of mental breakdown a few years ago. And she'd been very vague about James.

The police had looked into the family's strange disappearance, she recalled them at her house, asking questions, as if she'd have any idea what the hell Nicole's lunatic dad was thinking. The man packed up his family and ferreted them away in the middle of the night, and then disappeared himself four years after that. Who knew what he might have done? She'd have to look into the investigation, if there was one. The Orsonville Police Department back then was tiny, not that it was much better now. Depending on how they handled it, the county and state guys might never have gotten involved at all. But with the confirmation that he was using an alias, making the family keep running … Laura was certain she could make some headway. She could always call on her sister for help if necessary. Jenny was a Homicide detective with the county; it was what got Laura thinking about an alternative to the grueling regime of factory work when she'd felt Charlie was old enough for her to go back to school. She was pleasantly surprised to find she loved the work.

Several days later at the Iosco County Sheriff's Office, Laura stood at the printer waiting for the spread sheet she'd formulated. She'd meant to start working on this immediately but life always seemed to get in the way. She eagerly watched the paper roll out of the printer, ready to get to work. The dates she'd entered from seventeen years ago were September 23, 24 and 25: the date Nicole and her family had been discovered missing and one day before and after. She recalled that it was September when it happened, because it was just before Laura's birthday. She and Nicole had been planning a big slumber party. She'd had the program correlate all misdemeanors and felonies within the county during those three days, sorted in descending order of proximity to Nicole's old address on Maple Street.

Nicole was due in town late tonight and she hoped to have some small piece of news to share, if she was able to start wading through this paperwork. At least, Laura thought, being here in Orsonville might trigger Nicole's memories and help fill in some of the blanks.

The printer finished its job and spit out the final sheet. Laura grasped the fairly thick stack of papers, noting that there were twelve pages, with three or four infractions per page. She strode toward the lab, her home away from home, stopping to grab a cup of muddy looking black coffee on the way. After all these years, she could only imagine the relief and closure it would bring to her friend if the events of that night could be unraveled and John Murdock held responsible. She dropped the report on her desktop to begin.

CHAPTER EIGHT

Nicole's father's shouts carry right through the comforter and pillow, seeping under her fingers into her ears. She thought she was dreaming at first, but is dismayed to learn that's not the case. The yellow smiley face clock on her bedside table reads 11:24 pm, and Nicole can dimly make out Daniel's cries from the other side of her wall. She wonders if James is awake too. She flips onto her other side and peers out her window to Laura's dark bedroom window across the driveway. She sits up to inspect the other visible windows of the Miller's house, relieved to find them all dark. So they haven't woken the neighbors yet.

She hears a glass shatter against a wall out by the living room. Her mother's voice is a high-pitched whine. Cracking her bedroom door reveals her mother perched on the edge of the kitchen chair, coat still on and purse in her lap, face upturned to John Murdock with naked fear.

'I'm sorry, John, I lost track of the time; I didn't know--' her mother's voice trails off as her father cuts in.

'Didn't know what? That you have three kids to think about? That you don't need to be running around at night? Where the hell were you?' She can hear the fuzzy edges to his words two rooms away.

'We were up at the church trying to finish up the crafts for the fundraiser this Sunday,' Nicole strains to hear her mother's reply. 'I thought I'd make it home before--'

The return serve from her father—'Before me?! What are you trying to pull Irene? You keeping track of me?' --covers Nicole's swift footsteps to the door next to hers and the click of the latch as she quietly closes it, snapping on the small table lamp near Daniel's crib. Miraculously, James lay sleeping soundly in his bed on the opposite side of the room. She shushes Daniel as she picks him up, wrapping him in her arms and stroking his tired head on her shoulder. He takes a few final gasping, hiccupping breaths before settling down enough to tell her, 'Want Mama.'

'Shhh, baby, it's okay, Nicki's here now.' She kneels on the floor by the crib and spreads his soft blanket out with her free hand. She lies down with his bear under her head for a pillow and he snuggles into the crook of her arm. She fumbles through the crib slats for his pacifier. Daniel instantly shuts his eyes, tucking his head into her side as he drifts back down to sleep. She gently rests one hand over his exposed ear as she catches the next, maybe the last, phase of the fight from the dining room.

Her mother is trying to reason with him, 'Didn't Nicole have the kids in bed when you got home? I didn't mean to cause a problem. We were talking and I guess it got late,' she finishes lamely.

'Stupid bitches, lost track of time,' her father mutters. 'Tell you one thing, Irene, this is the last of your late night outings, I'm sick of it.'

Her mother's answer comes in a lower tone now, 'Why should you care anyway? You're never here for me.'

The sharp smack followed by a heavy thud jolts Nicole and she reflexively starts to sit up, but Daniel has his little fist clutched in her nightgown and he whimpers at her. Nicole can feel the skittery pattern of her loud heartbeat in her throat as a wave of nausea washes over her. How can she just lie here and do nothing? Her eyes are on the top of Daniel's strawberry-blond head. She thinks of the cordless phone, now unreachable, in her own bedroom. Maybe Laura's family will wake up. Maybe that would be a good thing now, she thinks. She can't see out the window in the boys' room from this angle, and now the baby's breathing is slow and regular, but he's curled into her, making any attempt at escape a bad idea.

She hears the front door slam, her father's car start, and then silence. Is she dead? Did he finally kill her? What if she's lying there, bleeding? Dying? All by herself? Nicole, in full blown panic mode now, uses trembling hands to uncurl each of Daniel's fingers from her nightgown and is about to ease away from him when she hears her mother's soft footsteps tiptoeing past their bedrooms on the way to her own. She thinks, well, she's up, she must be okay, and then thinks, how screwed up is my life, that when my mom can get up and walk to her room on her own rather than lying unconscious on the dining room floor, things must be okay?

The baby's cries jar her, but suddenly it's not Daniel, and her eyes snap open. Nicole lands back in the present and feels the soft plastic of the airplane seat armrests digging under her fingernails. She is on the flight to Detroit. Daniel is grown, not a baby anymore but her baby brother who now towers over her.

She swallowed hard and then took a deep breath, waiting for the panic squeezing her chest to loosen. Movement to her right prompted her to turn her head and she saw the toddler across the aisle wailing in his mother's arms. She forced a smile at him and the rubber bands around her chest began to give way. These dreams had become more and more frequent since finding Laura. She'd asked her therapist for help dealing with them, but so far all the doctor had offered was that Nicole must allow the memories in.

Nicole rubbed at her eyes and yawned, shaking her head a little.

"Good nap?" the teenage boy on her left asked her.

"Mmm—no," she answered, still feeling disconnected after that uninvited walk down memory lane. She and Laura talked on the phone almost every day lately. They'd reminisce about all the crazy things they did together, the crushes they had, sleepover parties, going roller skating every weekend. Later, she'd find herself replaying the darker scenes in her head without even meaning to.

That fight they'd had that night … there were only a few more like that afterward before they moved away, and she had a nagging feeling there were holes in her memory. She remembered that Danny was only about a year and a half old at the time of that fight, because it was just two months later that all three of them had been removed from their home. It had lasted nine days, and for Nicole, it wasn't long enough. There had been, of course, another blow up between her parents, similar theme, but this time Laura's dad had woken up.

He'd actually had the nerve to come and pound on their front door. She never knew what got into James that night, but he flew out of the bedroom and had that door open before she registered what was happening. She'd hurried down the hall but her father beat her to the door, and she saw him grip James by the back of the neck, placing his other hand on the door jamb to prevent Mr. Miller entry, if he had thoughts of trying. She stood helplessly in the living room, watching the meaty fingers of her father's right hand press into James' eight year old neck, as he lied to Laura's dad. She never heard his end of the conversation, but she watched her mother come to stand a little behind her father and nod in agreement to the lies. Yes, they realized it was past two in the morning. No, they didn't mean to be so loud, they were just having a little disagreement, you know how it is, blah blah blah. Mr. Miller finally gave up and left, and her father waited a beat or two before taking James' arm with his left hand, never releasing his grip on his neck, and dragging him back to his room. She still recalled the look on her brother's face as they pushed past her. It wasn't pain, it wasn't fear, but something in his eyes that said, 'maybe next time.'

Child Protective Services was on their doorstep the next day. They were smart, they came early, just after James and Nicole had gotten home from school. They cornered her weak mother who astounded Nicole by totally covering for her father, saying he'd just had a bad day at work, he was a good man, of course he'd never hurt them. But then the social worker and her assistant took each of them into her parent's room in turn, and Nicole did not lie. James did not lie. And the deep purple bruises around the back of James' neck spoke volumes.

They had gone with the social workers then, James staring out the car window away from Irene, who was standing on the porch sobbing hysterically. Nicole held poor whimpering Daniel in her lap and met her mother's stricken gaze unflinchingly. She thought it was probably the first time she'd ever thought to place any blame on her mother for how they lived their lives. Somehow it was disconcerting not to see Irene as the three of them, as a victim. If one of her parents was the bad guy, then the other must be the good guy, right? She wouldn't have drawn two messed up parents, that just didn't happen. But Irene's chance to protect them all had landed right in her lap, and she'd let it fly away.

Laura had said, 'something bad must have happened,' that forced her father to make the family run away. Nicole had always known that too, but had never been able to learn more. On a few mornings, when her father was in a joking mood and hadn't been drinking yet, she tried to ask him, but all she ever got in the way of an answer was 'I was just tired of that Michigan weather,' or 'what, you don't like Boise (or Denver, Phoenix, Houston, etc)?' And once she'd mentioned it in the heat of anger. She'd been dragging her feet after finishing her 5 to 11 shift waitressing, dreading the thought of having to get up for school the next morning, and found him nearly passed out on the couch, stinking of whiskey and cigarettes, with Daniel crying and her mother still at work. She'd actually had the nerve to shake him awake and confront him.

'Hey!' she shouts, just to knock him out of his stupor. 'Wake up, can't you hear Danny crying?'

His head rolls around and his puffy red eyes find her. 'Huh?'

'Why did you have to bring us here? Why did you have to ruin my life? Why did you have to move us away from everything I knew and loved?!'

'You're just a kid, shut the fuck up. Get out of here,' his voice is still groggy.

'I hate you! You're an alcoholic Daddy. I hate you,' she tells him, instantly bathed in a stinging hot flush from head to toe at what she's dared to say.

He sits up and looks at her, almost calm for a moment. Then he is on his feet, his big hands are on her upper arms, and then she is on the floor against the wall. Her head hurts. He is already lying back down on the couch.

She never spoke to him again about why they'd left Michigan, or about why they kept on leaving every time she was starting to get comfortable somewhere. But she'd always known it must have been something really bad, and somewhere in the back of her mind danced the knowledge of what her father was capable of.

That was confirmed for her when she was nineteen and John Murdock shot and killed a man in front of his wife and youngest son. Daniel had been too traumatized to give more than a cursory account, and her mother refused to say a word. Nicole had eventually been allowed to see the security footage, which showed her father approaching the man in the parking lot of a local convenience store. The man backed away with one hand reaching for his back pocket and the other hand in front on him, a gesture of appeasement. Murdock shot the man with a gun that he pulled from under his jacket, and Andrew Clayton was blown back hard onto the ground, darkness blooming around his head on the concrete. The black and white images on the screen showed her father calmly reach down and take Clayton's wallet, then climb into his car with his wife and seven year old Daniel. Daniel, small face pressed to the window of the car during the incident, had slunk down into the back seat as if he was no longer even there.

Murdock was gone within hours and, for all intents and purposes, vanished into thin air. He abandoned his car a few miles down the road, leaving a distraught Irene and nearly catatonic Daniel in it, and police quickly got wind of a stolen car a few blocks away. John Murdock made the common criminal mistake of driving his newly acquired stolen car across the state line into New Mexico, thereby involving the FBI. The ensuing manhunt yielded nothing, and the investigation that seemed to go on for years never turned up anything more than an occasional possible sighting of the man at odd locations in the lower states and finally Mexico, sightings that all proved to be dead-ends.

The FBI monitored Nicole's family's activity and questioned each of them extensively. What they didn't understand about Nicole's father was that he would never dream of contacting any of them after he left. She thought the authorities were probably counting on him missing his family, but she knew the truth. He would be glad to finally be rid of them, and he was most likely too drunk, where ever he was, to experience any pangs of homesickness. The only other good thing that had come out of such a violent act besides losing her father was getting her name back. When the FBI got involved, the fake names her father had assigned them had come into question, and they were able to revert back to their real names at last.

The fasten-your-seat-belt signs came on overhead and she heard the speaker crackle as the pilot made his landing announcements. "We will begin our descent into Detroit Metro Airport in approximately eight minutes. We're arriving slightly ahead of schedule thanks to good tail winds. The weather today is partly cloudy with a current temperature of 38 degrees. We hope you enjoyed flying United Air and look forward to meeting your travel needs again soon."

Nicole tossed her empty cup and pretzel wrapper into the flight attendant's bin as he glided down the aisle with his cart, then turned to watch out the window for their descent, and caught the teenage boy in the next seat staring at her. He blushed a rosy pink, cleared his throat and hastily readjusted his gaze to the window across the aisle. She suppressed a smile.

"It's chilly tonight, huh?" she said to him.

"What? Oh, yeah, I guess. Wonder if we'll get snow early this year?" Now he met her eyes again and she guessed he was only about sixteen or so.

"I hope not. It can wait till I go back home," she smiled, wondering if the woman to his left was his mother. He looked a bit like James at that age, she thought, which instantly woke the tightly curled coil of anxiety that always lay deep in her gut, ready to spring when it came to her brother. The police hadn't turned up any sign of him. There had also been no trace of the stolen Hummer. Harry said he guessed whoever it had been sold to had repainted it and got it out of the Dallas area; most likely, it wouldn't be found unless it was stopped for some traffic violation. Nicole had spoken to the police detective in charge of the case and given him the contact information for the guy she knew used to be James' dealer, but she was told last week that the dealer had known nothing—said he knew nothing—and the police didn't have enough to push him at the moment.

She knew it was a bad idea, but she'd decided to go anyway. Roman Lynch had been the man she'd dealt with when she was in her own deep pit of addiction, and she carried the guilt over James hooking up with him because of her like a ten-thousand pound stone on her heart. She'd tried heroin for the first time at the generosity of one of the girls she worked with at the strip club, and it hadn't taken long for it to get its claws into her. She remembered feeling that she'd been searching her whole life for something to dull the pain of her existence, and it couldn't have come at a better time. Not much seemed to matter when she was high. She had deluded herself into thinking no one knew what she was into, and one night as she'd pulled up to Roman's house in her old rattly Dodge Charger, James startled her by sitting up in the backseat. She'd let out an involuntary shriek.

"Hey, hey, Nicki, take it easy. I just wanted in on the fun, that's all. You got a much better handle on this than I do. Half the time I can't even find my guy." He gave her his charming grin in the rearview mirror.

"James, goddammit, get out of here. I don't know what you're talking about. I'm just stopping by to see a friend on the way to work." Her irritation with him was uncomfortably mixed with the itchy anticipation of what she knew lay on the other side of that front door.

He put his hands up, shrugging. "Okay, so I'm wrong. So what? I'll just come in with you, take you to work when you're ready." He paused, and she could see his mind was working on an angle, a way to talk her into letting him stay. "Come on, Nic, please?" He sounded like a kid to her, not the 21 year old he'd recently become. "I've never even been in Hot Tamales; I promise I'll just stay a little while. I bet you can get me in free."

Nicole's skin had had a life of its own for at least the past six or seven hours, crawling and tingling and achy. She felt like she might vomit any moment, and she was sure her heart was about to pound right out of her chest. She knew she'd die if she didn't get in there and see Roman soon. She glanced back into the rearview mirror. "Fine. Let's go."

She turned back to face James abruptly before she knocked on the door. "You stay in the front room. Sheryl's probably here, you remember her? You just stay and talk to her while I go check on something. You better be there when I'm ready to go." She thought for a second that she heard her father's threatening voice rather than her own as she spoke the words. Then she knocked and they were in and that was that.

Thinking now about how James had come to be introduced to Roman, that heavy black door in her memory tried to wall off the horrible feelings reawakened in Nicole. Guilt and remorse seemed to be the color of her skin lately. Especially since watching James sit so defeated on the floor of her ridiculous sunshine yellow room, in her ridiculous too-huge house. No amount of effort on her part would ever make up for how she'd failed her brother.

When she decided to go try to find Roman last week, she told herself that she owed it to James. A little voice whispered the logical truth: that if James had never met Roman, he still would've continued down the road he was already on, just used a different connection for his supply. But he hadn't. He'd used Roman, and along with Roman's fantastic skill as a businessman came all the other little endeavors the man had his fingers in. Didn't have enough money for the fix you needed? No problem, the first time. It was on the house. A second time? A third? Don't worry about it. Just do this little favor for me, he'd say. I got a friend, just moved here, doesn't know a soul, real lonely. Just go out with him for a night on the town. Dinner, dancing, whatever. He's a nice guy. Or, look, my cousin's ex stole her car, all you have to do is get it back for her. Here's the address, this is when he'll be gone, she doesn't have the key anymore so just hotwire it, no big deal. Lots of favors for Roman. Nicole had only been desperate enough to do a couple favors for him, and now she squeezed her eyes shut, forcing herself not to think about them.

She didn't tell Harry she was going. She went last Tuesday morning after Harry left for work. She waited only until eleven, when she knew Roman and his pals would be just starting to get up for the day, but would all still be at one of three houses she knew of as hang outs. The first house was a dead end; the windows and doors were boarded up, and when she poked her head in through a broken board over a front window, she saw the house was empty and deserted. The second house turned up an associate of Roman's whom she was surprised to see was still among the living and not in prison.

She shoved her shaking hands into the pockets of her denim jacket as she met the gaze of a man aptly named Hugo, his hulking frame filling the doorway. She'd dressed down for this task today, leaving all of her jewelry at home, hair in a ponytail, no makeup, jeans and a t-shirt and old tennis shoes on. He knew her right away.

"Well, if it ain't Nicki," he shook his head. "Look at ya." He made no move to let her in. "What do you want?" His voice was gruff but not unkind.

"I'm looking for my brother," she answered, and was thrilled to hear her own voice come out strong and unwavering. "James. You seen him lately?"

"Nope, can't say I have darlin'," he drawled. "Now, what you been up to? Didn't I hear you went and married a cop or something like that?"

"No," she said, not elaborating. "Listen, Hugo, James is in trouble. He needs me. Can I talk to Roman?"

"Roman ain't here sweetheart," he winked at her. "Even if he was, I don't think he'd be too happy to see ya, if you know what I mean."

She fought the suicidal urge to push past him and demand to see Roman. She'd never make it past this mountain of a man. "Okay. Can you get him a message? Please?" She knew she sounded desperate and she didn't care. "I'm really worried about James, and I need to find him. Please."

"I'll give Roman the message." He nodded, as if agreeing to himself to actually do it. "You need to get ahold of James. Got it."

She quickly pulled an old grocery list from her pocket and flipped it over, writing her cell phone number on the back. "Please ask him to have James call me, if he sees him. It's important." She handed the paper to the big man and cupped his forearm with her other hand. "It means a lot to me, Hugo, thank you," she told him earnestly, feeling the weight of her past fall away in view of the person she'd worked so hard to become. She wasn't the sullen, indifferent junkie this man remembered anymore. People do change, she thought. Maybe James can.

Hugo gave her a curt nod. She turned to leave and hadn't taken the first step when she felt his enormous hand close around her upper arm. Her heart stopped for a second and she forgot to breathe as she forced herself to turn back to face him.

He gazed at her through cool blue eyes in silence for what felt like an eternity. She could see the muscle in his jaw pulsing. She began to feel lightheaded and reflexively sucked in a deep breath, willing herself not to faint. The bond they'd shared three years ago had obviously taken a hit with James' current downward spiral. Nicole realized that Roman must know she'd sent the police to check up on the activity here after her brother stole Harry's car. Hugo finally spoke, not loosening his firm grip on her arm.

"Don't come back here again," he told her in his gravelly voice. "Next time, things might not be so nice for you." He watched the color drain out of her cheeks and added, "I know what you been through, Nicki. I don't wanna see you hurt. Get out of here, and don't come back, please, okay?"

She nodded, unable to find her voice. He let go of her arm and she tried not to run as she made it down the steps back to the safety of her car.

The plane rolled smoothly onto the tarmac at Detroit Metro and the "no electronics" sign blinked out, so she turned on her phone and checked her email to make sure there were no problems at home. She'd stopped by her mother's nursing home and given the staff a huge plate of cookies as well as all of her contact information and travel dates, and asked to be notified of any problems or changes, or even if her mother just wanted to talk to her. She'd left the nursing home and driven to Danny's group home, where she pretty much repeated the process, and was pleased to find that he was up for going out for dinner with her before she headed back. It was the nicest evening she'd had with him in a long time. He was doing so much better now. He seemed to be on the right combination of medications to control the schizophrenia, and he was working two days a week and taking a few college courses as well. He asked about James and Irene, and even nodded calmly when she tentatively told him that James was gone again. Nicole was relieved to see no new messages since yesterday. Things had been fairly uneventful lately, she was sure Danny and Irene would be fine.

She gathered her things and followed the stream of travelers into the terminal, feeling a strange mix of excitement and fear as she thought of her return home after all these years. Laura would be waiting for her at baggage claim. And then it was on to Laura's house, which she'd said was a mere three blocks from where they'd grown up, where Laura's parents still lived. Nicole had been so elated this past week planning and packing for the trip, she was dismayed now to feel that familiar knot in her stomach, letting her know that in spite of her best efforts, she couldn't hide from the fact that this trip was more than just a happy visit with an old friend. It was a homecoming of sorts, to a place where she'd left a frightening amount of horrible memories behind.

CHAPTER NINE

Laura's day had had already been a busy one, and it wasn't even half over yet. She'd gotten Charlie to school, made it to court for a case she was giving evidence testimony in, finished up in the lab, and finally zipped in the door to set about cleaning house for Nicole. She didn't know why she was so nervous. It was only Nicole, and they'd talked or emailed nearly every day since she'd left Texas, but she had a feeling that Nicole probably lived in a very nice house and she wanted her friend to like her own little home. She changed the sheets on her bed, putting on the brand new dusty rose comforter set she picked up yesterday, along with a few new raspberry colored throw pillows. She wished she had a real bedroom set, with the matching bed, dresser and nightstand, like the ones she always envied in magazines, but it just wasn't in the budget.

She finished tidying the bedroom, dusted around the knick-knacks on her dresser, cleaned both bathrooms, vacuumed and swept, and even set a dish of chocolate candies and a new cinnamon-vanilla scented candle on the bedside table in her room. She tossed a set of clean sheets for herself onto the pull-out couch in her office before firmly closing the door on her clutter.

She finally climbed into the shower, at last slowing down enough to think about this evening. Steve had invited her to dinner. He'd called last night and told her that he had something important to talk to her about, and he had dinner reservations at The Embers, the nicest restaurant in the county. He pointed out that she didn't have to pick up Nicole from the airport until after 10:00, and he really needed her to come, especially, he said, since he knew that once her friend was here she'd be pretty busy.

Now she couldn't stop wondering what all this was about. She and Steve did not, as a rule, go out on dates much anymore. Not ones that involved dinner reservations, anyway. Weekdays were busy for both of them. When they did eat out, it was usually at the joint in town for burgers or nachos and a few rounds of pool. She actually liked this system. It meant Charlie could come with them if he was interested, and, it being such a small town, was a nice way to catch up with everyone while they had a drink or two waiting for a table. She and Steve had not gone out for a pre-planned dinner anywhere in months.

Laura knew what the most obvious explanation was, but she didn't want to assume, and she also wasn't sure she was prepared to deal with it. What if he proposed? Although they'd been dating for a couple years, she just wasn't sure if she imagined herself with him in the long term. But then again, she thought, nobody's perfect. She knew from her married sister and other friends that everyone had little issues and problems in their relationships. She could be waiting the rest of her life for Mr. Right.

She took extra care in applying her makeup in the vanity, choosing a glossy pink lip gloss to go with the smoky eyeliner she'd traced around her eyes and fluffing up her hair. Not bad, she thought, before crossing the hall to look through her closet and considering changing her mind about the "not bad." Which dress wouldn't show the ten unwanted pounds that always seemed so prominent around her middle? She looked longingly for a moment at the silky red dress that Nicole had bought her before deciding on a safe black wraparound that didn't pinch or bunch anywhere and made the most of her good cleavage and legs. She grabbed a pair of black strappy sandals and revised her opinion once more as she checked her reflection on the way out of the room, pleased to realize that her satisfaction with her figure seemed to improve slowly but steadily as she grew older. Sure, it'd be nice to be thin like Nicole, but she was finding herself more and more comfortable in her own skin.

The drive to the restaurant flew by too quickly while she waffled back and forth in her thoughts, wondering whether she was right about what Steve wanted to discuss, and if so, what she would say. She knew he was a good man, but it drove her crazy that he always seemed to coast, accomplish only what he absolutely had to by applying the smallest amount of effort possible. The live-in situation with his mom was a perfect example. Bonnie was just as able-bodied and energetic as her own mother, and when Laura was feeling petty she told herself that Steve only stayed so he could continue to have her cook his meals, wash his laundry and basically take care of him. When Laura was feeling generous, she was more likely to take the stance that he was simply being a good son, looking out for his mother. And then Bonnie would do something to aggravate her again, like the two days in a row last week that Steve had to cancel his snow-blower shopping plans with Laura because his mother decided they hadn't been spending enough quality time together lately.

On Wednesday he told her, "I'm sorry, Babe, but she's been working on dinner all day, I just can't run out now. Tomorrow, okay?"

And the next day there was another Bonnie excuse. "Fine," Laura told Steve through clenched teeth. There was no way she was going to be the bitch who denied her boyfriend's mother time with her son.

She went snow-blower shopping herself on Friday in order to catch the end of the sale. She paid extra for delivery, thinking angrily she'd be damned if she was going to beg Steve to use his truck to get it home for her. He appeared in her driveway on Saturday afternoon to inspect the machine, telling her she paid too much and she should have gotten the Toro instead. She suppressed the urge to sock him one.

He must have picked up on her hostile vibe because he eagerly offered to go into town and grab Chinese for their dinner, and returned an hour later with their food as well as two movies she'd wanted to see. He even attempted to watch the first one with her after dinner, falling asleep halfway through. When she nudged him awake at ten o'clock so he could head home, he went into the hallway first and she found him changing the light bulb she couldn't reach. The part of her that knew it was possible he was still kissing up to her was overpowered by the part of her that was gratified to see him remembering a promise, no matter how insignificant.

This was the image in her mind when she walked into The Ember's lush lobby to meet Steve for their date. She handed her coat to the maître de and followed him through the restaurant to a cozy table nestled into a corner by a glowing fireplace. Steve had arrived before her, and he stood as she approached, giving her a quick kiss and actually pulling her chair out for her. The waiter glided over and she ordered a White Zinfandel, and Steve asked for another beer. She smiled across the table at him.

"Nice place, I've never been here before."

"Yeah, it's got a great reputation. The prime rib is supposed to be really good," he said, and then, as if noticing just now, nodded his head appraisingly at her appearance. "Wow, you look gorgeous."

She chuckled self-consciously. "Well, I figured why not get dressed up, just for fun? So what's new? How's work?" She felt very odd; they'd just seen each other two days ago, and this fancy restaurant, with the "something important to talk about" hanging over them, was making her feel awkward.

"Oh, fine. We might get that new account, it'll mean more work for me but that's all right, it's been slow lately." Steve now worked for a computer software company as an online support person. Much of the time, he was able to work from home, with occasional trips to a nearby satellite office.

"Well, that's good," she said. "I hope you get it."

"So," he clapped his hands together abruptly, startling her, "I want to talk to you about something."

She nodded, "that's what you said on the phone. Is everything okay?"

Now he chuckled nervously, which was not like him. "Fine, fine! Laura," he began, reaching across the table to take her hand, "we've been together a while now and lately I've been thinking…."

She nodded encouragingly, finding she couldn't speak at all around the huge lump that seemed to have lodged itself in her throat. She picked up her wine glass, hoping a sip might calm her nerves.

"Well, I've just been thinking that we spend a lot of time together, we do everything together, and you know I love you, and--"

He stopped suddenly as Laura was gripped by a choking fit, her swallow having gone down the wrong way. She coughed and wheezed in air, rapping her chest in attempts to clear her throat, and felt tears run from the corners of her eyes as her face turned red and she struggled to stop choking. Steve half stood, then sat again uncertainly, then finally stood and came around to her side, patting her between the shoulder blades.

"Are you okay?" he asked her, continuing to pat her back as the coughs finally slowed and she took a shaky breath in, nodding her head and staring hard at the candle centerpiece, knowing all eyes in the restaurant must be on them. He went around and took his seat, leaning on the table toward her. "Are you all right, Laura?"

She gave him a weak smile. "Yes," the word came out in a croak, and she cleared her throat one more time. "Yes, I'm sorry, Steve," she said, shaking her head and rolling her eyes at her timing. "I'm sorry, you were saying?"

He rubbed the back of his neck and smiled at her, taking her hand again. "I think the time is right, Laura," he paused, and the moment was heavy with anticipation. "I want us to move in together."

She blinked at him. Another moment crawled by, and she thought, did he really just say that?

Her lack of reaction must have been disconcerting to him, as he reached over and took her other hand in his, giving them both a little squeeze. "I know it's a big step, but I think we're ready for it, and it just makes sense all around, don't you think?"

"Steve," she said, and then closed her mouth. What could she say? It was hard for her to believe this man had known her for two years. He'd never once spent the night at her house, as she firmly escorted him to the door before midnight every time. They'd never gone away together, not even for a weekend.

"Steve," she started again, "I can't do that."

"Why not? If it's a question of where, we can work that out. If you moved in with me, it'd probably be easier, then I could still watch out for my mom, but I'd consider your place too…."

Laura squinted at him, almost wanting to laugh. "Steve, I can't move in with you!" She glanced around, not meaning for her voice to sound so loud. This was just so ridiculous.

He looked puzzled. "Laura, lots of people live together these days. It's not a big deal. I'm sure Charlie would be fine with it."

She shook her head. There were so many reasons why she wouldn't be fine with it. Most obvious was that moving in together after dating for over two years felt like a step backward to her. "I don't think it's a good idea. For one thing, Charlie would have to change schools if I moved in with you. Have you even talked to your mother about this?" Laura heard the bitter emphasis she involuntarily placed on mother.

Steve nodded eagerly, clueless. "I did! She's fine with it. You know I've got two bedrooms, and you can have my side of the garage, I'll use the carport. Mom said she won't mind."

He looked genuinely hopeful and all she wanted to do was wipe the smile off his face. When she'd thought he was going to ask her to marry him, she wasn't even sure what her answer would have been. Now it irritated her that this development was making her so angry at him.

"Steve." She pulled her hands from his and locked eyes with him. "Listen to me," she said, thinking, this is like trying to reason with a toddler. "I will not move in with you. You cannot move in with me. It will never happen. Ever," she emphasized the last word.

He was quiet, and she felt a twinge of sympathy as she watched him deflate somewhat. "I get it," he finally said.

"You do?"

"Yeah, I get it. You thought I was going to ask you to marry me, didn't you?"

"No!" she shot out, the lie leaving her lips before she could stop it. "Of course not! And that's not what this is about. I'm not trying to pressure you. I thought we were fine the way we were." She watched him scrutinize her silently.

"I haven't even thought about marriage," he said quietly, almost to himself.

She found she was clenching her teeth and forced herself to relax and take a deep breath. How in the world could he not have considered the idea of marriage in all this time? Laura couldn't begin to imagine living with his mother. And she knew right then and there that she could not imagine Steve living in her house. He'd given her startling clarity with his faux proposal.

She took a large swig of her Zinfandel, this time having no problem swallowing. It was uncomfortably quiet at their table. She sat back in her chair and let her eyes rest on the crackling fire, and Steve did the same. The waiter eventually materialized with their prime rib, and she pushed hers around her plate for a while as Steve attacked his with gusto. She nibbled a little of the meat and some of the rice pilaf, but found her appetite was ruined. Now, as she watched Steve polish off every last morsel while avoiding looking at her, she just felt empty. It was time she was honest with herself. She knew he loved her. But they were too different, and at different points in their lives.

Steve finished eating and pushed his plate to the side, leaning back in his chair and stretching. He found her eyes and smiled tentatively at her. She returned it with her own small smile.

"Hey, Babe, let's walk over and grab a cappuccino at that place you like. Let's forget about all this, okay?" He waved at the waiter for their check.

"Listen, Steve," she said, "I don't know. I think we want different things. I think--"

He cut her off, "No, Laura, don't get upset over tonight. It was all a big mistake. It'll be fine. You're right, things are great just the way they are," he told her, standing as if to usher her out and delay any further conversation.

She went along with it, and walked with him the two blocks to the coffee shop in tense silence, but she felt dismayed at how the evening and their relationship had deteriorated in front of her eyes. Outside the coffee shop, both of them holding their cardboard cups, she faced him before they went their separate ways to their respective cars.

"Steve, I need some time. I think we need some time apart," she told him as kindly as she could. Her words came out in tiny puffs of smoke in the cold night air.

He didn't look surprised, just defeated. "Laura, if it's marriage you want, maybe it's something down the road for us. I'm just not ready now," he said, shaking his head.

She took his hand and held his gaze. "It's not that. I swear to you, Steve, that's not it. I just don't think we're right for each other, I think we both know it. We've been nice and comfortable, coasting along, but I don't think this can ever really go anywhere. I'm sorry," she told him sadly.

He stared at her wordlessly for a long moment. His shoulders slumped a bit and he sighed heavily and shook his head. "I can't believe you're doing this. Is it just because I live with my mom? Because I can fix that, we can figure it out."

She stood on her tip-toes and kissed him one last time, kindly. It was a short, tender kiss, and she placed her hand on his cheek. "It's not only that. I just don't think it's going to work for us." She took a couple steps back and wrapped her scarf once around her neck, trying to give him the cue that they were finished here. He was a boy, she realized. He was a boy in a grown man's body. She needed a man. Or no one at all.

He frowned. "I think you're wrong," he told her angrily. "You're making a mistake. You were lucky to be with me." He set his cup of coffee down on the brick ledge that ran the length of the row of little shops and pulled his gloves on. "Well."

She cleared her throat. "I'm sorry Steve," she said quietly, feeling just that, very sorry that she was hurting him. She was bracing herself for the rest, the sadness and pain she remembered feeling when she and Charlie's father had broken up. She knew it was coming and part of her welcomed the thought. Maybe then she wouldn't feel so guilt-ridden at hurting Steve, once she was miserable as well.

They parted and walked in opposite directions to their cars. The entire two block walk back she searched internally for the grief, the sense of loss that comes when a long love affair is suddenly over. By the time she got back to the car, she realized that all she felt besides guilt was relief. Why had she spent so much time in a relationship that she must have known on some level was not a good fit?

She buckled in, turned up the heat to dispel the chill in the air, and flipped through the radio stations until she found one playing upbeat classic rock favorites. She cranked the volume, and by the time she pulled up to the curb at Detroit Metro Airport, she'd talked herself out of the major portion of the irritation she felt with herself for putting up with Steve's juvenile crap for so long. Next time, if there was a next time, she'd just have to be smarter.

She scanned the clusters of people with luggage waiting for rides, not finding Nicole. She was right on time. The flight came in at 10:10 pm and it was 10:20. Nicole was probably still on her way to baggage claim. Laura pulled out into traffic and slowly circled around once, reappearing at the curb five minutes later and firmly putting all thoughts of Steve out of her head for now. This time her perusal of the travelers along the curb revealed Nicole, red curls whipping about in the wind, a sharp black coat cinched tightly at her slender waist. She was peering into each waiting car and looked a little anxious. Laura threw her car into park and jumped out, running over to her with a huge grin. Nicole saw her coming and opened her arms, and both women were flung into a happy, spinning, bouncing embrace.

"You were lucky to be with him? He really said that?" Nicole shook her head and took a sip of cocoa. They were comfortably settled on Laura's sofa and it was just past midnight. Nicole's bags had been deposited in Laura's room, and both women were far too excited to sleep.

Laura nodded. “Yep,” she paused a moment. “I feel sorry for him though. He’s not a bad guy. I just … I hope I did the right thing.”

“Well, now, I think you did love him, right? But we’re not 22 anymore, I’m sure you’ve thought of that. What about long term? Can you see yourself with him?”

Laura shook her head slowly. “I don’t know why it took me so long to figure it out. I should have known he wasn’t right for me a long time ago, we’re too different. There were so many things about him that drove me crazy. I kept thinking it’d change, he’d change, grow up….”

Nicole tucked her legs under her and wrapped the blanket from the armrest around her shoulders, turning to face Laura better. She rested her arm along the back of the couch and squeezed Laura’s shoulder lightly. “Maybe you were just seeing him the way you wanted him to be. Tonight he opened your eyes for you. You know, you never once even mentioned Steve the entire time we were texting or talking on the phone. I didn’t know there was a Steve. What does that say about your feelings, hon?”

“I know. I know you’re right, I know I wasn’t happy with him. It’s just--why do I feel so … alone … now that he’s gone?” She didn’t miss him. She wasn’t sorry about breaking up with him. So why was she suddenly sad?

“Oh sweetie,” Nicole soothed in her low Texas drawl, “you wanted him to be the one. Now you know for sure he’s not. It’s never easy saying goodbye to what might have been.”

Laura sat quietly, nodding. She knew Nicole was right. Finally she said, “It wouldn’t have worked between us. I know I’m better off.” She smirked a little at Nicole. "I can do better, right?" She tossed her head and rolled her eyes, mocking herself, shaking off her delayed dismay the best she could.

"There ya go! Better than a guy who isn't ready for marriage, forgets to think about your son, has a lazy streak a mile long--from what you said, now, no offense--and is still suckling at his mama's bosom? Ya think?"

Laura laughed and shook her head. "Okay, you nailed it. Anyway, I didn't want to spend your first night here whining about my disastrous love life. How have you been? How's Harry? Is there any news about James?"

"No, nothing. It's only been a little while, but I have a feeling we won't hear anything until next time he needs something. I haven't told Danny about him stealing our car, I don't see the point. It'll just worry him more, and really, nothing's changed. James is still a junkie and now he's a car thief too." Her voice sounded uncharacteristically hard.

"He's had a hard life. I'm sure some of this is beyond his control, the James I knew was a good person," Laura said softly.

Nicole's eyes flashed. "A lot of people have a hard life. Even if you do screw up, you pick yourself up and start again. It's not so bad, what he's done, it's not irreversible. Why can't he be stronger? He's giving up, and I can't stop him."

Laura sat without speaking for a beat, then opened her mouth and closed it again. She wanted Nicole to see that James was possibly just lost, struggling, that he needed help and maybe he'd be all right one day.

"What? What do you want to say?"

They'd always challenged each other like this, Laura remembered. Never any trouble talking about the hard stuff. Laura had depended on Nicole for that level of honesty, and she knew Nicole felt the same.

Nicole frowned at her. "Say it."

"I just … I was just going to say, you can't judge him too harshly, you don't know what it feels like to be fighting the demons he's fighting. He can't want to be like this. I mean, I can't even imagine being so physically dependent on a drug that it makes you do things like steal from your family."

Nicole continued to frown at her, and Laura resisted the urge to back pedal. She watched, stunned, as Nicole's eyes filled with tears.

"I can. I can imagine because I've been there." The words came out in a whisper, Nicole's mouth set in a thin, quivering line as she watched Laura for her response.

"Oh," was all she said, unable to keep the shock out of her voice and struggling to rearrange her features into a more benign reaction.

Nicole's shoulders slumped and she squeezed her eyes shut, rubbing them with a thumb and forefinger, the gesture eerily reminding Laura of her friend's father. "I'm sorry," Nicole said softly. She looked again at Laura. "I'm really sorry. I wasn't going to tell you like that." Her chest heaved with a deep, hitching sigh. "I know you're right about James. I'm just tired. I'm so tired."

Laura pulled Nicole into a hug. “Don’t apologize. I’m sorry. I’m sorry you have had this life, so much darkness to deal with. I don’t know how you’re even here, talking to me.”

Nicole shrugged. “I had help. And Harry and I are trying to help James, but he won’t--or can’t--take it.” She shook her head, deflated. “Oh, I think I need to get some sleep.”

“I know,” Laura said, “I didn’t mean to keep you up, or for this to get so … heavy.” She waited until Nicole met her gaze. “I’m glad you’re here.”

CHAPTER TEN

Nicole's first day flew by and turned out to be more enlightening than either woman had counted on. She woke that morning with nothing more in mind than reacquainting herself with their tiny town. After an indulgent sugary breakfast at Millie's Diner, they planned to head out to a local ranch where they'd both taken horse-back riding lessons as kids. Their riding plans were waylaid when Nicole walked up to the counter to pay their bill. That red hair was like a beacon: she was instantly recognized by a good number of the restaurant patrons. The town was a throwback in that respect. The little diner, the town hub during daytime hours, held only four small booths on each wall. The rest of the space was taken up with several large twelve-seat tables. It was common practice to join whatever group was already there, most of the town was acquainted with each other anyway.

Laura found it an ideal way to pass the time and have some lunch. She'd noticed that at the other restaurant in town, part of a chain, the townspeople played musical chairs, catching up with the news, who was dating whom, who got kicked off the PTA for overt drunken behavior, or who the next town clerk might be. The seating at Millie's just seemed to make more sense.

To Nicole, who'd not only left Orsonville but lived in almost twenty other locales in the past seventeen years, this approach to dining was foreign and disconcerting. She purposely steered them toward a booth when they'd come in. They sat rather inconspicuously and enjoyed small talk and pancakes until she got up to pay.

A few old acquaintances politely stopped Nicole to say hello, and they'd almost escaped when she felt a light tap on her shoulder and turned to find Sissy Donovan, arms held wide, huge glossy pink grin on her face. She looked like she was about to burst.

"Nicole, I can't believe it," she all but shrieked. "What are you doing here? When did you get in? Where are you staying? Come here right now!" she demanded and pulled Nicole into a quick hug, then pushed her back to appraise her. "Oh, you bitch, I am so jealous, look at that bod, how do you do it? The kids ruined my figure," she rested her French-manicured hands on what Laura supposed she thought were wide hips but were easily narrower than her own. "I've missed you! What in the world happened to you?"

Laura politely murmured that she needed to run next door to the pharmacy, looking apologetically at Nicole, and left her with Sissy. Laura didn't mind leaving them. Sissy had been in the popular clique a lifetime ago in school. Nicole had effortlessly floated among all of the little segregated groups, always dragging Laura kicking and screaming along with her.

She walked at a leisurely pace along the sidewalk, taking the long way around the block to stop in at the post office on her way to the drugstore. She'd never be able to move from this town, she thought. The pharmacist, the grocer, the video store clerk, librarian, bank teller, gas station attendant all knew her by name; plus she'd miss the convenience of having everything within a two block radius.

It struck her now, standing in line at the drugstore, that it had grown too quiet around her. She glanced over her shoulder with an odd prickly feeling and caught the clerk from the liquor store nudging and leaning in toward the older woman beside her whom Laura recognized from the school. Both were staring at her and their eyes darted elsewhere as she gazed at them. She frowned, turning back around. Was she being paranoid, or were the pharmacist and his assistant unusually quiet as well? Normally there was a steady banter behind the raised counter. This had to be because Nicole was back, she thought. But how in the world could the news have traveled so fast?

She stepped up to the register when it was her turn, set her bottle of multivitamins on the counter and smiled warmly at the cashier, a plump woman in her mid-sixties who'd been behind that register since Laura was a child. Ruth gave her a perfunctory smile and no small talk, no 'how are you today?'

She looked back to find the line of six people behind her whispering and consulting each other. It stopped abruptly.

She threw her hands in the air as she addressed the queue of people behind her and the three behind the counter as well. “You people are unbelievable! All this just because Nicole Murdock is back in town! Is the sneaky, hushed behavior really necessary? If you want to know something, say so!”

Instead of shame or embarrassment appearing on the faces of the patrons, confusion seemed to be the universal emotion.

Finally Ruth asked, “You mean Irene’s girl, Nicole? Back in town? When did that happen? How is she, bless her heart? Are the boys with her?”

Laura stood, deflated and bewildered, and leaned a hand on the counter, moving to one side so Ruth could help the person behind her. She shook her head. “If you didn’t know about Nicole, then what’s all this about? And don’t say nothing, ‘cause the second I walked in here you all shut right up.”

She was looking at Ruth for the answer. She was reasonably certain the woman would have it, as she seemed to know nearly everything about everyone in this fishbowl of a town. Now Ruth’s manners returned, and she reached across the counter to give Laura’s hand a little pat. “We’ve heard about you and Steven. I’m so sorry.” She patted her hand once more before returning to her task and ringing up the next customer.

Laura blinked rapidly at Ruth. Her throat closed. "Thanks," she croaked, before turning toward the door, muttering a quieter 'unbelievable' on the way out just as she heard the remark, "Poor guy, I heard he proposed and she dumped him!"

Laura felt her face flush hot and bit her lip to stop an angry retort. She exited as if she hadn't caught the ignorant snipe. Stupid, small minded small town, she thought. She could definitely do without this crap. She scoffed at her Mary Poppins idealism only moments earlier. If it weren't for Charlie and how well adjusted he was at his school, she'd move away in a heartbeat.

She couldn't imagine how they all knew about the breakup less than eighteen hours after it occurred. Most likely Steve had gone over to his buddy Ron's house to whine about what a bitch she was, and Ron and his wife had seen fit to broadcast the albeit skewed news. Laura was still fuming when she saw Nicole rounding the corner, heading toward her.

"Hey," she called, smiling. "You didn't have to take off, you know."

They met and Nicole pivoted so they could walk back toward the car. "I know. I just needed to grab something from the drugstore."

"So where is it?"

"What?"

"Whatever you went to get?"

Laura looked down at her empty hands. In her haste, she'd left the vitamins on the counter. She let out a frustrated little growl and rolled her eyes. "I forgot it. I'm big news today, I guess, at least until everyone gets wind of your return. Steve's already been spreading the news that we broke up, and his poor-me act is going over big."

"Oh, hon, I'm sorry. You know, that's the bad thing about this town--"

Laura cut her off. "I know. Believe me. Nothing happens around here without it getting chewed up and spit back out by the rumor mill. I'm making sure Charlie gets the hell out from under this microscope as soon as he graduates."

"My goodness, woman, change your mood! You know it's not that bad. Anyway, Sissy actually had a great suggestion. She asked if we've been by to see my mother's friend Helen Bourdain. Remember? She lived right over on Second Street … "

"I know, I remember your mom always going over there to knit or play bridge or whatever else all those church ladies were up to at the time. Didn't your mom go, like, every Thursday or something for a while? They had some women's group. I don't think we ever paid attention enough to know what it was."

Nicole nodded. "You're right, I do remember a standing weeknight appointment, she'd get dressed up and talk about the ladies teaching her to crochet or something. Sissy's mom is still close with Helen, and I guess Helen has always worried about my mother, about what happened to her." They reached Laura's car and sat chatting, letting the heater warm up while the car idled in the parking lot.

Laura exhaled, tapping her fingers along the steering wheel. "I wonder if Helen knows something. Like you said, those ladies in the church group were close. Want to go see Helen?"

Nicole answered without having to think about it. "Yes. Can we go now? Shouldn't we call first?"

"Probably." Laura made a quick call to her mother, who still had the roster of all of the neighborhood association members, and jotted down Helen's phone number. She held her cell phone out to Nicole. "Do you want to make the call or should I?"

Nicole and Laura were welcomed into the older woman's spotless home twenty minutes later. "Girls! Come in, come in! Dave," she called over her shoulder to her husband, "put on another pot of coffee, would you?"

"Yes, Dear," came the response from the kitchen.

Laura offered an apology for stopping by without much notice and Helen waved it away, leading them into the living room. "You have no idea how happy I was to hear from you two."

Nicole smiled at Laura. "I'm going to gain 20 pounds before I go home, I can already tell." Laura rolled her eyes and Helen laughed.

"You could use it," she patted Nicole's hand. "I was so worried about what became of you, you and your brothers. Your mother and I were very close, you know. Is she…." Helen didn't seem able to finish the sentence.

Nicole quickly reassured her, "She's in Texas, she's fine." Helen caught the hesitation in her voice and looked at her questioningly. Nicole shrugged a little, meeting the woman's eyes sadly. "She's sick, Mrs. Bourdain. She has Alzheimer's. She's in a wonderful facility. Most of the time she's fairly content. I don't believe she remembers very much of what we all went through."

Helen was nodding. "I'm so sorry, Nicole. Maybe it's a blessing that her memory has failed," she added quietly.

Nicole couldn't disagree, in spite of the knowledge that all of this would be so much easier if her own mother could simply explain her past to her in pieces that made sense.

Laura leaned forward a bit. "We thought that, since you and Irene were friends, you might be able to help fill in some of the holes for Nicole. We're trying to unravel what might have led to the family disappearing, and possibly track down her father."

A dark cloud passed over Helen's features at the mention of John Murdock. She caught it and cleared her throat, composing her expression. "You … you want to find him?" She kept her voice level but there was fear in her eyes.

"I want him to be held accountable for what he did to my family."

Helen nodded again, looking at Nicole with new respect. "I'll tell you what I know about your mother during that time. I wish I could tell you what happened the night you disappeared." She shook her head. "I thought about it the next morning, of course, we all did; trying to remember small details of the few days before, anything unusual, anything that might help find you. The police back then, Nicole," she softened her tone at this, "they just weren't that concerned with your family up and moving away like that. Sure, it got looked into, with the house standing empty and all, but what it came down to was the authorities assuming your dad got a new job somewhere else. They figured he wouldn't want to wait around trying to sell the house for less than what he paid for it. Times were tough back then. But I--we--were worried. I hated to think of you and those little boys out there somewhere, without a soul to watch out for you but your poor mother." Helen paused.

Her husband had come to stand quietly in the doorway and now he spoke. "I had a cousin who was an officer with the Village of Orsonville back then. When a week or two passed and nothing was being done, I asked him to look into it personally. He couldn't find a thing. There were four automatic teller withdrawals the first two days you were gone, three of them from out of state, which took the bank account down pretty close to zero. And after that, there was nothing. I had him check again a few months later because Helen was so concerned, and there was still nothing. Considering the way your father got when he drank, I asked Lou to go over the police blotter for that night, which I'm sure the other detective had done too, and he even widened the territory an extra ten miles to Perry, but it was fairly uneventful. A couple bar-fights, a dui, a domestic dispute or two, but nothing that raised any red flags, and nothing he could tie to your dad."

Nicole was amazed at the concern these friends of her mother's had had for her family. "Wow," was all she could manage, taking it all in. "Well," she said after a moment, "I think that all makes sense, except I'm surprised they didn't find anything to connect him to from that night. And

I'm sure your cousin wouldn't have found any trace of him. I've told Laura he made all of us change our names, more than once actually, and I know he always found work 'under the table'—being in construction made that easy to do." She shook her head and gave him a grateful smile. "I can't tell you what it means to know how hard you both tried to find us," she extended the thanks to Mrs. Bourdain as well.

Helen took Nicole's hand now. "There's something else you should know," she said, glancing at her husband, who nodded his unspoken encouragement.

"I still don't know if this is important or not, but it's weighed on me all these years, especially the possibility of your dad having found out."

The room suddenly became much smaller around Nicole. She could see something coming, a dark storm closing in on the horizon, moving much too fast. She wanted to stop it, or at least get the hell out of the way. If she just opened her mouth and told the woman to stop, stop talking, she might halt the moment in its tracks. She didn't need additional reasons to be disillusioned in her parents. But she sat, frozen, and listened.

"This is not something I ever wanted you to know, but it may be important." Her pause was heavy with trepidation. "We think your mother was seeing someone."

Nicole blinked at her. "Seeing someone. Like a doctor?" She knew as she said it how stupid it sounded.

"Another man. I think it had been going on for a while, but as far as I knew, they were just good friends. Your mother said she enjoyed talking with him. It might well have been just that, I can see how your mother would've needed a … friend, some attention," she said gingerly, concern furrowing her brow as she gauged Nicole's reaction.

The silence seemed to stretch on, from a minute to two, until Nicole wasn't sure she could break it. She swallowed hard, closed her eyes for a long moment. She felt hot tears sting the back of her eyes and fought them. Not now, she thought. She hid behind that black shield, embraced it. Not now. She knew she couldn't hide forever, but for now she would. When she'd regained her composure, she directed her question to Helen's husband. "Did your cousin know about this? Did he look for leads related to this?"

Dave nodded. "We told him what we knew. But even with that, nothing turned up. And no one but Helen even seemed to know anything about it. No one in this fishbowl of a town," Laura's eyebrows went up at this, "could seem to recall even seeing your mother around much unless it was with your dad or you kids."

Nicole nodded. "I had no idea. I just…." She turned back to Helen. "Do you know who it was? Please. If you know anything, even a first name, you have to tell me," she pleaded.

Helen shook her head. "I don't. I think your mother took me into her confidence because she needed a little help with what to tell your dad on a few occasions. She asked me to cover for her, if he were to ask about our church events and such. I'm sorry now about how I reacted. I made sure your mom knew I disapproved. She didn't tell me much after she knew how I felt."

Nicole felt let down, like she'd just glimpsed the beginning of the end of this, and then had it snatched away. Was she making more of it than it deserved? Not if Daddy knew about it, her voice, the voice from her childhood, answered in her head. Abruptly, she stood, looking at Laura.

Laura took the cue and stood as well, setting her empty coffee cup on the tray. "Thank you so much Mrs. Bourdain," she told the woman sincerely.

Nicole gave the woman a quick hug, saying, "I really appreciate your honesty, thank you. It might help."

Nicole was quiet in the car for a long time, stewing over the new information and all of the unsavory possibilities now running through her mind. In all of her imaginings of what had happened to her family, she'd never expected something like this, and definitely not from her mother.

"Are you okay?"

Nicole sighed. "Sure. Story of my life," she shrugged, "for real. It's always something. I think I've made my mother an innocent victim for far too long."

Laura reached over and squeezed Nicole's hand. "Nothing your mom could have done justifies your dad's actions. Not that night, and not before or after."

Nicole nodded. "I know that. You know, you're very lucky to have what you have." Laura knew exactly what Nicole was talking about. "I can't deny the fact that I've missed out on something vital where family is concerned."

"You have. Without a doubt. But you have a second chance, with Harry." Laura paused, weighing her words. "Have you thought about whether you'll have kids?"

Nicole was silent. As far as she knew, she'd never have a chance at a fulfilling parent/child relationship. She leaned back into the front seat and turned her head, facing away from Laura. She might never have her own child. Maybe she wasn't meant to. Maybe whatever sick, diseased part of her dad had made him the way he was was also in her. Maybe she shouldn't ever be a mother.

She bit down hard and squeezed her eyes shut. Not now, she thought. That feeling crawled over her chest, rubber bands tightening around her ribcage, and she tried to choke back a sob that found its way through her clenched teeth. Nicole pressed her eyes but couldn't stop the tears that finally streamed down her cheeks. Her shoulders shook with mute sobs and she covered her face with her hands, so ashamed. She had a beautiful life now, didn't she? A husband who loved her. How selfish to want to bring a child into her screwed up family history. Addiction, abuse, mental illness. Secrets and lies. What could she hope to pass on to a child of her own but misery?

Nicole pressed her forehead to the cool car window and felt Laura's hand on her shoulder, rubbing in slow, soothing strokes. The car had stopped. Nicole wanted to sink into the passenger seat and disappear. She couldn't give voice to all of this. She wouldn't tell Laura about her fear, of becoming a mother or never becoming a mother. Of becoming her father. There was no solution. She had no idea how to be a parent. Maybe it would never matter. She kept her skin on the cool glass, the sobs finally starting to slow.

"Hey," her friend said. "Hey, it's okay. It's all going to be fine. I promise you, Nicole," she whispered. "This is a lot for anyone to handle. We'll figure it out. I'll help you."

Nicole breathed in a deep, broken gulp of air and slowly turned her red, tear streaked face to Laura.

Laura hadn't seen this Nicole since that last day, on her porch steps. The look in her eyes was agony, torture. Defeat.

Laura grabbed her and pulled her into her arms, afraid. She didn't want to see this Nicole. This Nicole was gone, healed … but she wasn't. Laura hugged her friend tightly.

Nicole spoke first. "Okay, all right now." She chuckled. "That's enough," she sniffled, drawing back a bit. "I'm okay, really."

Laura rummaged in her purse and produced a tissue for her. "Jeez. I don't know," she studied Nicole. "I think maybe you don't understand what that word means."

Nicole smiled in spite of herself. "Yeah."

"Tell me what you're thinking," Laura said.

Nicole swallowed hard. She couldn't answer.

Laura squeezed her arm lightly. "Please. Please let me help you."

Nicole shrugged. "We can't get pregnant. Harry and I. We've been trying and it's not happening."

"Oh." Now this made more sense. "Well, for how long?"

"Two years."

Laura smiled. "That's not so long, you know. I mean, I'm sure it feels that way. But a girl I work with just got pregnant after trying for five years!" That didn't sound as encouraging as it had in her head, Laura thought. "My point is," she rushed on, "you can't give up. And they can do a lot now to help you. Have you seen a specialist?"

Nicole shook her head. How could she tell Laura what she was really afraid of? When she couldn't even admit it to herself without falling apart? "No."

"Well there you go. That's your next step. So many people go through this, Nic. You'll be a wonderful mommy someday. I know it."

Nicole closed her eyes and nodded. She opened her mouth to tell Laura, to say the words aloud, but they wouldn't come. She felt sick. "I hope you're right," she said instead.

Laura watched her worriedly, waiting for more. She knew there was more, she just didn't know what it was.

Nicole cleared her throat and turned once more to look at Laura, and she knew the subject was closed.

"Sorry. That was just--" Nicole sighed and shook her head. "I know I'm lucky to have what I do. Danny's doing better. Harry is amazing. And now you. I have to remember I'm lucky."

"You had no other family, did you? Grandparents, aunts, uncles … . I don't recall ever seeing any other family around when you lived here."

"My mom's parents lived in Prague until they died twenty years ago or so, and my father's parents both died before I was born. The only family left here is his sister."

"I forgot all about your aunt. Is she still around, then? Didn't she live somewhere the other side of the state?"

Nicole nodded. "I've thought about looking her up while I'm here. This is terrible, but I don't even know if she's still alive. We rarely saw her when we lived here, and the last time I spoke to her was a month or two before we moved. She used to be in Benton Harbor, about three hours from here."

"Well," Laura said, "We can try to find her, if you want. I can get you an address and phone number."

Nicole was quiet for a moment before responding, considering. "I'd like to think about contacting my aunt, I'm not sure yet that it's a good idea. She wasn't the nicest person when I knew her as a kid. But I'll do it if you think it'll help us figure out what happened here." She felt a chill run up her spine, a small measure of anticipation, knowing that she could actually make some headway into the greatest mystery of her life.

CHAPTER ELEVEN

Nicole had been staying with Laura for exactly a week the morning the flowers arrived. Nicole answered the door as Laura was in her office/make-shift bedroom going back over the spread sheet she'd formulated again, looking for a way into the puzzle of that night. She needed a few quiet hours and she knew something would jump out at her, a starting point. For now she and Nicole were on their way to the outlet mall to do some browsing.

She heard Nicole call from the front room, "Somebody loves you," in a sing-song voice.

Nicole appeared in the office doorway bearing a gorgeous arrangement of pink roses. "Laura's got a boyfriend," she chanted, looking for a moment like the twelve year old Laura remembered, possibly chanting those same words, when she'd gotten her first crush on a boy named Tony Barzetti.

"I can't believe him," she muttered. "He waits a week and sends flowers, like that's going to take care of everything? He just doesn't get it! He wasn't even listening!"

"These are from Steve?" Nicole's eyebrows went up. "I, uh, kind of got the impression he was a tad peeved with you last time ya'll chatted. You know, right before he blabbed to the whole town about your breakup?" She began searching for a card, pulling one out from beneath the wrapping. "Well, now, let's see," she began, sliding a fingernail under the flap before Laura snatched it out of her hand.

"Of course they're from Steve. This is classic Steve. He can't make a decision until someone kicks him in the ass and forces him to, and even then he takes his sweet time. I tried to explain to him that it wasn't just about the marriage issue. He thinks he can put a Band-Aid on this and everything will just miraculously be solved!" Laura tore the envelope the rest of the way open, muttering, "If he thinks he can just send flowers and suck up--"

She stopped abruptly, reading the card. Nicole stood in the doorway waiting, her anticipation growing as Laura flipped the card over to continue reading on the back. Crimson began to creep into Laura's cheeks until she was blushing from one side of her smile to the other and then some. Nicole bounced up and down a little, jamming her hands in her pockets to keep from ripping the card out of her friend's hands. When Laura finally looked up, Nicole grabbed the small card and read:

Laura, Don't know if you remember me, but I haven't been able to stop thinking about you since we met at the airport. I was the annoying guy trying to no avail to get you to go out with me. I would really love to see you again. The offer to have coffee still stands, anytime. Just call me. Yours, Adam

His phone number was squeezed into the space at the very bottom. Nicole raised her eyes to Laura's, clearly excited.

"This is the guy? This is Airport Hottie? God, listen to him! He's absolutely smitten! 'Just call me yours, Adam.'" she finished in a breathy voice, placing the emphasis in all the wrong spots.

Laura couldn't keep the grin off her own face, and she silently told the inappropriate guilt tugging at her conscience to take a hike. She wasn't betraying Steve. She deserved to be happy about this. She could feel the heat emanating from her cheeks and forced herself to take a long, slow breath, still smiling like an idiot. She felt like a teenager again, this was crazy. It was just flowers and a card. But she'd pushed Adam to the back of her mind very shortly after they met and hadn't allowed herself to think about him since that day. Now, with the aroma of the roses wafting around her, a snapshot of the man's intense blue-eyed gaze appeared in her mind. Why would a nice, intelligent, strikingly handsome man like Adam be interested in her? She might as well have "expired" stamped across her forehead, she thought. Her haircut was the ten-dollar special at Fantastic

Sam's, her clothes were ten years old and so out of style they'd be back in fashion soon, she knew she wore that perpetually exhausted my-life-is-my-kid look without even meaning to. But now this, his words....

"You're doing it again," Nicole broke into her thoughts. "You're a million miles away, hon. What's going on in there?" She gently tapped Laura's temple, smiling.

Laura shrugged self-consciously, "Nothing. I don't know. It's … it's weird, don't you think?"

Nicole shook her head and couldn't help rolling her eyes up to the ceiling. "You are incredible, you know that? You're exactly the same as you were in ninth grade. I know what's going on in there: Why would he like me? I'm too old, fat, ugly—help me out here, hon, what am I missing?" She was joking but Laura could read a trace of irritation in her tone.

"No! That's not what I was thinking! I was just wondering why he would track me down like this after what? Almost a month? We only spoke for a few minutes."

"Well apparently you shared a moment, darlin', get a clue. He made an impression on you, you told me about meeting him before you ever told me about Steve. And I believe this," she waved the card and jostled the flowers still in the crook of her arm, "means you made a big impression on him. Why *wouldn't* he be interested? Take a look in the mirror once in a while, for God's sake!"

Laura's gaze went to the mirror over her bureau.

Nicole let out a frustrated little groan as she threw her hands up in the air, turning toward the kitchen to put the roses in water. Calling back over her shoulder, she said, “I was speaking figuratively. Give yourself some credit—aside from the fact that you’re a very pretty woman, you’ve got brains and personality to spare.”

Laura, still feeling a little disoriented, followed her into the kitchen to protest but thought better of it as she watched Nicole trim the stems of Adam’s roses and arrange them in a vase.

Nicole finished and looked up at her. “Now, would you please get over yourself already so we can go bra shopping? You promised we’d go check out the new mall days ago. And on the way we can discuss when you’ll call Adam and what you’ll say.” She flashed her dazzling smile at Laura as she swished past her to the front door.

If the two women had known what would be waiting on the front porch for them when they arrived back home, they might have chosen to stay and shop for more than just bras and shoes. As it was, the trip did take the majority of the day.

It was already dark at 7:00 when they rolled into the driveway to find a figure sitting on the shadowy porch steps.

He stood when they came to a stop, and as he approached, Laura sighed, “It’s Steve. What is he doing here?”

She stepped out of the car and he paused about five feet away. “Hey Laura.”

“Steve.” She waited, aware that Nicole had gotten out as well and was quietly gathering their packages from the back seat.

"I need to--I wondered if I could--" he stammered, his eyes darting to Nicole.

"Steve, this is Nicole. Nicole, Steve." Laura's mother had raised her to have good manners, no matter what the circumstances.

Steve nodded briefly at Nicole before focusing on Laura again. "Laura, I need to talk to you, could we--" he tipped his head toward the house.

Laura hesitated. "What do you want, Steve?"

"I just want to talk to you, please. Could you hear me out?"

Laura's eyes went to Nicole, who gave a barely discernible shrug with raised, questioning eyebrows. It was her call.

"All right, let's go in," she said, noting that the house was dark, which thankfully meant Charlie wasn't back from dinner with her parents yet, although he would be soon. She didn't prefer a scene on the front lawn, and she had a feeling Steve was going to be heard one way or another.

She hung up the coats and turned the thermostat up a touch to dispel the chill in the air. Nicole deposited their bags in Laura's bedroom and stopped back in the living room, finding Laura perched on one arm of the easy-chair, her arms crossed over her chest, while Steve sat stiffly on the couch opposite her.

Nicole announced, "I'll be in the kitchen."

"Well," Laura said to her former boyfriend.

"Laura, listen, I know things got blown out of proportion the other day."

"Uh-huh. Nice number you did on me in town. You've got everyone's sympathy vote, you know."

"I didn't say anything!" he said defensively. Laura merely cocked an eyebrow at him, a trick she'd learned long ago to help weed out Charlie's little white lies. Not surprisingly, Steve seemed to respond to the same tactics she used on her teenage son.

"Look, I miss you. I think we should give it another try. It was a stupid fight. It didn't mean anything. I was a jackass, and … I really miss you, Babe," he leaned forward earnestly, and she was surprised to find sadness in his eyes.

Now she took in the scruffy beard he was sporting, the faded and stained jeans with holes in the knees, his flannel shirt wrinkled and misbuttoned so that it sat askew on his frame. His mom's slacking on his laundry, she thought, and instantly regretted the mean-spirited jibe, even if it did remain unspoken. He looked like he hadn't slept or showered in days.

She gave in and went to sit beside him on the couch, resting her hand on his forearm. "Steve, what's going on with you?" She didn't like seeing him like this.

"I've had a bad week," he grumbled. "I'm not sleeping, I'm not eating … I just miss you Laura," he appealed to her. "I need you. Please come back. I'll change. Things will be different, I promise."

Laura rested her elbows on her knees like him and pressed her eyes with her fingertips. Why was he doing this to her? She couldn't stand seeing him this miserable. But she had not been happy with him. How would things be different?

"Steve, I can't come back. I miss you too, but there were too many problems, I really think we're not right for each other. We don't make each other happy."

"But you do make me happy," he protested. "And I know we had problems. But I'm going to move out. I've already been looking at apartments. And I'm going to be more reliable, you can depend on me now, I promise."

His brown eyes searched hers desperately as he made his plea. He took her hands in his and she stared at them, his strong tanned hands folded around her paler ones.

"We've been together a long time, Babe, give me another chance."

She felt her reserve softening in light of the two years they'd spent together. What had they really fought about other than his mother issues and his immaturity? If he was going to work on these problems.... She met his sad eyes without speaking for a long moment. She knew he did love her.

"I need to think." She saw a burst of hope flash across his features and was quick to squeeze his hands, saying, "Steve, I said I'll think about it. I'm not saying yes. I just don't know," she shook her head, feeling her gut churning unpleasantly. Damn food-court nachos, she thought.

He stood abruptly, his hands up in front of his chest, fingers splayed wide. "I know, you're not saying yes, okay. But you're saying maybe. I'll go. You think. Please. And I mean it, it'll be different, I'll be different." He paused, then leaned in and kissed her on the cheek, giving her a whiff of body odor covered ineffectively with Chaps cologne. He was out the door before she could say anything more to him.

Nicole tactfully remained in the kitchen until Laura came and sat at the little table with her, dropping her body heavily into the chair and sighing. She looked apologetically at Nicole.

"I'm sorry, my life is usually not so dramatic. If you'd caught me a couple weeks ago, you would've been bored to tears!" She gratefully took a sip of the hot tea Nicole had made for them.

Nicole laughed and shook her head. "My gosh, what are you going to do? How do you feel about all that in there?" She waved her hand toward the living room.

"I don't know ... when we broke up, I was so relieved. It felt like something I'd needed to do for a long time. We never seemed like a good fit, you know?"

Nicole nodded, "I know what you mean. Like, you liked the idea of him, but when you're with him, it's not the same?"

"That's it exactly! When I was with him, he irritated the hell out of me most of the time! I was constantly disappointed in him. He never thought about me or 'us' first ... I think maybe it was the same way with him, now that you put it like that. He liked having the girlfriend, but only when it was convenient," she mused.

Nicole was quiet. She struggled to keep her thoughts to herself. This was Laura's love-life, Laura's potential future. She had to come to her own conclusion. At least she's on the right track, she thought.

"But he's not a bad guy," her conflicted friend said. "We were together a long time. He seems like he really has changed a little already."

A tiny exasperated sound escaped Nicole.

Laura looked sharply at her. "What?" she demanded.

"All right, I can't help it! You've got to take a step back and look at the big picture, Hon! When were you ever happy with that guy? Why didn't you ever mention him to me in all of our chats? Why do you set the bar so low? Give yourself some credit, have a little self-confidence for once. He's not good for you, Laura, and you deserve better, you deserve somebody great." She looked at her, adding, "maybe somebody who's got his act together, is motivated enough to pursue you, seems to know what he wants...."

Laura shrugged, not offended or even surprised at the outburst. "I don't know what to do. And it doesn't help, hearing from Adam, 'cause now he's in the back of my mind." Her mind raced with thoughts and possibilities she wouldn't have considered a week ago.

"What if I just meet Adam for that coffee? That'd be all right, wouldn't it?"

Nicole couldn't help laughing. "Honey, you're a single lady. You can do whomever--I mean whatever--you want," she winked at Laura.

Laura blushed and snickered. Shaking her head, she said, more to herself than to Nicole, "No, I can't. I need to figure out what I want. I don't want to be thinking of falling back on Steve if Adam and I don't hit it off. I need to sort through all this and figure out what I want before I call Adam."

"You always were too sensible for your own good. Just don't wait too long to call Airport Hottie, you seem to have really clicked with him."

They left the empty coffee cups and talk of romance in the kitchen when Charlie arrived home, and it wasn't until nearly three in the morning that Nicole got the phone call which would ultimately change her life forever.

CHAPTER TWELVE

Nicole grabbed the cell phone before the second ring, out of a deep sleep, well trained from years of worrying about Danny, her mother, James--all the people in her life who seemed to hold a precarious position in the land of doing-just-fine, thank-you-very-much. She fumbled it, dropped it, and did a slow slide out of Laura's fluffy, flowery bed straining to reach it under the night stand.

"Hello," she said breathlessly, finally attaining a sitting position on the floor by the bed.

The gruff voice on the other end could be mistaken for no other, she recognized Hugo instantly and felt her heart give a sickening lurch as she knew, was certain, that James was dying or already dead.

"Nicki? I'm calling about your brother."

She heard her own sharp gasp as he paused, and struggled to breathe normally so that she could ask him what she needed to.

"Please. What's happened to him?"

"I took him to the hospital, Nicki. He showed up here yesterday, wantin' a fix and freaked out of his mind. Don't know what else he was on, but I ain't ever seen him like that--"

She cut him off, she couldn't help it. "Hugo, is he alive?" She began to sob, couldn't help that either. "I'm sorry, just tell me, is he--"

"He was alive when I left him. He got shot, got into it right out back with some punk kid been hanging around here, didn't even care about the gun. I'm sorry, Nicki. He's at Dallas General. I took off once they rushed him in. Sorry I couldn't do more, but you know how it is. Roman will kill me if he knows I talked to you." He paused again. "You need to get home fast. I told him you would come," he added, more gently.

She nodded, her face hot with tears, and then remembered to answer him. Drawing in a shaky breath, she whispered, "Thank you. Thank you for taking him. I'm coming home right now." She heard the click on the other end. She felt the strangest combination of disgust for the lifestyle that may have gotten her brother killed, and immense gratitude for Roman Lynch's right-hand man, who may have just saved her brother's life.

Nicole stood and was nearly floored again by a powerful wave of nausea. She sat quickly on the bed and bent at the waist, willing it to pass, she didn't have time for this, and only dimly registered that it was the second time it had happened this week. She mentally pulled herself together. She needed to go home, had to get a flight, get a ride to the airport, should she wake Laura yet? She picked up her phone and did what now came naturally whenever she needed help: she called Harry.

He answered on the sixth ring, mumbling a sleepy "mmm?"

"Harry," she said, her voice breaking. He heard it, that catch, and was fully alert.

"What's happened? Are you all right?"

"I just got a call, James has been shot." She stopped cold, thinking, damn, now how am I supposed to know that? He'd be furious if he knew she'd been in contact with her old cohorts, had gone anywhere near that life again. Harry would never fully understand her connection to Hugo.

"Shot? When? Where is he? Who called you?"

"He's--" her thoughts raced. "He's at Dallas General, they called, he had my number in his wallet. It happened tonight. Harry, I have to get home. Can you get me a flight, quick?"

"Let me make a call. Talk to you in a minute."

In the time it took Harry to arrange a charter flight from Lansing to Dallas leaving in an hour, Nicole had packed up her suitcases, tidied Laura's bedroom, and zipped quietly around the house gathering loose odds and ends of hers. She wasn't due to leave for two more days and had gotten pretty comfortable. She took the call from Harry, then tiptoed down the hallway to Charlie's room to slip a hastily written goodbye note under his door, and headed back toward Laura's office.

When she'd roused her friend and given her a chance to get her bearings, Nicole perched on the edge of the futon and, doing a lousy job at maintaining her calm, briefly explained why she was leaving at 3:30 in the morning.

Laura pulled her into a tight hug and consoled, “He might be okay, Nic, it sounds like the guy got him to the hospital pretty quick, right? Call me as soon as you know anything.”

Nicole nodded, swallowing hard.

“You’ve got to get to the airport,” Laura exclaimed, jumping out of bed. “Let me get my keys--”

“Hon, it’s all taken care of, there’s a car out front,” she gestured as she stood and headed toward the doorway.

“A car? Oh, okay, got it.”

Nicole shrugged, “Harry spoils me. I could have called a taxi. I’m sorry to cut our visit short like this, we were having so much fun, and I wanted time to see what you came up with about my dad….” her voice trailed off.

Laura followed her out to the car in her pajamas and handed Nicole’s carry-on bag to the driver. “Call me, so I know you’re okay.”

Nicole squeezed her hand through the window, “I will. Thank you, Laura,” she called before putting the window up as the sleek black Cadillac rolled quietly down the street.

The drive to the airport and the two and a half hour flight into Dallas seemed to take years. She was flooded with relief to see Harry waiting as she stepped onto the tarmac. They were seated comfortably in the limo, speeding through the dark night to Dallas General Hospital, before Harry told her.

"There was no James Murdock brought into the ER tonight."

She searched his face, worried for a moment that Hugo had given her the wrong hospital, until it hit her: he was probably a John Doe, or whatever they called them. She could bet he didn't have any ID on him, certainly not a wallet, when he was left in the ambulance bay. Her expression spoke volumes, apparently, because Harry continued.

"There was a John Doe, though, registered earlier tonight. I went by and checked on him. James went into surgery twenty minutes ago, Nicole. The doctors won't tell me anything other than he's lost a lot of blood."

Harry's eyes were dark tonight, so dark the iris nearly swallowed the pupil. His concern for her overpowered his anger at being lied to, but she wasn't off the hook. Those twin lines were there between his eyebrows. She opened her mouth to tell him and then stopped.

"Nicole, you'd better start talking, because anything you have to say has got to be better than what's going on in my head right now."

She met his accusing tone head-on, her pale green eyes locking onto his nearly black ones. "I gave my cell phone number to Lynch's guy before I left for Detroit. I went there and asked him to please call me if he saw James," she told her husband unflinchingly. "He's my brother. No matter what else, he's my brother, and we protect each other. We have to. I should have been here. Maybe he tried to see me. Maybe if I'd been here…."

Harry's arms went around her instantly as she collapsed without warning into harsh, uncontrollable sobs.

"I can't let anything happen to him, this is all my fault! We didn't survive my father to lose him like this," she wailed, drawing in big jerky breaths as she fought to calm down.

Harry held her, stroking her back, silent. Her breathing slowly became more even, and he took a tissue from the console and wiped her eyes and cheeks for her. He cradled her jaw, his face inches from hers.

"None of this is your fault. You can try all you want to protect him, Nicole, but you can't live his life for him."

She closed her eyes, laid her head on his chest. She could hear his heartbeat under her ear. His chest was warm through the brushed cotton of his shirt. She kept her arm wrapped around his middle, soothed by the rhythm of his heart and his strong arms enveloping her.

Images of her own past played against the dark screen of her eyelids like a bad silent movie. Why James and not her? How many times had she been at Lynch's when things got rough, somebody got too paranoid or too desperate and the situation got out of hand? Why had she escaped the worst of it, the things she'd seen James through these past few years, when she'd been an even easier target for disaster?

She squeezed her eyes more tightly shut, trying to will away the one memory that would never go away: the night she was attacked and raped after work four years ago. There had been a gun then, too. She tasted the metallic, nauseating fear on her tongue again as she remembered the barrel pressed against her throat while one of the regular customers at Hot Tamales battered her, the sickly sweet stench of liquor oozing from his cruel mouth, from his clammy skin. At the time, she'd been so terrified that at one point she'd sworn it was her father glaring down at her, and she was sure she was going to die, or maybe--mercifully--was already dead.

It wasn't until he'd finished with her and was panting stupidly on top her that she was able to reach the knife she always kept in her purse. She drew back and plunged it as hard as she could into his left side. The sensation of the blade halting a bit through the skin and then sinking into warm, wet meat set her to shaking uncontrollably. As he flailed about trying to remove the knife, it was all she could do to get out from under him, onto her feet and run, run as fast as she could on legs made of jello. She didn't stop to retrieve her torn panties or the shoe she'd lost in the struggle. She didn't stop until she'd run the thirteen blocks to Roman Lynch's house, straight into the huge, capable arms of Hugo, who, without a word, had gently wrapped her in a blanket, helped her into his beat up old car and driven her to the hospital.

The time between Hugo carrying her into the ER, waiting with her until he was certain she would be okay, and when she met Harry, was still fuzzy. She hadn't even known there was anything visibly wrong with her until the next morning when the nurse helped her into the bathroom and she caught sight of herself in the mirror. Her left eye was swollen shut, the right one was red from a burst blood vessel, her lip was split in two places, and her face looked twice its normal size. Her hair was matted and felt greasy from the asphalt behind the club, where she'd been walking to her car when that monster grabbed her. She took in the deep purple color of most of her face and the ugly black stitches just under her collar bone that must have been put in while she was unconscious, hanging onto her IV pole for support. Her knees seemed to dissolve and she felt like she might throw up.

When the nurse had successfully gotten her back to bed and was busy with the IV, Nicole finally noticed the quiet, solemn man in the suit standing in the corner. She was able to read the kindness in his eyes before turning on her side, her back to him, trying to regain her composure. She couldn't stop shaking. Her face was soaked from tears that ran like stinging rivers over her battered cheeks. As vain as she knew it was, no one had ever seen her like this before. She'd never felt this terrible, this dirty and worthless before in her life, not even growing up with John Murdock for a father. Whoever this man was, she didn't want him here. He carefully placed a chair a good three or four feet from her bed and sat down.

He waited until her sobs weren't audible anymore and the shaking in her shoulders had stopped. Clearing his throat, he spoke in a low tone to her back. "Miss Murdock, my name is Harry Peterson, and I'm an attorney with the Public Defender's office. There is a detective in the hallway who'd like to take your statement about what happened last night." He paused, but Nicole couldn't bring herself to face him. "Just so that you know, the man who attacked you was picked up outside the club shortly after you were brought to the ER. He's in intensive care--the knife wound punctured his lung." Something in his voice made her gingerly turn over and meet his eyes. There was little change in his expression, but he gave her a little nod that helped alleviate her fear: what would happen to her now for stabbing the asshole?

"You acted in self-defense, no question about it, and it's a good thing your aim was good. This might be the same guy who raped and nearly killed another woman a month or so ago at a different bar--you may have heard about it, over in Nixon?" He paused, watching her, before continuing. "We got an anonymous tip that we might find the guy behind the establishment last night. He'll be an unwilling guest of the state as soon as he's well enough to leave the hospital."

Anonymous tip, Nicole thought. Hugo. Her heart swelled with gratitude for her unlikely champion. She finally spoke. Her voice sounded hoarse, and her swollen lip mushed the words together. "What about…." She didn't know what she wanted to ask first. Will I be in trouble for stabbing him? What if he lies and denies everything? What about the heroin in my jacket? Her eyes darted around the small room, looking for her meager belongings.

Harry nodded his encouragement. "What about what?"

"What if it's his word against mine? He had a gun. I couldn't get to the knife until after…." Her eyes filled with tears again and she wished with every ounce of her beaten body that she could erase the last twenty-four hours. The last twenty-four years.

Harry opened his hands, palm down, in front of him in a calming gesture. "We already have enough forensic evidence that it won't matter what he tries to say happened." He couldn't keep the pity out of his expression. They both knew what he meant. "They may try to charge you with possession, but we can deal with that."

Nicole's face fell and she dropped her head, trying not to think about how they'd gotten the forensic evidence. Her mind seemed to go on standby mode in crises, long-trained by her father. She had no recollection of last night after Hugo had leaned down and carefully kissed her forehead, the fluorescent lights of the ER making her eyes hurt. And now she'd be charged with possession. She supposed it could be worse, though it was hard to imagine. She felt like she'd been run over by a truck. And that was only her body. She thought it would a long time before she could meet her own eyes in the mirror. "I'm sorry," she whispered, not knowing why she was apologizing to this man, feeling foolish the minute she'd said the words.

He reached out as if to pat her hand, but stopped, letting his hand settle instead on the side rail of the hospital bed. "You've got some work ahead of you, if you're up for it. We can set you up with a treatment program. You might surprise yourself." He stood abruptly.

She looked up at him through her good eye, very aware now of how grotesque she must look. "Thank you, Mr. Peterson."

"Harry, please," he told her, smiling for the first time.

Nicole nodded, acknowledging the work involved in getting clean. "I will try. I can't--" She stopped, swallowing, trying not to cry, especially when the tears stung her cuts so much. "This isn't--this can't be me, it's not me. I need help. I'll really try," she told him earnestly, not understanding why she felt so compelled to make him see the good in her. She only knew she'd been on this road for far too long, fueled initially by the need to support her family, then by the need to get her next fix. Look what you've become, she thought. This is the end of the road.

The promises she made to herself and the support and faith that emanated from Harry were the driving force behind her rehab, behind the hard uphill climb to beat the heroin, then the Methadone addiction, and to put that destructive lifestyle behind her. She'd been clean and sober a full year before Harry asked her out on a date.

Nicole had realized two or three months into her recovery that she was falling in love with her lawyer. She'd fought the feelings at first, telling herself it was just gratitude at finding someone who believed in her. It was in Harry's office, while going over her testimony one last time before their court date, that she felt the true depth of her feelings for this intelligent, handsome, caring older man. He'd leaned over her to point out something in the paperwork, and she found herself looking for an excuse to just touch him.

From then on, she tried hard to hide her emotions around him, knowing for certain that he was out of her league (just look at how he'd come into her life, she told herself). She was painfully aware of the attention he seemed to draw from the female associates in his office. There was no way a former drug-addict stripper could compete. But she did catch herself gazing a little too long into those dark changeable eyes of his, or studying his firm build under those rich Italian suits while he wasn't looking. The court date came and went, Chuck Waisner was convicted and sentenced to ten years for the charges against him in

Nicole's case and the other woman's, and eight months after she'd met Harry, she was faced with the prospect of never seeing him again.

He took her to lunch to celebrate the sentencing, and before the salads even arrived she suddenly reached across the table and laid her hands on his forearms; she couldn't take it anymore. She had to tell him. "Harry, I need you to know something."

He pulled his arms back a bit and took her hands in his, the intensity of his gaze rattling her resolve.

Her heart raced and her mouth felt like a desert as she quietly told him, "I don't want to say good-bye to you." It was all she could think of to say, after the many times she'd rehearsed how she'd convince him to give her a chance, to see her differently than just an unsalvageable junkie or crime victim.

She was surprised to see color creep into his cheeks as he cleared his throat. "Nicole, you're not my client anymore. Our professional relationship is over," he began.

Now it was her turn to flush, as she stammered, "I know that, but I was hoping--I wondered if we could--I know I'm not the type of girl you normally would--"

He cut her off, squeezing her hands a bit as he said, "I'd really love to get to know you better, Nicole. You're an amazing woman, and I'd like to see where this might go, if you're at all interested." He tipped his head, adding, "I know I'm a good deal older than you, so if that's something you'd rather not get into, I understand."

Nicole hadn't realized she'd been holding her breath until it came out in a joyful little laugh. "Harry! You have no idea." Impulsively, she stood and leaned over the small table, resting one hand on his warm, rough cheek, and kissed him on the mouth. It was a slow, gentle kiss at first, quickly gaining intensity and surprising them both.

She pulled back self-consciously and sat, scooting her chair in and smoothing the napkin back onto her lap. It took forever to work up the nerve to meet Harry's eyes, and when she did, she was overwhelmed by the heat she found there.

Harry leaned forward onto the table, taking her hand again. His voice was deep and quiet. "I need to see you Nicole. I think we'd be good together. But," he paused, causing her instant worry, "you should finish your rehab program. Get to your one-year mark. Make sure this is still what you want. You're young, beautiful, smart; you have a lot of choices. If you still feel the same way about me by then, well, then I'm in. I'm all in." His smile reached the corners of his eyes and she felt as if she'd just been hugged by this man.

"I know I will. But four more months? Seriously?" Now she tilted her head, stroking swirls around the skin on his wrist while his hand still enveloped hers, stirring his arousal against his better judgment.

He wouldn't budge on that point, though, and looking back, it just told Nicole in one more way that Harry always had her best interests at heart. She knew then, as she knew now, pulling up to Dallas General to see James, that she was lucky, pure and simple. She was lucky she realized she'd hit bottom before she wound up dead. She was lucky Harry had found her and somehow believed in her. She didn't know if James would be so lucky.

CHAPTER THIRTEEN

As sad as she was to see Nicole go, especially under the circumstances, Laura decided to take good advantage of the entirely free day stretching ahead of her. She was already off work because of Nicole's visit. Her kitchen table was now covered with various pages of the sheaf of papers she'd printed and brought home with her from work. She'd promised Nicole she would work on getting her some answers as to what prompted John Murdock's abrupt flight from their little town, and she meant to find at least some preliminary answers today. By the time Charlie got up for school, she had the possibilities narrowed down to a much more manageable number. While Laura's forte was dealing with the origins of crime scene evidence, what she couldn't figure out on her own, she could ask for help with.

The way she had it worked out, she was looking for some occurrence that Nicole's father could hypothetically be linked to, most likely on or around the day of their disappearance. She knew the kind of man Murdock had been. She remembered hearing his bellows and shouts late into the night more than once. But as horrible as she now understood Murdock to have become at times, she knew that he would not have uprooted his family and left a paying job behind over something trivial.

The unsolved crimes that had occurred in Iosco County the night of Nicole's disappearance and the night before were varied and geographically spread out. She'd thrown out everything from the day after the disappearance except for a report of a vagrant turning up dead from a knife wound. The time of death had been put in the early hours, shortly after Nicole stated they'd left, but she knew the medical examiner could have been off by a couple hours, especially with the technology available seventeen years ago. This might have looked promising to Laura, but the location was at the far west end of the county, nearly an hour away from Nicole's residence, and it didn't seem right to her. She knew Murdock had mainly frequented the two local bars. She couldn't figure how he would have turned up way over on the other side of the county, but she kept the vagrant on the list anyway as a remote possibility.

She had four other infractions listed. There was a hit and run two towns over, only twenty minutes from Orsonville and the Murdock's house.

There was also a bar fight in nearby Hancock that had resulted in the victim losing an eye and sustaining a broken arm. When he gave his statement at the hospital, the man said he'd been attacked by three large men, and John Murdock could've easily fit the description of two of them.

Add to that the bar, The Shady Lady, was one that many Orsonville residents seemed to patronize, as it was just a few miles into Hancock. Laura was sure Nicole's father must have been there at some point. Unfortunately, there were no helpful witnesses who claimed to have seen anything useful.

There was an officer shooting which had gotten quite a bit of media attention at the time, but had failed to yield the capture of the man suspected. From what she could tell, it looked like a routine traffic stop gone bad. The officer had radioed in the license plate number of the car, and when dispatch was unable to reach him again after twenty minutes, the cars they sent out to the site found the officer down. He was DOA at the local hospital. Laura knew how intense and immediate the response would have been; but the car and the man it was registered to had never been found. She didn't see how Nicole's dad would be involved here either, but it was a significant unsolved crime from the target date, so she kept it.

The crime she isolated from the day before the disappearance was what she considered the strongest possibility. There was an unsolved shooting in Parker, which was about thirty minutes away from Orsonville. A detective Smyth had noted in the file that the victim, Bill Connor, had been shot in the head while sitting in front of TV. The time of death was placed between ten p.m. to two a.m. that night. The victim was a heating and cooling contractor, single, and neighbors said they thought he had a girlfriend, but no one had really gotten a good look at her. According to the file, there had been no forensic evidence to give detective Smyth a decent starting point, and the investigation had pretty much stalled until it had gone into the cold case files. After learning of Irene Murdock's probable tryst with another man, this one had jumped off the page at Laura.

She remembered Nicole's mother as a quiet, mousy woman. It was hard to reconcile that memory with the idea that she would have betrayed a man as volatile as John Murdock. And now Laura found her mind offering flashes, glimpses of the few domestic violence scenes she'd been called in to collect evidence on when things went south of bad. She never failed to be surprised by the intricacies of marriage, especially deeply troubled marriages. Whatever the reason for Irene's affair, Laura was determined to learn the truth, in the hopes of peeling back a layer or two covering the long-buried mystery of Nicole's disappearance. And there was the added benefit of the chance to have a part in nailing a very bad guy for something big, seeing as he'd never pay for the multitude of damaging little crimes against his own family.

Laura knew that she would start with the Connor case. The file mentioned a sister who still lived in Parker. Laura placed a quick call to her own sister Jenny, a Homicide detective with the County Sheriff's Department. She explained that she was trying to shed some light on what had happened to Nicole's family that long ago night, and had found a possible connection to Nicole's father. She didn't need to remind the Jenny of the type of man John Murdock was. She did provide a few details on the apparent wake of wreckage he'd left in his path. Jenny had no problem spending a little time looking into things. Laura covered the basics for her.

Connor had been found shot in the head in his own living room. There were no witnesses, no family except the sister and the man's elderly parents nearby. Coworkers, friends and family all denied knowledge of anyone who'd want to harm Connor. In fact, no one questioned seemed to know anything about whom the man had been involved with. No forensics ever entered into evidence. Laura paused as she read that aloud to her sister. With a close range gunshot wound to the head, how was there no trace evidence? Jenny read Laura's mind and asked which detective had been assigned to the case back then.

Jenny, older than Laura by five years and in the Homicide division for the last two, chuckled on the other end of the line when Laura told her it was a detective Smyth. "Well, that explains a lot. Smyth wasn't worth two shits. This isn't the first case of his we've had to reopen. Let me see what I can find." Laura smiled into the phone and thanked her sister profusely when Jenny said she'd call soon with an update.

Laura figured if the Connor case was a dead end, she'd move on to the hit and run. But everything about the way the man had died seemed off to her. She already had it all worked out in her head: Irene had met Connor either at their church or maybe he did a heating and cooling call for them once. They'd hit it off. Irene began a series of late-night liaisons with the victim, coming directly to his house, as the man was a bachelor and lived in another town. The lateness of the hour when Irene would visit probably had more to do with her own constraints as a wife and mother of three than with trying to maintain any secrecy; she would have been reasonably confident that news of her activities couldn't make it back to her husband.

In Laura's theory, John Murdock had found out. She didn't know how yet, but he'd found out and followed her one night. Something nagged at her from the original detective's report, something she couldn't put a finger on. The description of the scene was that there hadn't been a struggle, so this meant that Murdock had the self-restraint to wait until his wife left before going in and doing the shooting. He'd most likely had possession of a gun already. That was another thing she hadn't had time yet to check into, whether the man had ever purchased or registered a gun.

She assigned herself that as her next task, to be done first thing tomorrow morning when she was back in her lab. Her work so far today had taken up most of the time Charlie was in school. Laura leaned back in her chair and glanced at the clock: he'd be home in less than an hour. They had a very important appointment to keep and she knew there was no way Charlie was going to let her out of her promise.

She locked the van in the parking lot of the Farm and Fleet store and walked beside her son, taking in the signs plastering the front windows. Today and tomorrow were free adoption days set up through the local chapter of the Humane Society. With the recent cold snap, the animals were inside; in warmer weather there would be cages lining the storefront. Charlie had been campaigning for a dog for quite a while. If she was honest, Laura thought, he'd been trying to convince her to let him get a dog since he could talk. She had no illusions as a single mother about what she could handle and what she couldn't. Her steadfast argument against a dog had been simply that she had no time to take care of a pet. Now that her son was a capable fourteen, her argument wasn't holding much water anymore.

He was old enough to handle the responsibility, and she believed he would keep his vow to do a good job, so desperate was he to adopt a dog. She stopped him before they went through the doors and he fell in love with every animal inside.

"Listen Bud, please go in there with an open mind. You know you can't take them all home. We talked about what type of pet would work well in our house. I hope you know there's a chance today might not turn out to be the day. We are only just starting to look. We can go to the animal shelter in Lansing this weekend if there isn't a dog in there with your name on it, okay? I promise it'll happen. But you need to make the right choice, don't rush it."

Her sensible son nodded and shrugged. "I know Mom. Don't worry. Maybe we'll find our dog today, maybe we won't." He flashed his brilliant smile at her. "Can we go in now?"

***

Adam Caufield stood diligently at his post, watching the steady flow of shoppers and browsers funnel through the maze of cages. He volunteered twice a month with the Iosco County Humane Society, getting all of the adoptable animals up to date on their vaccines, clearing and screening for health problems and doing his best to make sure that each animal here had at least a few notations on personality, health, special feeding requirements, and so on. He'd learned over the years at these events to easily differentiate between the casual browser and the person seriously looking to adopt a pet. He spotted a definite adopter toward the back of the light crowd of people ambling slowly past him.

The boy she was with stopped at a cage and was talking to a Labrador mix, drawing his mom down toward him for a better look. She straightened up, smiling, and Adam felt the commotion around him dissipate. His airport mystery woman. Right here, fifty feet away. She'd been in his thoughts so frequently since meeting her last month, it was jarring to actually see her in person. He'd given her his card, and there had been no response yet to the flowers he sent yesterday, making him wonder if he'd chosen the wrong Laura Miller from the phone book. He'd started to think he was chasing a fantasy, had told himself he was ridiculous for being infatuated with someone he'd shared the space of twenty minutes with.

Adam was not a man who believed in fate, destiny or divine providence. He dealt in facts, science, absolutes. But this was surreal. He hadn't been able to stop thinking about this woman for more than a few hours at a time, and now here she was. If the hand of God had reached down and smacked him on the ass, it wouldn't have felt any clearer than the sensation he had standing in the Orsonville Farm and Fleet on Pet Adoption Day. He gently placed the puppy in his arms back into its cage without any awareness of the action and started toward Laura. He would convince her to give him a chance, have a conversation with him. He had no idea why she hadn't called him and he didn't care. His future was already intertwined with hers.

CHAPTER FOURTEEN

Laura stared stupidly up at Adam. He was so completely out of context that it took her a moment to regain her composure. He'd just strolled over and called her by name, smiling widely, obviously happy to see her. She stared into his sea blue eyes, mute. He saved her by speaking first.

"I was hoping you'd remember me," he told her, and his low, smooth voice sounded like rich, steaming coffee to her, warm and inviting.

Boy, do I ever need to get laid, she thought, and felt her cheeks burn at her own silent audacity. Get a grip, girl, she told herself, he's just a guy!

"Of course I remember you, Adam," she answered, adding, "The flowers you sent were beautiful, thank you."

"I wasn't sure if you'd gotten them." He nodded to Charlie, who was watching the interaction with interest.

"Oh, uh, Adam, this is my son Charlie; Charlie, Adam."

Charlie had a devilish glint in his eye Laura did not like. She wondered briefly if he'd overheard her nickname for the man during Nicole's visit. She tried furiously to send him a don't-you-dare message with her gaze.

Charlie returned Adam's smile and put a hand out. "Nice to meet you. Do you work here? Funny, I think my mom has mentioned you." He feigned concentration, trying to remember.

Laura would've kicked him if he wasn't her son. Adam graced her with a small half smile, hopeful. "Really? That's great. And as a matter of fact, I do sort of work here. Not for Farm and Fleet, but I volunteer for the shelter. Are you looking to adopt a dog, Charlie?"

Having gotten Charlie onto a subject he was invested in, Adam gestured at the rows of cages. "Want me to show you a few of the best ones here?"

Laura fell into step behind the two of them as they toured the rows. Charlie did fall in love with two puppies, as she'd anticipated, but neither seemed quite right for them. She was pleasantly surprised when, after over an hour, Charlie looked at her and said, "I think I'll wait. I want to be sure." He shook Adam's hand again, "It was nice meeting you Adam, thanks for your help. I'm gonna go check out the baby goats outside, Mom."

Laura was left standing alone with Adam. She glanced over his shoulder at the dogs, then to her right at the livestock fencing, studied her shoes for a bit … and finally looked at him. "Thank you, that was really nice of you." She buttoned her coat, switched her purse from one arm to the other. That's exactly what he is, she thought. Nice. That's all. She turned to go.

"Hey, Laura," he leaned in toward her, and she caught the faintest hint of a subtle, spicy scent, "would you have dinner with me tonight?"

Her mouth was suddenly too dry to speak. She wondered if he could tell she was trying to suck in her belly. "I, ah, no, I can't," she stammered, thinking, why can't I? "Charlie's waiting, I have to go, I'm sorry," and she wished she would just shut up. What the hell was she doing?

Adam looked genuinely disappointed. He tipped his head to the side a bit and captured her gaze with those intense blue eyes. She noticed that little cowlick again at his temple and wondered if his jet black hair was as soft as it looked.

"Okay!" she burst out. Then, flinching at her own volume, a quieter "Okay. We have a few more errands to run," she lied. There was absolutely no way she was going out with him looking like this. She needed time. "When are you done here? I can come back later, we don't live far." He was so close she could see the very light spattering of freckles across his nose and cheeks.

He looked immediately relieved and smiled. "How about 6:00?"

She nodded, thinking how much easier it was to dismiss this man when he was just Airport Hottie in her memory than when he was inches away, focusing all his attention on her.

Fate smiled on her as Charlie informed her on the way home that he'd already planned to stay over at a friend's house tonight. Laura had plenty of time to change out of her ratty jeans and tee, and her bed was now littered with half her closet in the quest for something to wear. She knew nothing about this man. She hadn't a clue how to dress. It finally occurred to her to choose something that she was comfortable in. She settled on a nicer pair of jeans and the cool black boots she'd found on clearance with Nicole, a clean top, and darted back into her bedroom at the last minute to add dangly silver earrings.

She spent the short drive back to Adam trying to calm her nerves. The butterflies kicking up a ruckus in her stomach would have to settle down or she'd never make it through the night. She didn't remember feeling this nervous about her first date with Steve, but then she'd already worked with him for a long time at that point. Steve popping uninvited into her head sent her an extra wave of queasiness, and she wished she'd made a solid decision about their relationship before running into Adam.

They left Laura's car in the Farm and Fleet parking lot and Adam drove them to an Italian restaurant he said was his favorite, just this side of Lansing. The hostess showed them to a table near the fireplace, which left not much to look at but your dining partner, Laura thought, wishing she was better at small talk. When the waiter brought Adam's beer and her red wine, she sipped it and asked him how he decided to become a veterinarian.

"I've always loved animals. You know how most kids think they want to be a vet when they grow up? I guess I never really grew out of it. I went to school right here at MSU. Been doing it for ten years now, and I still love it. What about you? Did you always know you wanted to work in law enforcement?"

The wine was starting to do its job and she relaxed a bit as she said, "I actually planned to become a lawyer, but I got a little sidetracked along the way. I'm lucky to finally be doing something I enjoy with the job in forensics."

"Then we're in the same boat, aren't we? I don't think most people get to do what they really like." He paused, thoughtful. "What made you decide to go back to school?"

"Oh, ah, I had Charlie pretty young. His dad isn't in the picture, so I didn't have time for school until a few years ago." She smiled, glad to let Adam know up front what her priorities were.

"That must have taken a lot of drive, you should be proud of yourself. Charlie is what … thirteen or so? You must have been really young, just a kid yourself."

She had to laugh. "Old enough to know better. I was 19. Charlie is fourteen--wow, I can't believe that," she shook her head.

"Well, motherhood's been good to you. I had you figured for no more than thirty."

"Really? Uh oh, so I guess the date's over?"

"Yep," he pushed his chair back and half stood before laughing with her and taking his seat. "No, actually, that's great that you're a bit older than I thought, it means the ants are probably out of your pants by now."

She couldn't help laughing again. "I've never heard it put quite that way, that's perfect." She paused as the waiter set another glass of wine in front of her and swapped Adam's empty Labatt's for a full one. He reappeared seconds later with their appetizer, a dressed up garlic bread smothered with mozzarella and sundried tomatoes. She carefully broke off a slice and tasted a bite, rolling her eyes, "Mmmm, you've got to try this. It's incredible. How did you know I love Italian food?"

He shrugged. "Lucky guess. What about Italian men?"

She looked up at him quizzically. "Italian?"

"Half. Half French."

"What kind of French-Italian name is Adam Caufield?"

"I was adopted."

"Oh." Her cheeks burned. "I'm sorry, that was very insensitive. Really, you were adopted? How old were you?"

"I was a baby. My parents were always up front with me about my heritage. They'd tried without success to get pregnant before finally adopting me, and then a year later they had my brother, followed by three sisters and two more brothers. You'd love them, they're a unique bunch. My youngest brother lives in Florida and the rest of us are still all around here."

"Wow," Laura breathed. "Big family! How was that, growing up knowing you were adopted?" She knew this was a personal question, but the wine made her braver, and Adam seemed so open and easy talking about his life.

"I don't know. I don't have a frame of reference to weigh it against. My parents are amazing. I used to wish that I'd have a marriage that lasted the way theirs has. My mom is just one of those people who are natural mothers. Nothing much seems to faze her. I think they felt that telling me about my background was the best way for me to feel secure in the family, if that makes any sense. Like, I belong to them, they chose me, and it was their responsibility to tell me where I came from."

"And you've never wanted to meet your birth parents?"

"Why? Whatever their circumstances, they did the best thing they could have done giving me up. I've got no complaints." He smiled at her. "Especially not tonight."

Their entrees arrived then, and by the end of the meal Laura was very glad she'd taken a chance and accepted Adam's invitation. She'd already learned that he loved dogs, had two horses he kept at the clinic stable, and lived in an old farmhouse from the 1850s that he'd renovated. She finally opened up and gave him more than the basics, covering her recent break-up, and she'd even, after the second glass of wine was gone and the bill was paid, told him about the nickname she and Nicole had given him.

"I am shocked!" He stopped walking and looked down at her. They were now strolling just off the college campus, past little shops, night-clubs, cafes, among what must be hundreds of others out on the unusually balmy November night. Adam shook his head at her. "I had no idea you were such a shallow tart. If I had known what you were interested in me for--"

"You'd what? Have asked me out sooner?" she joked, laughing at his mock indignation.

"Hey, I did, you forget. Now, when you call your friend Nicole to tell her all about our date, will I still be Airport Hottie, or do I get to have a real name?"

"What makes you think I'll be calling Nicole with details of our night?" she flirted back.

He grabbed her hand and pulled her through a small crowd of people around the corner they'd just reached. "Sorry about that, right here," he nodded at a door in a small alcove to their left. "I want to show you something."

She followed him, curiosity piquing her interest. Once inside, she saw that it was a condensed jazz club of sorts. Tiny white lights covered the ceiling and traced paths on the walls, and there were scattered small round tables and a few couches and soft, overstuffed chairs throughout the room. The stage was only a slightly raised platform in the corner, but on it was a gleaming baby grand piano. A man stood at the mic playing the most amazing saxophone she'd ever heard. The woman at the piano was still, her eyes closed, fingers resting lightly on the keyboard. Adam's large warm hand rested at the curve of her waist as he steered Laura to a table along one side with a dim lamp in the center, and the woman came alive and began to play, turning the lone sax solo into a melancholy, bluesy jazz creation. Laura, who hadn't listened to much of anything except her kitchen radio in years, realized suddenly how much she missed real music.

It stirred her emotions and made her heart feel full, a power she'd forgotten it had.

She looked at Adam with wide eyes, feeling very young and naïve, and put her lips close to his ear to tell him, "I love it." There was that spicy, masculine scent again, mingled with the heat from his skin, and she reluctantly sat back.

When the set was over and the two musicians wandered over to the bar for a drink, Adam brought his chair closer to hers and tipped his head, gazing at her with those liquid blue eyes. "I'm glad you love it." He nodded to the waitress circulating and she made her way to their table. He ordered two caramel cappuccinos and a "special," which she had to ask about. "You'll see," was all he said.

The coffees were delivered along with an enormous chocolate fudge brownie with ice cream and glazed pecans crushed over the top, and she shook her head, giggling. "Chocolate is my favorite, especially brownies. My sister and I figure we've built up a chocolate tolerance so high, the average person would pass out from overload." She pinched his arm. "Are you sure you're real? It's almost like I made you up."

"Ouch!" He rubbed his arm in feigned injury, smiling at her. "Um, shouldn't you pinch yourself to make sure? Here, let me help," he reached over and she jerked her arm back, laughing.

"No way! Why would I want to wake up from this?" She picked up the forks and handed him one. "You're helping me with this." A fleeting thought drifted through her mind and she willed it away; who had he last shared one of these "specials" with?

As his car headed toward the expressway to take them back to the Farm and Fleet in Orsonville, she wished the store was farther away. She didn't want to leave this man yet. He was kind and funny, and they had this rapport, this back and forth volley thing that she couldn't remember having with anyone ever, not even a lifetime ago with Charlie's dad. The clock in Adam's Mountaineer read 12:22 am. She blinked and read it again, then reached into her purse and checked her cell phone, hoping she hadn't missed any calls from Charlie. The screen on the phone told her nothing but the time, no missed calls. She dropped the phone back into her purse and turned toward Adam, studying his profile.

"Adam, I'm so glad I ran into you today," she said softly.

He met her eyes before focusing back on the road. "So am I. I've been thinking about you for over a month." He gave her a mildly embarrassed smile.

"I've been dragging my feet," she admitted. "I don't know how long it would have taken me to call you after those flowers. Too much indecision, fear, whatever. It was stupid."

"Don't be hard on yourself. It worked out, right?" He fell into silence for a moment. "Hey, do you want to see where I live?"

Laura was quiet, not sure how to answer. What did that mean? It was their first date, she could only imagine what he'd expect if she went to his house with him this late at night. Had she been wrong about him, about the kind of man he seemed to be? She was sure she hadn't given him the impression that the evening would end with sex, for crying out loud, this was their first date! Her inner turmoil must have been apparent on the outside as well, because he reached over and took her hand.

"Laura! I only meant: do you want me to show you where I live, that's all. Man, you had this look like I was going to kidnap you and steal your virtue or something." He squeezed her hand. "I'm just not ready to let you go yet, I was trying to stall."

Her cheeks flushed and she was glad the inside of the car was dark. How had this man randomly come into her life? They'd shared the same thoughts so many times during the evening, she felt as if he already knew her, she was so comfortable around him. When he looked at her, especially when he touched her, even now, just holding her hand in his, her pulse quickened and all she could think of was being close to him, touching him, burying her hands in that silky black hair.

She found her voice and tried to lend a little lightness to her tone, saying, "And I was just wishing my car was a longer drive away. Where do you live? Is it far?" And with those words, even though she knew they were just going for a drive, she couldn't help imagining what it would be like to go inside with him, to let him kiss her, to kiss him back and lose her restraint.

They stretched their evening by another hour, by the time he'd driven her down two long country roads east of Lansing, sitting in the car for a time under the willow tree in front of his house while he told her about the history--the house had originated as the first Lutheran church in the area, and had the first working well--and the renovations he'd done. She noticed he said "we" at times, as in "we wanted to keep the original stairway," but Laura wasn't ready yet to ask if the "we" was a girlfriend or ex-wife. She felt too good, too cozy and appreciated and too damn *good* to ruin it with details. What did it matter anyway? Of course he had a past, everyone did. She did. She hadn't gone into details about Steve. So she listened to the story of the house and to the timbre and cadence of his voice as he spoke, her hand in his and their knees almost touching, basking in content.

They made it back to the store parking lot, and he stood with her outside her car, both of them now breathing out little puffs of smoke into the much cooler night air. Laura shifted her weight from one foot to the other, rubbing her hands together.

"Boy, the temperature sure dropped, didn't it?" All the awkwardness from the beginning of the evening had come right back to her now that it was time to say goodbye.

"Come here," Adam reached his arms out and pulled her gently to him, wrapping his arms around her and rubbing her back. "Better?"

Laura smiled into his neck, breathing in his warm, intoxicating scent, the lapel of his coat tickling her cheek. "Mmm hmmm," she nodded, hugging him back, thinking, what a brilliant move, use the cold to get a hug. She couldn't have planned it better if she'd tried. After a while she pulled back, just enough to tip her head and look up at him. His face was inches from hers and he kissed her, tentatively at first, softly, and then more sure once he felt Laura press into him and kiss him back. He tightened his arms around her, sliding one warm hand along the back of her neck and into her fine blond hair. She stroked his muscled back and her pulse quickened at the feel of his firm chest and legs against her as he molded his body into hers.

The kiss deepened and she knew he wanted her as much as she did him. Her heart raced and she forgot to breathe, and she couldn't tear herself away. A soft moan escaped her and it seemed to be almost too much for Adam. He nearly lifted her off her feet with his embrace, and then loosened his grip and pulled back, drawing in a ragged breath. He gazed intently down at her and it was all she could do not to tear his clothes off and wrap herself around him right there. Talk about passion unleashed, she thought wryly. This is what she'd been missing all these years.

She curled a hand around one firm forearm and placed the other on his chest, feeling his heartbeat and unable to calm her own crazily racing heart. "Thank you Adam, I've had a wonderful time." She was hit with a sudden heavy sadness that she had to leave him.

He pulled her gently back into him with one arm around her waist and kissed her softly, his thumb lightly skimming the hollow under her jaw. "When can I see you again?"

"Soon. Call me, okay?"

He watched her get into her car, and she lowered the window to say goodbye. He rested his elbows on the window frame and kissed her one last time. "I will. Are you going to make it home okay? You're not too tired?"

She laughed. “No, I’m not tired at all.” She couldn’t stop smiling at him. She hadn’t felt this alive in years. She might never need to sleep again.

CHAPTER FIFTEEN

Nicole sat with Danny in the family waiting room of Dallas General. Harry had already come by this morning before work, and she knew he'd be back again in the evening with dinner. This was the pattern they'd established over the last six days James lay unresponsive in the ICU. Last night they'd been informed by Dr. Sanchez, the attending physician handling his case, that her brother would need a kidney transplant if he hoped to survive. The dialysis was no longer enough to provide the filtration that his kidneys weren't able to do since the shooting.

Dr. Sanchez stood at the end of James' bed with clipboard in hand, making his evening rounds, and explained that the first bullet had nicked the right kidney after blasting a hole through his liver, and the second bullet pretty much destroyed his other kidney along with a good portion of large intestine. Now the "good" kidney was failing. Nicole, recalling the scant few nursing courses she'd made it through before taking up exotic dancing full time, thought that the damage to that kidney was probably worse than they'd thought. She imagined the surgeons hard at work over her brother that first night, racing to stop the hemorrhaging from the liver, cleaning up the spilled contents of the intestine and hoping to prevent peritonitis or worse, removing what was left of the bad kidney. The right kidney would have been small potatoes at that point, she figured, as long as it retained enough functioning capacity. The lead surgeon had told her six days ago, "We'll have to wait and see. We may not know the extent of the damage for several days."

Score one for the brilliant surgeon, she thought bitterly. Add one more thing to the odds stacking up against James ever recovering. Now she sat next to Danny on the uncomfortable couch in the waiting room, waiting. She and her youngest brother had both had their blood taken early this morning for HLA typing to see if James might be able to take one of their kidneys. Nicole felt drained, utterly deflated, as she looked at the clock for the thousandth time and glanced sideways at Danny. I wonder if we should bring Mom today, she thought, unable to voice the question.

She just didn't know how her mother would handle seeing James this way. She knew that Irene needed to come, especially now with his condition so unstable. Nicole squeezed her eyes shut as she imagined her mother, tiny and slumped in her wheelchair, trying to make sense of her son in the big hospital bed, still attached to the ventilator, surrounded by lines and tubes and machines. The obtrusive white and blue ventilator tubing that jutted out of his mouth and distorted his features into some grotesque mask that hardly resembled her brother was a constant reminder that he wasn't even breathing on his own yet. How could Irene bear to look at him?

Nicole's stomach knotted and churned as she wished again that she wasn't responsible for making these kinds of decisions. She wished her brother was out of here, maybe still at her house, doing fine and weeks into his sobriety. She felt a pang of guilt as she even wished for her own soft, comfortable king-sized bed instead of the hard, crinkly hospital cot she'd been sleeping on this past week. Nicole had only left the hospital once, on the second morning, to pick up some things from home.

Harry had taken the list she jotted down and tried his hardest to gather everything she needed, but he'd failed miserably when it came to the little detailed items, like her pore cleanser, the right lounge pants, the latest Cosmopolitan she was in the middle of. Nicole waited for Danny to arrive that second morning. She hated thinking about the possibility, but he needed to have an opportunity to say good-bye if it came to that, even if it might be detrimental to his own stability. She knew that Danny was stronger than she gave him credit for. She'd seen it repeatedly growing up, and recently as well, in his struggle to find his way back to normalcy, sanity. He could handle this. She reasoned that he would never have left her in the dark about something like this had their roles been reversed.

Danny had taken her chair at James' bedside, and Nicole drifted through the hospital wing to the elevator, stopping at the nurses' station to inform them she'd be back in an hour. She kept her head held high as she walked the rest of the hallway, positive those nurses were gossiping as she went. She couldn't stand the looks they gave James when they came to attend to him. His track-covered arms were a glaring confession of the lifestyle he'd led. The nurses, at least the majority of them, came into her brother's room with preconceived notions of whom they'd be taking care of that day, just some poor junkie who'd finally gotten his due. She could read it in their faces. They rarely spoke to her, and when they did, it was to say, "what a shame," or, "we see so many like this." Nobody looked beyond the emaciated body, the tattooed and pierced skin, the flat purple lines running up and down his inner arms, to whom he might have been: somebody's brother, somebody's son, a boy who'd tried from too young an age to be a man when there was no real man to teach him how.

So for six days Nicole sat holding his hand in hers, with her back straight and her expression composed, making eye contact with all of them, telling them silently that it didn't matter what they saw or what they thought. James Murdock was loved, and worthy of their skills, if not their respect. She told them aloud that she'd be staying until he woke up, until he was better. If there was a chance James might not receive the best medical treatment and care because of who they thought he was, then she was damned well going to make sure he got it because of who she was. She worked in the adjacent hospital, and she was married to a man who was now running for congressman, not to mention had given nearly a million dollars to the children's hospital in the last year alone. If it took using Harry's name to get James well, to give him a chance to be the man she knew he could be, then so be it.

Dr. Sanchez appeared in the doorway of the family waiting room. Danny stood up anxiously and glanced at Nicole. The doctor flipped through the pages on his clipboard and began, “All right, we have the results of the typing, and the good news is that you are a match for James, Mrs. Peterson.” He nodded at Daniel, “The HLA markers are not the same between you and your half-brother, Mr. Murdock, I’m sorry. But it’s a step in the right direction that we at least have one compatible donor,” he said, rifling through a few more pages on the clipboard, missing the wide-eyed stare Nicole was sharing with Daniel. ‘Half?’ his eyes said to her. Dr. Sanchez continued obliviously, “However, we have a small problem, we always run some routine--” He broke off mid-sentence and cleared his throat at the two, neither of whom was paying any attention to him now.

Nicole and Danny both slowly focused their gaze back on the doctor. “I’m sorry,” Nicole told him, “you were saying?”

“Yes, well, we routinely run a few other tests when we do the HLA typing, and your blood count came back a little off. Has anyone ever told you you’re anemic?”

Nicole frowned and shook her head, “No, and I just had a complete physical about six months ago. Everything was fine.” Her gynecologist had done a thorough exam and a ton of lab work--she remembered them taking four or five tubes of blood. Everything had come back normal. “Well, can’t I just go eat a couple steaks, take some iron, or something? How long would it take to get my blood looking better?”

“That is pretty individual, but assuming the cause is simply diet related, it may not be an issue. We do need to rule out a couple things first, though, a few specific types of anemia, any other possible causes ... there’s no chance you’re pregnant, is there?”

Nicole opened her mouth to answer no, and shut it again. The morning Hugo called her at Laura's house played over in her mind, having to sit down quickly to stop the room from spinning she was so dizzy. And before that, she'd been shopping with Laura and suddenly had to lean on the cart, she felt so light-headed and nauseous. Laura had gotten her over to the cafe where she shed her coat and dropped into a booth, certain she was either going to pass out or throw up. The frozen Coke and pretzel Laura placed in front of her helped immensely, and she'd accepted her friend's analysis that the whole thing was from Nicole skipping breakfast.

Now, looking at Dr. Sanchez, she said, "I'm ... I'm not sure."

He nodded briskly, adding to the orders in front of him. "We'll run a pregnancy test too, then."

"Well, what if…." God, how could she be in this situation? Was she actually going to hope she was pregnant, now that she might be the only person who could save James? Life couldn't be that unfair, she thought. "What if I am? Is there any way...?"

Nicole knew it was a stupid question, but she couldn't help herself. The little bit of medical knowledge she had from school and from her current job did nothing for her now. She wanted this nice doctor to tell her that of course she could still help her brother, the baby would be fine.

He shook his head sympathetically. "I'm sorry, no. It'd be extremely risky. No surgeon I know would attempt it. Let's not get ahead of ourselves here, though," he told her, patting her arm. "It may be simple nutrition-related anemia. If you go down to the lab now, we'll have the results back before dinner time. I'll come find you."

With the doctor gone, Nicole sank into the lumpy couch next to Danny, neither one speaking. She finally turned to look at him, not knowing what to say. She noticed for the first time that he had a full beard growing in, maybe a week or two old. He must be at least a half a foot taller than she, and she was on the tall side at 5'8". He still had that white blond hair he'd had as a kid, and pale, pale blue eyes. When had her baby brother grown up?

He'd been committed to the state psychiatric hospital at just nineteen and diagnosed with Bipolar Schizoaffective Disorder. It had taken over a year for the doctors to get him on what they felt was the right combination of medication so that Danny could 'come back to himself,' as the doctors put it. They explained that he'd probably had a predisposition for mental illness, and the stress of college could have been his trigger. Nicole's own opinion was that in Daniel's case, predisposition or not, the stress of college, combined with repeated physical abuse, witnessing your father kill another man, and growing up with virtually no parent other than a floundering older sister, was the more likely trigger. Everyone had a breaking point.

Six months of intensive one on one and group therapy once he was on the right meds had helped facilitate the transition to the group home he lived in now with six other adults who were overcoming various problems in the quest for independent living. He seemed so well now, so healthy, that it was easy to forget how far he'd come in the last two years or so. Her visits with him had been so focused on his health, his progress, somehow she'd missed all the signs that he'd become a man.

Why hadn't they asked the doctor about the test results, how accurate they were, how he could so flippantly call Danny her "half-brother?" They could be wrong, she thought. Danny returned her gaze, his eyes bewildered and filled with tears. He's only 21, she reminded herself. He's been through so much, and he's still learning who he is.

"Did you know?" he asked her, giving voice to the fear that not only had his world just been turned upside down, but maybe his sister had known all along.

"No!" She grabbed Danny and hugged him tight. "Of course I didn't know, you goofball," she tried to laugh and found herself fighting tears too. "It doesn't change anything, you know," she pulled back and looked him in the eye. "All it means is that you're lucky. You aren't really the son of a murderer." She gave him a small wry smile.

Danny sat back and drew a few deep breaths. "Did Dad know? Do you remember anything?"

Nicole shook her head slowly. "I remember Mom was so in love with you. She'd talk to you all the time, have whole conversations with you, even before you were born. I thought she was nuts, talking to her big round belly, but she said you could hear her." She paused. "I'm sorry honey. I wish I could say I remembered something, like things getting worse or Dad seeming like he found out. Things were bad for a long time back then, and they'd gotten worse, but I can't pinpoint when."

He nodded. "I can't believe Mom would have cheated on him," he reflected.

"I know," she said, "but I don't know if I can blame her, you know? The whole situation was terrible." Helen Bourdain's words came back to her: 'I can see how your mother might have needed a friend, someone to talk to.' Danny's real father.

Danny spoke. "I've always wished I could remember more ... I can't recall anything before the shooting, did you know that? And I was seven when Dad shot that man. I should be able to remember more."

Nicole simply nodded, having no argument for that. "I think you're lucky you can't. All you'd be remembering was us running, Dad drinking, Mom slowly disappearing. I don't even know how many states and names we went through." She offered him a platitude. "They might be wrong, you know. We could have them redo the test."

Danny shook his head. "I'll talk to Dr. Sanchez later when he has more time. I'd be surprised if the test was wrong." He was quiet. "I wonder what Mom would have to say."

Nicole raised her eyebrows. "You'd ask her?"

Danny shrugged. "Why not? This family has been all about repressing and suppressing and covering up. Maybe it's time we started dealing with our crap out in the open." He met her gaze evenly with his calm, clear blue eyes.

She leaned in and kissed his scruffy cheek. "How did you get to be the wise one? You're the baby."

He laughed and looked down at her. "Not anymore. Go get your blood taken and see if I'm going to be an uncle." He hugged her around the shoulders, reading her mind. "You're not James' only option, Nic, take some of that pressure off yourself."

She looked at him in confusion. "I don't think Mom is healthy enough."

"We might be able to track down Aunt Emily. And there's always the transplant list, if…." Nicole heard the unspoken end of the sentence as if Daniel had said it. If James would even qualify, with his history of drug abuse.

Neither sibling mentioned the other person who might be a match for James; neither wanted to think just now about the implications of their father being found, or the virtually non-existent chance he would even want to help his son.

She stood suddenly. "All right, I'm off to the lab. I'll meet you back in his room?"

She walked with Danny down the hall toward the ICU, stepping into the elevator just as her brother's day nurse was getting in to go down to the cafeteria. Lucy was one of only two nurses Nicole liked so far in the ICU. When she came in to tend to James, she always spoke to him as if he were awake. She told him what she was going to be doing as she went along, whether it was changing out the IV bags, suctioning his airway, or drawing blood off his central line. She made conversation with Nicole and Daniel almost as an afterthought.

"Now, this won't hurt a bit," she'd tell him, hooking up the nebulizer to administer a breathing medication, "and when you wake up, you're just going to have to take over some of the reading your sister's been doing for you. She's already gotten you halfway through the new Stephen King book. You can give her a break and read to her for a while. She's got your room all set up for you at home, she even told me about the big old TV in there, with any movie you could ever want to watch. And your little brother was here this morning to see you, he's almost as handsome you, lucky kid," she'd chuckle.

Now, Nicole smiled warmly at her, "Going to get some lunch?"

"Oh, if you can call it that," Lucy rolled her eyes. The nurse told Nicole that she'd seen the HLA typing results, and wished her luck with her blood tests. The worry must have been crystal clear on her face, because Lucy gave her arm a little squeeze and said, "Hey, let's just focus on one thing at a time. For now, James' vitals are looking better this morning, and I know it helps every time you and Daniel sit and talk with him. I believe he knows you're here."

Nicole nodded, a little twinge of excitement humming in her chest as she thought about the remote possibility of a tiny baby growing inside her, and that old familiar James-related coil of dread on top of that if it meant she couldn't help him. "Thank you. Go have your lunch. I'll see you back up there."

She found the lab, had her arm poked for the second time that day, and returned to the intensive care unit. Lucy was already back on duty and keeping an eye on the monitors while she worked.

Nicole pulled a chair up next to Danny and tucked the tag into the back of his shirt. For so many years she'd been his mother, and she'd been so unqualified. She hated to bring this up, especially now, but she had to. "I think we should bring Mom in."

Danny was silent for a moment. "Are you sure?"

"No," Nicole said, "but he's her son, and I think she needs to see him. All she ever asks about when I visit her is you two. Seeing him like this might be better than never seeing him at all. I know it's terrible timing, though. I can wait 'til you're not here, if you want," Nicole offered sympathetically. "It would be understandable if you didn't want to see her right now."

Instead of answering, Danny stood and walked to the foot of James' bed, shoving his hands in his pockets. Nicole watched him take in the big picture, the I.V.s and tubes and bandages and ventilator. He sighed heavily and shrugged. "It's shitty timing. But you're right, she needs to come, and ... I don't know how long ..." He couldn't finish the sentence.

Nicole nodded and said softly, "I know. He feels farther and farther away from me every day." She held his limp hand in her own and absently swiped at a few tears that escaped her red eyes. All she wanted was for James to open his eyes and look at her. See them waiting for him here. See that they needed him, that he had to find a way to survive. She stroked his hand and curled his flaccid fingers around her own, swallowing around the painful lump in her throat and watching his chest rise and fall with the clicking rhythm of the machines. Wake up, she thought. You are part of this family. We need you. We'll fix this. We will. We will, over and over in her head, a silent prayer. She rested her head on the bedrail and closed her eyes.

Danny braced his hands on the footboard. “Could you bring Mom today? I haven’t seen her in over two years. For a while I just couldn’t. I should have visited these past few months, I guess.”

“No, hon, you had more than enough to try to deal with. Don’t be so hard on yourself. Listen, if I go pick her up now, she’ll still be pretty lucid, it’s only one o’clock. The Alzheimer’s doesn’t usually make her too confused until nighttime.”

Daniel gave his sister a small smile. “You’ve really thought this through, huh?”

“Well, yeah, especially since last night when they said the dialysis wasn’t working well. But here’s how we’ll do it. I’ll be back within an hour. I know you’ve missed at least a few days of work, being here. This is a good job you’ve got. I don’t want anything to mess that up. If you can stay while I run and get her, you could grab a taxi back home and make it to work tonight.”

He shrugged. “It’s not a big deal.”

“Yes, it is. So is school. If you’d rather deal with Mom at another time, just take off in an hour or so. You won’t even have to see her.”

“Nic, how’s it going to make any difference at this point *when* I talk to her about my genetics? That doesn’t need to happen today. I’d like to see her. I’ll hang around.”

Nicole stood and on her way out, cupped his cheeks in her hands, making him stoop a little. She kissed him on the forehead and shook her head at him. “I have no clue how you turned out so well, darlin’,” she told him.

He nodded at her, his expression serious. "I do."

Nicole brushed off the compliment, knowing she didn't deserve it. Daniel had always been the sweet one. She stopped to tell Lucy she'd be back in a bit with her mother before heading out. She was so nervous every time she left, whether it was to get coffee or go to the lab or now, actually leaving the hospital for the first time in days.

She got her mother loaded into the car and the wheelchair stowed in the back, merging back onto the expressway before her mother asked her where they were going.

"I'm taking you to see James, Mom. He's in the hospital. I know he'd want to see you."

"Is he sick? I hope those doctors know what they're doing, James is a good boy. He'll be all right," she nodded to herself.

Nicole decided to wait until just before going in to try to prepare her mother for what she'd see. She stopped outside the ICU and came around to the front of the wheelchair, holding the hand-rests and dropping down to meet her mother's eyes. "Mom, I want to tell you what you're going to see when we go in there. James is very sick. He's hooked up to a breathing machine, and he's getting lots of medications through an IV. But he's doing a bit better today. The doctors think he may wake up soon." She told this lie to try to soften the shock Irene would feel seeing her middle child like this.

Irene, clear eyed and focused, nodded without saying a word.

"Are you ready?"

"Yes," she said. "I miss my boys."

She pressed the automatic door opener on the wall and wheeled Irene in. Lucy was just finishing changing James' bandages as they came around the curtain. Danny was nowhere to be seen. The nurse put the last strips of tape across the large bandage over James' belly and efficiently pulled and straightened the bedclothes so he was neatly tucked in again. She shed her gloves and turned to smile at Nicole and Irene, tucking a chunk of her silky dark bob behind her ear.

"Hello, Mrs. Murdock," she said, bending a bit to address Irene. "I'm Lucy. We're taking good care of your son." She looked over the older woman's head to Nicole. "I'll be right at the desk if you need anything." Nicole watched her go to the sink to wash her hands, wishing she'd stay. Now what? What should she say to her mother? She couldn't offer any more platitudes.

Irene surprised Nicole and placed her hands on the wheels of her chair, rolling herself over close to James. She carefully picked up his slack hand and held it to her face as big fat tears rolled down both cheeks. No matter what else, James was her child. As imperfect a mother as she'd been, Nicole had to believe she did the best she was capable of. She drew a chair up next to her mom and rubbed her back in big, slow circles, hoping to soothe her. "The nurse says he knows we're here, Mom," she whispered. "He can hear us. You can talk to him."

Irene nodded, staring at the bony notch between James' collarbones, her eyes shiny with grief. "Oh, Jamie, what have I done to you," she said in a voice so heavy with sorrow Nicole felt her own throat tighten and her eyes burn. "You were so young, just a baby. Aunt Emily was going to help me leave, we had it all planned. But he found out ... he always found out, he stopped us. I thought he was going to kill us. And then…." Irene wearily laid her head on the bed next to James, still holding his hand.

Nicole realized she'd been holding her breath, not wanting to make a sound and break the spell. Her mother was recalling a time that Nicole knew nothing about, maybe a time before Danny was born. And Aunt Emily must have known--she was going to betray her own brother by helping his wife run away?

"Then he was sorry, he was always sorry, too, wasn't he? And he needed us, I know he did. He said he'd take the gun to himself if we left, and I couldn't do it. I'm so sorry, Jamie. But I knew he meant it. And later, after Danny, I was ready for that," she said so softly Nicole had to strain to listen. "I knew he'd threaten to kill himself, except by that time I just didn't care. Isn't that awful? What kind of awful person doesn't care that her husband might kill himself? But it didn't matter. None of it mattered in the end. We even had the airplane tickets for the five of us. We were finally going to be free. But he found me, and--" her voice broke and she covered her head with her free hand, shaking with sobs.

Nicole sat, stunned, as she watched her mother's anguish in confessing her sins to her son. She wished she understood more of it. The Alzheimer's was slowly killing all order in her mother's thought processes. Irene had apparently meant to take her and her brothers and run away from her abusive monster of a husband, had even had a solid plan. But why five plane tickets? Was the fifth one for Aunt Emily? Or for the man her mother had been having the affair with, Danny's father? She pressed a tissue into her mother's hand and used another for herself.

Irene lifted her head now and looked intently at James, taking in the marks on his arms, the sinewy, knobby elbows and wrists, the pale yellow cast to his skin. "I messed everything up. I should have been more careful. You might have gone to college. You'd never have been mixed up in the drugs. But it was all over. I knew he'd do what he said and come after us. I had to protect you, all of you. Maybe I was wrong. Maybe we all would have been better off, better than this." Her face was lined with regret as she gazed sadly at her son and sobbed, "I only wanted to keep you three safe."

As if on cue, Danny rounded the curtain carrying Starbucks coffees from the cart in the lobby. The scene stopped him in his tracks. He looked helplessly at Nicole and raised his eyebrows, as if to say, 'what's going on?'

Before she could get a word out, their mother turned in her chair, her tear streaked face focusing on Daniel. Nicole and her baby brother watched as the grief was replaced by shock, and Irene inhaled sharply, breathing, "My God," before her eyes rolled back and she slumped over to one side in her wheelchair.

CHAPTER SIXTEEN

Laura's mother sat across the little kitchen table from her, patiently chopping carrots into tiny pieces for the veggie pizza that would be the appetizer for Thanksgiving dinner. They sat in comfortable silence, Laura mixing the onion, celery and seasoning into a big bowl of stuffing as Jane glanced up at her daughter. "So, what have you heard from Nicole?"

"I haven't," she answered, standing to carry the turkey over and begin stuffing it. "What is it, 10:00 already? I've got to get this in," she murmured, picking up the pace a bit. "I've tried calling, but haven't heard from her in days. Why the hell won't this thing stay shut--" She frowned in aggravation as she tried to force the legs into the wire holder, careful not to wind up with turkey juice all over her blouse. She gave one last mighty tug, and the entire fifteen pound bird slid neatly out of the pan and onto the floor with a sickening splat.

Laura stood with her hands palm up at waist level, fingers splayed, looking like a surgeon whose patient just died on the operating table. She blinked back tears and finally bent to start the clean-up, her face hot with embarrassment. Why couldn't anything be easy?

Jane came into her line of vision, rescuing the turkey and plopping it into the sink. "A little hot water rinse and he'll be just fine. I won't mention his escape attempt if you don't," she added, watching her daughter out of the corner of her eye.

Laura couldn't stifle a snort of laughter, and then was overcome with a giggle fit and sat down on the floor. When she regained control, she sighed and rubbed her forearm across her eyes. "I hate not knowing how Nicole is. I hate not knowing if her brother is getting better. I hate leaving Charlie. And I already miss Adam." She shook her head, looking at her mom. "I'm pathetic."

"You're a long way from pathetic. Although ... sitting in a pool of turkey drippings isn't helping your case much."

Laura shuddered and stood quickly, grossed out all over again and going to the cupboard to grab the bleach. She poured some on a wet dishtowel and carefully wiped down the linoleum floor and table legs. "You deal with that stupid bird. I've had it with him," she told Jane.

Her mother already had the turkey back in the pan and the legs pinned together. "You're a good friend, a good mother. Isn't it nice to have so many people in your life to care about? What time does your flight leave tomorrow?" Her mother could always put things in perspective for her.

"Dad's taking me to the airport at seven tomorrow morning. I don't even know if Nicole has gotten my messages, if she knows I'm coming."

"Do you know what hospital her brother is at?"

"Dallas General. And I have her home address, but I've got hotel reservations, just in case. I just have a bad feeling ... I can't imagine why she hasn't called."

Jane nodded. "I'm sure there's a good reason. You be sure to call and let us know you're fine when you get there and find her, Laura." She closed the oven door on the turkey and noted the time on her watch. "You know Charlie will be fine. He'll miss you, but you'll only be gone a couple days this time." She paused, then asked, "And what about this Adam?"

Laura's cheeks went instantly pink and she wished she hadn't said anything. "What do you mean?"

"Well, all I know is he's a veterinarian and you've had a handful of dates with him in less than two weeks. When do we get to meet him?"

Laura shook her head at Jane, "Not for a while, Mom, I can't do that. I don't even know if it's serious, I can't bring him home at this point." As much as she wanted Adam to meet her family and spend time in her home, she couldn't risk having her son getting to know and like him if they weren't going to last long term. She'd thought she had that with Steve, but she knew her judgment was off there. The way he handled things last week when she went to talk to him, to be clear that they should both move on ... she felt a pang of guilt for how upset he'd been.

"Well, whatever you think is best," Jane said, handing Laura a large pot of peeled potatoes. "Put some water in here and start 'em to boiling. I'm going to run home, I promised your dad I'd go to mass with him today before we have dinner."

She took the potatoes, suddenly remembering her clothes were covered in turkey juice. "I've gotta go change, I'll see you after church," she told her mom and headed toward her room. Laura deposited her disgusting clothes into the hamper and pulled on a burgundy sweater and black pants. With her mother gone, Laura hefted her suitcase onto her bed to finish packing before the early flight tomorrow. She picked up her phone to try both Nicole's cell and house phones once more, with no answer, then impulsively dialed Adam's number. True, they'd only been on a few dates, but they'd spent nearly every night on the phone after Charlie was in bed. The first conversation, the night after their impromptu date, lasted over two hours.

She felt just like a teenager, so much so that she could recall perfectly what it felt like being eighteen and talking on the phone almost all night with Charlie's dad, about nothing and everything, and mainly just so they could hear each other's voice. It was a strange sensation to have these feelings reawakened in her thirties. She knew that she was a bit infatuated with Adam; had known that since he held her in his gaze that day at the airport.

Infatuation aside, however, she knew every time they spoke that she'd found another part of herself she hadn't even realized was missing. His kindness came through in the topics they discussed, the manner in which he lived his life. She was able to see herself through his eyes as he paid her the occasional compliment, not pouring it on thick the way Steve had at times if he wanted something from her. Adam's comments were almost afterthoughts. He mentioned how she'd felt to him that night when he'd "finally gotten to" wrap his arms around her. And she couldn't forget the smoldering, intense gaze he'd given her when she met him for their third date wearing the Texas Red Dress (it would always be that in her mind) and strappy heels. Laura felt as if her own feelings for him were written all over her face, so she tried to keep her compliments to a minimum in an attempt to preserve her dignity, but she blushed even now remembering the end of their date.

She stood in the dark with him outside his car in her driveway, loving and hating their goodbyes. She stamped her feet a few times to knock the dusting of an early snow off her skimpy shoes and leaned back against the car, not caring about the faint salt stain it'd leave on her long black wool coat. His eyes crinkled at the corners and she felt his smile on her lips when he leaned down to kiss her. "What are you doing to me, lady?" he said huskily, when she came up for air after a time. Their faces were inches apart. The silky black cowlick at his temple drew her eye and she reached up without thinking, tracing the curl with a light touch, then gently running her fingers into his thick, soft hair, not missing for an instant the way his eyelids lowered and he leaned a bit into her hand.

Her other hand came up and then both arms went around his neck, tightly, as she drew him to her and kissed his lips and then his neck. With no conscious thought, she unbuttoned the top few buttons of his shirt so her lips could feel more of him, more of the heat radiating from his skin. Her breath caught in her throat and she buried her face against his chest, hearing his heart racing as fast as hers as his warm hands roamed her spaghetti-strapped back under the coat. She gingerly tasted his skin there in the firm smooth contour below his collarbone, and wanted more. It took a staggering amount of self-restraint to keep from wrapping her legs around his thighs and the hardness she felt pressing against her. He ran his hand around to her ribcage, his fingers brushing the side of her breast as he traced a path slowly down to her hip, pulling her more tightly against him. She moaned, a deep longing sound she had no control over.

After a minute or two, he cupped his hand under her chin and she resisted, her cheeks burning with mingled desire and embarrassment. "Hey," he whispered, finally getting her to look at him. When she met his eyes, she found passion there, but more than that, she saw a tenderness she didn't expect, especially in a moment like this. He relaxed his grip on her slightly and kissed her again, but softly now, first on the lips, then the forehead, one hand still resting possessively around her hip, holding her there.

"I'm sorry," she murmured, still surprised at her own impulsivity.

Adam laughed and shook his head at her. "For what? Why would you apologize?" He pushed a stray strand of blond hair out of her eyes.

Laura shrugged, "I don't know ... it's just ... Adam, you must know, you're just so ... I mean…." she stammered.

He waited for her to finish, and when she didn't, he chuckled again. "I'm just so…."

Now Laura rolled her eyes at him, finding the courage to continue. "You're just amazing, that's all. You're so great to be with, and on top of that, you're just…."

He looked at her expectantly, eyebrows raised.

"Well, you're not terrible to look at, you know," she smiled at him. "I'm pretty self-sufficient, I never felt like I needed a guy to be happy, but--I'm having such a great time with you," she laughed, trying to lighten the mood a little. "I guess I'm just waiting for the other shoe to drop. Does that make sense?"

He was quiet now, considering, and Laura thought, fantastic, nice going Ace, you just officially scared off the one and only guy you've been really smitten with in over a decade. He joined her leaning against the salty, icy SUV, and turned an odd expression on her.

"Okay, let me get this straight. You, who have single-handedly raised a child to be a well-adjusted teenager, who have supported yourself and your son in a house you pay for and take care of, who have a successful career that you found the time to go back to school for, who have such a big heart that even hearing some of the unwanted cat and dog sob-stories from my clinic makes you cry, you just can't figure out why in the world a nice, intelligent, handsome, modest guy would be interested in you?" He cocked one eyebrow, a hint of a smile threatening to break his serious expression. "I thought you were smart."

She jumped to her own defense. "I am! Adam, I'm not saying we don't hit it off, and I'll be the first to admit I'm proud of what I've accomplished." She paused. "I guess I'm just not used to this kind of attention, or feeling so strongly about someone--" she stopped herself and searched his face. "Okay," she said, unnerved as always by the intensity of his gaze and attempting to change tacks. "Okay, let me just ask you this, and don't be upset ... but I need to know. You lived in that old farmhouse with someone. Were you married? Was it a girlfriend? What happened? And how long ago? Why won't you talk about it? And how come you're not dating anyone now?"

His eyes widened at the barrage of questions. Clearing his throat, he said, "all right, those are fair questions. I was married. For nine years. We got divorced two years ago. I kept the house and she moved back home to Connecticut. No kids, no ties, haven't spoken to her since she moved the last of her things out two years ago." He made it all sound so cut and dry, Laura thought. But now she had that little nagging thought in the back of her mind: why did he get divorced? What was wrong with him--or her--that they couldn't stay married? Was that too personal a question at this stage in the game? Damn, she was so bad at this. Where was the handbook when you needed it, she wondered.

"And for the record," he elbowed her lightly, "I am dating someone, and I'd like to think it's getting serious, but you'd have to ask my girlfriend to know for sure."

Laura's idiotic heart did a little jig inside her chest at these words. She pushed off the car and faced him toe to toe, hands on his chest. "Oh, she'd definitely agree, I already checked with her." She stood on tiptoe and kissed him.

Now, in her bedroom, she put the call through, waiting impatiently for Adam's rich baritone voice to come on the line. She'd say she was just calling to wish him Happy Thanksgiving, she wouldn't stay on long. They'd spoken enough the night before to last at least the next few days. Anticipation changed to disappointment when his voicemail picked up instead. Oh, well, she thought, he did say he'd be spending the day at his parents' house, he was probably busy. She smiled thinking of all those siblings, and their spouses and kids, and the possibility of meeting them one day. She and Jenny had always wished they were from a big family.

The doorbell rang and Laura heard her four year old niece greet Charlie, and then a high-pitched whoop of joy when Charlie had probably, as usual, scooped Lindsey up and flipped her over his shoulder. Laura appeared in the living room just as the door flew open again and her sister stomped in, cheeks bright red with the cold, followed by her husband. Mike held an overfilled paper bag full of desserts and goodies, and Jenny handed Laura a warm casserole dish.

Hours later, dishwasher running and the scent of pecan pie still hanging in the air, Laura finally dropped into a chair across from her sister at her kitchen table and took a cookie from the overflowing platter. The rest of her family was settled in the living room, presumably overstuffed as their turkey had been. In the moment of quiet, she hoped to get an update from her sister on the Connor case.

Jenny's daughter zipped into the room overloaded with coat, hat, mittens and boots. "Daddy's taking me and Charlie night-sledding, Mama, get my stuff on!" The little girl dropped the pile at Jenny's feet and stood with her hands on her hips, dancing in place.

Jenny smiled and bent to help her daughter, "How about 'get my stuff on please?'"

"Puh-leeeeze," came the reply, and she did a quick twirl as Jenny tried to zip the snow pants that seemed premature for the third week in November.

Laura had to laugh. "Man, can I borrow some of that energy, Linds?"

Her niece just looked at her quizzically, slipping her arms into her thick winter coat and allowing her mother to loop a plush scarf around her face twice, careful to leave eyes exposed. The boots and mittens went on, and Lindsey was gone again in a flash, calling, "Thanks, Mama!"

When the front door had whooshed shut and the house fell suddenly even more silent, Laura brought two cups of coffee to the kitchen table and sat back down, smiling. "I think that is the definition of a whirlwind."

"I know," her sister agreed. "She's non-stop." She stared at Laura for a long moment. "Do you ever think about having more?"

Laura's eyebrows went up. "Where did that come from?"

"Nowhere. Just wondered, that's all," Jenny shrugged, taking a sip of hot black coffee.

Laura tipped her head a bit, gazing out the window. "I don't know. I never really thought much about it, but ... I think maybe it'd be nice, you know? I was never crazy about all the newborn stuff, but the twos and threes are so much fun. And Charlie would have a little brother or sister…."

Now she found Jenny looking at her curiously. "Wow, what's going on with you?"

"Nothing! What do you mean?"

Jenny chuckled. "Well, if I'd asked you about having more kids a few months ago, it would have been a flat-out no. So things are going well with Airport Hottie, huh?"

Laura nearly dropped her coffee mug. "You can't call him that anymore! He has a name. And that's not why! We're just dating! And we've only been out a few times--jeez!"

Jenny nodded calmly across the table from her and Laura was sure she could read her mind, that old line about the lady protesting too much.

"Touchy much? Settle down, all right? I'm just happy that you're happy, plus I didn't have to stare at Steve's face over the turkey this year, that's all."

"Steve's history, don't worry." Laura paused. "He was a mess when I went over there last week to talk to him."

Jenny nodded. "Mom told me he came over when Nicole was here and made his final plea. I'm proud of you for not caving."

"Hey, I wouldn't have," Laura defended herself, thinking about how she'd actually considered getting back together with him, and she felt a faint shudder pass across her neck and shoulders. "I knew we weren't going to work out, I just kept thinking things would change. It's probably the best decision I've made this year," she smiled at her sister.

"That, and wearing your come-get-me jeans to the airport last month to fly home."

"All right, quit it," Laura laughed.

"Okay, okay, so listen," Jenny said, changing tacks. "I checked into the Connor case for you, and I've got some new information. The man was definitely having late night liaisons with someone, whom the neighbors had never officially seen. He was single, close to Irene Murdock's age. You mentioned there was some speculation that Nicole's mother was having an affair. The lead detective on the case back then was a bit of a slacker; many of his cases went into the cold case files because he just didn't follow procedure that well, was lazy about the chain of evidence. Your theory added up, until I talked to the sister." Jenny recounted the interview she'd had with her.

Dorothy Frooter, a house-coated, plain-faced woman in her seventies, had been bewildered to find a detective on her doorstep, but once Jenny explained that she was just investigating all possible leads in a missing persons case, the woman relaxed and invited her in. She told Bill Connor's sister that the man in question had disappeared on the same night as her brother was killed. By then she was seated in the woman's bright, sunny kitchen overrun with geese. The salt and pepper shakers were geese in chef hats, the clock displayed two geese wearing aprons, and the wallpaper border was a parade of geese. The cookie jar on the counter was even a large goose that actually honked when Dorothy tipped the head back to place some cookies on a platter for the detective to go with the steaming hot tea she'd made.

Laura smiled at Jenny. “I’m getting the visual.”

“Well, the visual helps, because you won’t believe what this woman did. She covered up her brother’s suicide. He wasn’t killed, Laura. His sister walked in and found him with the gun still in his hand, dead probably only a little while.”

Jenny told Laura about how she had asked Dorothy Frooter if she knew who her brother was seeing.

“I’ve ... we, uh … we never met, no.” The woman’s hand went to the little gold cross at her throat, her gaze shifting to the left, and Jenny knew she was lying. She called her on it.

The man Laura had suspected Irene of having an affair with had been gay. Bill Connor had only allowed his partner to visit him at home late at night, after he’d hoped the neighbors had all gone to bed. Dorothy had learned at the funeral that the two had planned to move in together, but that would necessitate Connor coming out to his family. Dorothy had a heart wrenching conversation with the man who had loved her brother. Apparently, they’d argued the night he died. He’d given Connor an ultimatum: stop lying about who he was, or they were through. The boyfriend had dissolved into tears during this confession, according to Dorothy. He’d only meant to push Connor to be honest about who he was; he never imagined this outcome.

The woman’s fingers never left the cross at her neck during the retelling. She begged Jenny to keep this new information on what was thought to be a homicide quiet. Her parents were elderly and ill and must not find out their son had not only been gay, but also committed suicide.

Laura sighed along with Jenny at this. “Catholic?”

“Dyed in the wool Catholic. Twelve years of Catholic school for all the kids, mass every Wednesday and Sunday, fish on Fridays.”

Laura shook her head. She’d stopped being susceptible to the Catholic-brand of guilt years ago--must have been after having Charlie out of wedlock and realizing it didn’t make her a bad person, she thought. “Damn. Are you sure that woman was telling the truth this time? That it was a suicide?”

“She still had the note and the gun.”

Connor’s sister had taken the gun from his hand, wrapped it in a dishtowel, and put it away in her closet along with the note in his lap. She’d cleaned his hands with a wet washcloth, to get rid of the gun shot “residuals.”

“Gunshot residue,” Jenny had filled in quietly without meaning to.

Dorothy nodded at her. “I put his hands in his lap, turned on the TV, and unlocked the front door--I always came in the back way, you know. Then I called 911 and reported that I’d found him. I waited for the police officers and then everyone who came after that.”

She’d left the room then, reappearing and handing Jenny a very old shoebox. She sat stone still while Jenny pulled on gloves to lift the lid, and gazed out the window when the detective carefully unwrapped the gun. “There’s a note in the bottom,” Mrs. Frooter said quietly to the window.

Jenny lifted a corner of the dishtowel in the box, revealing a crisp-looking yellowed piece of notebook paper. The paper was brittle and faded as she carefully opened it.

'I'm so sorry. I can't live like this anymore. I love you all. Please forgive me.'

The four short sentences probably summed up years and years of turmoil.

"Well, shit." Laura stood to refill their coffee cups. "That is so screwed up. So avoidable."

"And so not an answer to what happened with Nicole's dad," Jenny agreed.

"I thought I had things worked out right for Connor's death connecting to him," Laura said, a little defeated. "There's a hit and run from that night, too, but I'm having a hell of a time finding anything new on that. There are a couple of others, a bar fight where a guy lost an eye, and an officer shooting with the suspect known but missing. Can't see how that one would fit, but it's in there just in case."

"The hit and run, was the person killed?"

"Horrible incident," Laura nodded. "But it was so long ago, and there weren't any witnesses. Happened right in the middle of town, on Main Street in front of the pharmacy. It was around 11:15 pm. That one'll be my next project if the bar fight doesn't turn up anything."

Jenny wrinkled her nose a bit and Laura caught it. "What? What's wrong with my logic?"

"Just thinking. You said Murdock killed a man in Texas, a few years after they left Orsonville. I don't know if I can see him going to all the trouble of uprooting his family and leaving Michigan just because he hurt some guy in a fight, even badly."

Laura nodded. "I know. That's bugging me too."

"What about the gun he used to kill the man in Texas?" Jenny asked.

"Nothing in the system matches the bullets recovered at the scene before or after the shooting, I ran it. That is also a little strange, because Murdock bought and registered that gun years before they took off. With his temper, I guess I'm surprised nothing else came up matching the gun or bullets to anything else at all. The officer shot on my list was killed with his own gun. Murdock's gun was either tossed somewhere between Texas and where he wound up, or he still has it. It was never found. Anyway," finished Laura, "Texas law enforcement would have already checked into any related incidents, too. But that gun is still in the back of my mind."

CHAPTER SEVENTEEN

'I want a divorce.' Nicole carefully opens her door a fraction of an inch to let in more of the conversation. Her parents are sitting at the kitchen table, one on each side, and her mother has just uttered the words Nicole has prayed for years she would say. She can't see all of her dad, only her mom, and her father's huge hands flat on the table, flanking his beer bottle. She waits for the explosion, the reaction, but it doesn't come. Not yet.

John Murdock takes a long pull from the beer and sets it back down on the table. 'How long?' His voice sounds quiet, soft, to Nicole. The beer in front of him is deceiving, he's not drunk, he's in complete control. It's an odd question, but she feels she knows exactly what he's talking about. It's a nagging feeling, just out of reach....

'How long what, John?' Her mother sits back a bit in her chair and folds her hands in her lap. She's still wearing her blue pantsuit, the

one she wears on Sundays to help out with the coffee and donuts after the church service is over.

'How long have you been screwing around on me?' A chill runs up Nicole's spine, the words are too calm. She'd somehow feel better if he was yelling. Things are always more predictable then. His hands on the table don't move.

Her mother fidgets with her wedding rings. 'I don't know what you're talking about,' she says evenly.

'Are we really gonna do it this way, Irene?'

'John,' she says, her voice cajoling now, 'there's nobody else. For heaven's sake, will you just let that go? You know things are bad, John, they haven't been right in a long time. We're better off apart.' She tries a different tack. 'It will be easier for you. We're just not good for each other anymore. I won't even ask for child support.'

Nicole actually hears her mother's sharp intake of air and sees the nearly imperceptible flinch before the table is overturned, spilling her mother out of her chair to the floor along with it. The muscles in Nicole's legs jump involuntarily with the urge to run out there and help her. She forces herself to remain still. Her brothers are still quiet in the next room. No one knows she is up.

She watches her father bend over her mother and lift her off the floor by an arm. He rights a chair with his foot and drops her into it. Her mother's eyes are dry, and for once Nicole doesn't see fear written on her features. Her face remains blank as she meets her husband's angry stare. A cold chill snakes its way down Nicole's spine. It is a mistake not to be afraid of her father. She holds her breath, waiting, watching the scene between her parents.

'I will find out who it is, Irene, I promise you that. You'll wish you never looked at another man. You think you can make a fool of me? Convince me that this is a good idea? What about the kids?'

This entire conversation is ridiculous, she thinks. Like he's worried about us?? The irony makes her furious. Her father has hurt his three children more than anyone in this world deserves to be hurt. Why would he even try to pretend to care about them now?

She hears his voice continuing, softer now, as he bends down over her mother, gripping her jaw in his big hand. 'You try to leave. See what happens. You think I won't do what I have to, to make sure my wife knows where she belongs? You still have to go to work, Sweetheart, you can't be with your precious kids all the time. Hell, I know Danny ain't even mine, wouldn't be any skin off my nose if something happened to him,' he shrugs, letting go and straightening up. He finishes his beer in two gulps, grabs another from the fridge and settles into the big easy chair in front of the television, where Nicole knows he'll be the rest of the night.

Irene shakily stands and sets the kitchen table back on its feet, brushing herself off. Nicole watches as she heads down the hall on the other end of the house to their bedroom, taking off her jewelry as she goes. Danny is not her father's son. Somehow she thinks she already knew that. She closes her bedroom door without a sound, holding the latch. She walks on cat's feet back to her bed and pulls the pink flowered notebook Laura gave her from under her pillow, flipping it open to write. Putting her thoughts down on paper makes her feel a little better; it started out as Laura's idea, and has turned out to be a good one. Writing in her journals makes it seem like it's all just a story, something happening to someone else.

Nicole's eyes flew open with the image of the pink notebook still burned into her memory. Her journals. How could she have forgotten about her journals? Her father had insisted she bring them along when he hurried them all out of the Michigan house in the middle of the night so long ago. He'd made her give them all to him when they'd reached the first motel, just over the state line into Iowa. She watched him load up the inadequate little trash can, pour a little whiskey in for good measure, take it out onto the sidewalk and drop a match into the notebooks. She remembered that he hadn't gotten all of them, two remained rolled up and tucked down along the inside of her backpack. She'd managed to separate them out at the last minute when she realized what he planned to do.

Laura had given her a set of ten when they were thirteen and her father's temper had really gotten out of control. "Just use them to write down your thoughts, how you feel. Sometimes it helps me figure things out, or makes me feel better, like I've gotten rid of whatever was bothering me," her best friend advised. Laura had been wise even at thirteen.

It seemed excessively silly to her at the time, a grown man so afraid of what his fifteen year old daughter thought of him that he had to burn the evidence. Now, looking back, she was sure he'd burned them because he thought of them as real evidence, a step-by-step account of all the terrible things he'd done. She recalled her dream, that feeling that she knew just what her father was talking about when he'd asked her mom the question, 'how long?' Nicole had suspected her mother was having an affair. She closed her eyes.

She'd even met the man. She frowned, trying to pull the memory from her subconscious, trying to bring focus to the man, the circumstances….

"Nicole," she felt Harry's warm hand on her shoulder and looked up into his worried eyes. "What's wrong? Were you dreaming?"

She shook her head. "Remembering. Trying to, anyway." She stood and stretched, her back sore from the uncomfortable chair by her brother's bed.

Harry handed her a fresh bottled water and kissed her. "Please go home," he said. "You've been here for days. You need to go get some real rest, especially now." He couldn't keep the twinkle out of his eyes or the smile off his lips as he dropped his gaze to her middle.

Her hand went to her flat belly and she leaned into his embrace, watching James out of the corner of her eye. Yesterday had been a big day. They'd weaned her brother off the ventilator. The doctors were uncertain if James would be able to breathe on his own, but he passed the spontaneous breathing trial well, and established a normal respiratory pattern once the tubing was taken out and the ventilator turned off. The relative silence in the room without the rasping machine was welcome and comforting. He'd yet to regain consciousness though. Nicole stubbornly refused to consider the possibility that he might never wake up.

The only bright spot at all was the amazing news from Dr. Sanchez that she was pregnant. And even that was colored with sadness, since it meant she couldn't donate a kidney.

Nicole had skipped right past elation to despair with the news of her positive pregnancy test. She'd been trying hard to convince herself that terminating the pregnancy was an option. Maybe she'd be lucky and get pregnant again, she thought. She shouldn't assume that just because this had taken two years, it couldn't happen again. She wanted to talk to Harry about it but she found she didn't have the words. Her baby was growing inside her while her brother was dying. Happiness and misery, joy and guilt. When would she ever know what it was to feel one solitary, wonderful emotion? She couldn't escape that ever present dread, always changing form but always there, dampening the clear edges of any real feeling she ever stumbled into.

"I'll stay with James for a while," Harry told her, taking her seat and opening his briefcase on the bedside table. "Please go home. Take a nice long shower, have something to eat. Maria made some turkey dish with the leftovers. It's in the fridge to be warmed up."

She nodded at him, giving his hand a squeeze and stopping to kiss her brother's forehead before she left.

She met Danny coming in as she was almost to the parking garage. "Hey, Nic! I did it! I found Aunt Emily!" A wave of relief washed over Nicole: maybe there was someone who could still help James, after all, she thought. Their aunt would have a fair chance of being a match for a kidney, according to the doctor.

"How?" she asked her little brother. "Where? Is she coming? Did you talk to her?"

He was nodding to all of her questions. "She was still in Michigan, on the west side of the state, near Benton Harbor. She's flying down tomorrow morning."

"Wow," Nicole breathed, hugging Daniel. "Thank you so much for taking care of that. Was she ... was it weird, talking to her after all this time?"

He shrugged. "A little, sure. But mostly she just sounded glad to hear from us, and eager to help."

Nicole arrived back home feeling like a wrung-out dish towel, she was so tired. She found a note from their housekeeper, Maria, who'd been putting in extra hours lately due to Nicole spending so much time with James. She followed orders and finished a large serving of Turkey Tetrazzini before trudging up the wide curving stairway to run a bath. Sinking gratefully into the large warm tub, she stretched her arms and legs and rolled her head around her neck, feeling all the little knots of tension and worry. Her eyes drifted closed and she tried to force thoughts of James in the big hospital bed out of her mind for at least a little while.

Instead, she saw her mother as she was in James' room, passed out in her wheelchair. Nicole hadn't brought her mom back in since that Sunday a few days ago ... the doctors were able to revive her, but it was unclear what had caused it. Nicole knew she'd been spooked at seeing

Daniel after so long, but that was an extreme reaction. When she regained consciousness, she was as disoriented as ever and Nicole drove her back to the nursing home in silence after she'd been kept for observation for a few hours.

Nicole soaked until the last possible minute, when the water was finally losing any trace of heat. She reluctantly toweled off, bundled up in her plush white robe, and crashed on top of the covers of their big four poster bed. She knew her hair was going to dry all lopsided and crazy but she couldn't bring herself to care.

She woke momentarily when Harry came to bed much later and gently scooped the bedclothes out from under her, covering her up, and fell easily back to sleep spooned up against him with his warm arm wrapped around her.

What seemed like only a few short minutes later, the sunlight streaming through the open curtains danced on her face and forced her to open her eyes. Harry was gone, most likely already at the office. She hurried getting dressed, unsure what was causing the rising feeling of worry and dread. She needed to get to the hospital. Leaving the dishes in the sink and the bed unmade, she tried to calm her nerves on the way there. The hospital hadn't called. James must still be the same, she was probably only jittery because her aunt was coming today, or from the pregnancy. When she stepped out of the elevator onto the unit, she knew she was wrong. There were nurses and doctors bustling in and out of James' room, checking his chart, flipping through paperwork. Terrified, her walk changed to a run and she skidded to a halt in his doorway, breathless.

James stared back at her.

"James!"

At the bedside, Lucy turned and smiled at Nicole before resuming her assessment, listening to James' lungs. "He just woke up a little while ago."

James held his hand out to Nicole.

She took it and hugged him carefully around the IV lines, crying and laughing, unable to stop smiling. She placed a hand on his cheek, searching his blue eyes. He was here. He returned her gaze and the smallest of smiles crossed his lips. She sobbed aloud and kissed his cheek. Her brother was back.

He closed his eyes and her breath caught in her throat for a second until he opened them again. "James," she whispered. "Jamie, oh my God, thank you, thank you."

Tears filled his eyes and spilled over onto his cheeks.

The monitor alarmed and Nicole jumped, looking to Lucy in fear, but the nurse nodded at Nicole and smiled. "Just his heart rate speeding up a little. He's okay, he's happy you're here," she patted James' shoulder gently.

Nicole didn't ask Lucy; she let go of her brother's hand only long enough to lower the obtrusive bed railing. She carefully climbed onto the bed next to her brother and rested her head between his bony shoulder and chest, hugging him. On some level she registered the monitor's beeps slowing, and she knew he was calming. She couldn't speak. She kept her hand over his heart, and thought she'd never felt such an amazing thing as this: her brother's heart beating steadily, strongly, under her fingers while he gripped her other hand.

Nicole would give him her kidney. She would give him his life, a new life, the life he'd been denied. She and Harry could conceive again. She knew immediately that she might be giving up any chance at all to ever have a child of her own. To be a good mother. To finally know the beauty of a parent/child bond. She kept her arm across her brother's chest, this scared little boy inside a broken man's body. If there was any way she could save him, she had no choice. She thought of the tiny baby growing inside her and squeezed her eyes shut. This was her decision.

She sat up a little and looked at her brother, not seeing the red rimming his blue eyes, the yellowing outside the iris, the chalky, grayish cast to his cheeks under his stubble. She swabbed at the twin trails of tears that leaked from the corners of his eyes and smiled at him. "James, you're going to be okay," she whispered. The little nagging voice in her head started up and she stomped it out. He would be okay and that was all. "I can help you. They're going to give you my kidney and you're going to be fine. We're going to be fine. Better than fine."

She spoke now to Lucy, who was staring wide-eyed at her. "Why isn't he speaking?" Her gaze went to James, then back to Lucy. "This is good. This is good, right?" Her question was challenging, defying the nurse to give her anything but the answer she wanted to hear.

Lucy hesitated only a second, locking eyes with Nicole. She regained her composure, nodding and reaching up to change the IV bag and recalibrate the pump for the new volume. "His throat is probably really sore from the ventilator. First thing on our list is to check his labs, which I was just about to do. Dr. Sanchez in on his way up now, too."

"Lucy has been taking such good care of you," Nicole told her brother, sitting now on the side of the mattress and trying not to jostle him. "How do you feel? Does anything hurt?"

Lucy efficiently set up her lab draw supplies on the other side of the bed and set to work taking several tubes of blood from the port on James' IV.

James opened his mouth and winced as he tried out a word. Nicole leaned closer to him. He whispered, "I'm sorry."

This made Nicole cry all over again. She kissed her brother's forehead. "It's okay," she whispered. "It's okay, you're going to be okay now," she told him quietly, meaning it. She held his hand and told him what she'd been afraid she wouldn't get a chance to. "I'm sorry, James, I'm sorry for everything. For not protecting you, for not being a better big sister, for letting you get into any of this. I'm so sorry."

He shook his head slightly. "Stupid," he whispered, rolling his eyes and pointing at both himself and her, his finger wagging back and forth. Nicole couldn't help a tiny sad smile as she agreed, nodding. "You've been the best sister," she heard his scratchy voice as he cringed from the effort. She didn't want to hear this. To hear him say she'd been. She was and would continue to be.

"Was Mom here?" His voice was a hair above a whisper but the shuffle around them had gotten respectfully quiet as Lucy and one doctor worked in the room.

"Yes. A few days ago. She's been worried too...." Nicole felt he might want to see her, but was hesitant to offer, not knowing if her mother's health could take it.

"Danny?"

She nodded. "Danny has been here every day. He's doing so great, James. You'd be proud of him." She went back to her original question. "Are you in any pain?"

Lucy gestured to the morphine pump next to the bed, and handed James a little button attached to a cord. "You're getting regular pain medication, James, but if you hurt, go ahead and push the button. It'll give you an extra dose, up to a set limit, when you need it." She gathered her clipboard and tubes of blood to go to the lab and exited noiselessly.

"Nothing hurts."

"Good."

"Could you bring Mom back?" Nicole's mind raced. Of course he'd want to see their mother. No matter her inadequacies as a parent, the three of them loved her just the same.

"Sure," she nodded. He had a right to see her, especially now. "Do you remember Aunt Emily? Danny found her, still living in Michigan. She's coming today, too, to see you." Nicole held the faint hope that maybe Emily would be a match for James. She didn't know how she would talk to Harry about her decision. How she would handle it herself.

She kept her eyes on James, determined to stay objective. Her brother came first. She was all he had.

James eyebrows went up at the news of Aunt Emily coming, but he didn't comment. The room was stifling and still for too long, so Nicole attempted to change the subject again. "Did you know Hugo was the one who brought you here, and called me to come?"

James was frowning now. "Why?"

"Why did Hugo--"

"Why Aunt Emily?"

"Because ... we didn't know if you…." She didn't know how to finish the sentence. She didn't want to tell him about the baby, about the need to test Aunt Emily. She didn't want to tell him that two days ago the doctors had come in to talk to her about hospice. About the possibility that her brother wouldn't survive. They'd strolled in here and started up the discussion with no preamble, taking her completely by surprise. It had taken her a full two minutes to even come up with a response, and then, when they'd tried to back up their suggestion with odds and percentages, she'd drawn an audience of nurses and staff with her emphatic answer. She'd told them to get the hell out of her brother's room.

Now she answered James' question. "Daniel told Aunt Emily what happened, and she wanted to fly down and see you, all three of us," she finished lamely.

James rested his hands on his hollowed out middle and turned his head toward the window. She knew then that her brother realized how sick he really was. She sat back down in her chair, right next to his bed, not letting go of his hand.

"James," she said softly. He looked at her. "Please trust me. Please try … give yourself a chance to get better. I know you can. We need you," she swallowed hard, a tear sneaking from one eye. "This is your do over, a new beginning," she whispered. James closed his eyes and held her hand.

CHAPTER EIGHTEEN

An eternity later, Dr. Sanchez made his appearance along with the clerk from the desk. The clerk addressed her as Dr. Sanchez perused her brother's chart at the foot of his bed. "Mrs. Peterson, there's someone to see you."

She rounded the corner into the visitor waiting room and was amazed to see Laura standing nervously with a huge bouquet of flowers spilling from her arms.

"Oh! My Lord," Nicole exclaimed, "of all the people I didn't expect to see standing here!" She flung herself at Laura and hugged her tightly, crushing some of the blooms. "How in the world--what are you doing here?"

Laura laughed. "I just thought you might need me," she shrugged humbly, as if she'd simply stopped in from a few blocks over rather than put her life on hold to fly across the country on the chance her friend might need some support.

Nicole dropped her thin frame into a chair. “I need you. I can’t believe you came. James just woke up less than an hour ago. I think it’s good, but--no one is saying anything. The doctor is in with him now.” She glanced at Laura, who’d taken a seat beside her.

“You said he was in a coma, so I’m sure it’s a good sign he’s awake. And you said he needs a kidney and no one’s a match so far ... I know it’s a long shot, but could they test me?”

Nicole nodded gratefully at her. “Of course, thank you. I think we actually have a match.” Nicole heaved a sigh. She would explain things to Laura, but she wanted to get back to James. “Daniel even found our aunt, she’s flying down this morning too. Oh my goodness, I have to call him!”

Nicole placed a quick, joyful call to Danny, who said he was waiting at the airport for Aunt Emily and would be at the hospital shortly. She and Laura worked out the details of Laura staying at Nicole’s house while they walked back down the hall. They decided to go pick up Irene soon.

“I also want to wait and talk to Dr. Sanchez before we go.”

The mood was gloomier on the way to the nursing home. Dr. Sanchez was less excited about James regaining consciousness than Nicole hoped. The preliminary labs they’d run had come back showing that not only was his remaining kidney barely functioning, he was also going into congestive heart failure. Even on dialysis, it would be difficult to treat. The infection from the perforated bowel didn’t help matters either.

They'd do everything they could, but so far the IV antibiotics and diuretics and heart medications weren't making much of a difference. Nicole explained that her aunt would be coming in soon for HLA testing, and that she'd decided to be James' donor if Emily wasn't a match.

Nicole was crushed when Dr. Sanchez haltingly told her that at this point, James was not stable enough for transplant, even with a perfect match.

Nicole peppered the conversation on the drive to and from the nursing home with half-hearted questions about Laura's life, Charlie, her family's Thanksgiving. Laura knew how worried her friend was when she neglected to ask anything at all about Adam.

Nicole and Laura pushed Irene's wheelchair onto the elevator, heading back up to the ICU, just as they heard Daniel called out, "Wait!"

Laura hurriedly hit the button to hold the doors and watched in awe as the grown up version of the toddler she remembered stepped in, followed by the woman who was obviously Aunt Emily.

John Murdock was there in the woman's features and it was jarring. Her lined face bore neither a trace of make-up nor any sign of extraneous care. She was only a bit shorter than Daniel, maybe 5'11", and solid, but definitely not fat. Her forearm next to his as they rode the elevator looked muscular and sinewy. A long, thick gray braid hung down her back and her faded peasant skirt swayed over worn gray work boots. Emily's hands brought a rush of memories back to Nicole. She stood still behind Irene's wheelchair, staring at her aunt's hands.

Emily Murdock's hands were rough, calloused, leathery looking, a little discolored. The nails were blunt and thick, and under each was a faint line of dirt that probably wasn't even dirt at all, but the stains of dirt. She and James had been once to visit her in Benton Harbor. Her little cabin was almost completely hidden by a multitude of trees, and she had a garden running around the entire perimeter of the house, where she grew, stored and canned everything she'd ever need to eat. She hunted for the rest. The entire time they'd stayed there with her, they hadn't seen another person. Emily had cut herself off from the world in that house.

"I'm so glad to finally see you both again," she told them, her voice quiet and low.

Nicole nodded and swallowed hard, pushing the old memories out of her head. "Thank you for coming, for trying to help."

"There hasn't been a day gone by when I didn't think of the three of you."

Irene sat silent in her wheelchair, staring straight ahead. Laura wondered if the woman thought she was in an elevator full of strangers; she seemed absent.

After a few beats of awkward silence, Emily cleared her throat a bit. "I hope I'm a match for James, it would mean so much to me if I could help."

Daniel spoke to Nicole. "I filled her in, she knows James woke up this morning. Maybe things will all fall into place," he said hopefully.

Nicole didn't have the heart to tell him what Dr. Sanchez said. She refused to believe that James couldn't somehow improve. After all, she thought, look at the odds he'd already overcome just by getting off the ventilator and waking up.

The elevator doors swished open and the little group found themselves standing in the wide white hallway. "Oh!" Nicole took Laura's arm and pulled her into the circle.

Laura had been trying to remain unobtrusive. This reunion of sorts seemed so surreal, and she was certain it felt strained and awkward to each of them.

Nicole hastily made introductions. Laura nodded, murmuring hellos. She spoke to Nicole in a low tone. "Would you like me to sit with your mother while you all go down first and see James?"

Nicole breathed a sigh of relief. "Yes. Yes, please, that would help. Could you just give us a few minutes, and then bring her down?"

Laura wheeled Irene into the quiet visitor's lounge. The woman looked at her blankly when she tried to make light conversation while they were waiting. She seemed oblivious to her surroundings. Laura got a reaction when she mentioned living next door to them years ago. She saw a flash of recognition in Irene's eyes.

She surprised Laura by reaching out to take her hand. "You were always such a good little friend to my Nicole."

The trio of Murdocks drifted down the long hallway, slender Nicole flanked by her big baby brother and her long lost aunt.

Emily hung back just outside James room. Nicole looked at her questioningly. "Are you all right, Aunt Emily?"

The large woman sighed, shoulders slumped. She shrugged, eyes cast downward. Finally she looked up and met the gaze of the niece and nephew she hadn't seen in years, had never attempted to find. "I know what you're thinking," she said.

Danny put a hand on her arm. "It's okay," he started. She shook her head at him.

"I know what type of man your father was. He was exactly like our father. Exactly the type of man he swore he wouldn't become. He did you a favor running away and leaving you all behind, you know," she said softly.

"We know that," Nicole answered. "As bad as things got after he left, it was better than having him around, I'm sure of that."

"He realizes that too," she said quietly.

Daniel stared at her. "You've heard from him." His whole expression changed, his brow knitted, and he felt himself move away from her. "You've heard from him and you've done nothing?"

Emily turned to him. "I get a postcard once a year around his birthday. They started after you left Michigan. There's no return address, only a postmark." She paused. "I've done nothing, you're right. You three are better off. John is…." she paused again, searching for the right words.

"A murderer," Daniel finished for her. "A child abuser. A man who beat the shit out of his wife and kids on a regular basis just because he could."

Nicole squeezed his arm, glancing at the nurse's station nearby. A few of them were looking in their direction. None of what they'd endured as children was this woman's fault.

Daniel shook his sister's hand off. "How long are you going to continue to do nothing, Aunt Emily? Do you know what we've been through because of him? James is in this condition at least partially because of him. Nicole has been through hell and back trying to take care of us because of him. Our mother is a tortured, timid shell of a person because of him. An innocent bystander is dead because of him."

Emily's face was flushed red and her breathing rapid, but she continued to meet his angry gaze. "I understand now. I suppose I always imagined…." She took a deep breath. "I thought once he was gone you'd all be fine, somehow." She laughed without meaning to, a nervous, humorless laugh. "How ridiculous. We weren't fine. We've never been fine. Our parents are dead, John's a monster, and I--"

Daniel's expression softened a bit as he listened to her, realizing she'd had a childhood similar to his own.

"Well, I," she finished, "have just let it all keep happening, haven't I? I'm done doing nothing. I'm so sorry," she beseeched Nicole and Daniel with tortured eyes. "I just thought, he was gone, and you were better off. I was wrong." She nodded to herself.

"I've been silent for too long. I'll do whatever I can to help, to help James, and to help you find John. I promise."

Nicole was heartened to see her brother's face light up a bit when Emily entered his room. She walked to his bedside without a word, folding his boney hand in her large ones. Fat tears rolled down their aunt's cheeks and she smiled, her features distorted painfully with sadness and regret. Nicole stood on the opposite side of the bed and wrapped an arm around Danny's waist. She leaned on him as he pulled her in, squeezing her shoulder.

Emily carefully bent over the bed and placed a hand gently on each side of James' ashy face, kissing his forehead. Lucy, always there when she was needed, slid a chair up to the bed and motioned for Emily to use it.

"You look just like the little boy I remember, Jamie," she smiled at him.

James forced hoarse words out, cringing. "I can't believe you came."

"I'm sorry it took so long. I've missed you so much." She tenderly stroked his matted hair off his forehead and James closed his eyes. "You've got to get better. I'm not going anywhere until you do."

James nodded. "Thank you, Aunt Emily." His eyes went to Daniel standing next to Nicole. "You grew up," he whispered.

Daniel moved to the side of the bed. "I guess I did." It had been over two years since he'd seen his brother. The man in the hospital bed was not the brother he remembered.

"Nicole says you've got it together," James winced as he spoke. Daniel tried to interrupt him, stop the painful effort, but James waved his hand weakly, continuing.

"I'm proud of you, Danny."

The weight of those few, simple words bore down on Daniel and the room blurred around him. His throat burned and his chest ached. He would trade places with his brother right this second if he could. He crouched down by the bed, inches from James. He gingerly hugged his emaciated frame, was startled when he felt James return the embrace with one limp arm.

Danny turned his face to James, cradling him carefully in his strong arms. "I love you brother," his voice broke at the end, the words barely more than a whisper. He kissed James' scruffy cheek and gently laid him back on the hospital bed.

Nicole fixed the bed coverings around him and smiled through her tears at him. He closed his eyes as he captured her hand in his and held it, not letting go.

The siblings and their aunt sat in silence, remnants of heavy words and unspoken thoughts drifting in the air around them.

Emily spoke after a while. "Hey … do you remember when we went fishing? I took you and your sister out in my little row boat and we sat for hours, waiting for a bite."

She had his attention now, James looked at her wearily. "Nicole wouldn't shut up," he whispered.

Nicole laughed. "You wouldn't stop picking on me! You pushed me out of the boat!"

"You hit me on the head with the oar."

"Oh yeah." She looked at him, chastised. "Sorry."

He rolled his head on the pillow back toward Emily. “And then we started catching them.”

Emily nodded. “One after the other. You wouldn’t stop. We had enough for the whole week. You would size each one up, and throw back any that were smaller than your hand.”

“She made me,” he motioned weakly to Nicole. “She kept naming the little ones.”

“And then it got dark. I told you we had to go, and you still didn’t want to give up. I only got you to put the pole away when I promised to take you back out the next day.”

James nodded. “You did.”

Emily smiled at him. “You were a great fisherman. Patient, determined. You found the joy in it. You’ve always been that way. And I always keep my promises,” she glanced up at Nicole. Her need to be forgiven, to be accepted back into their family, was written in her features.

James closed his eyes again, a faint smile now painted on his face. He looked so relaxed, more peaceful than Nicole could recall seeing him in ages.

The room fell quiet but for the whirring of the IVs, the steady blip of the monitors. After a time, Laura appeared at the doorway with Irene.

“Is now a good time?”

Nicole nodded, taking the wheelchair handles and thanking Laura. “Would you like to stay?”

Laura stood in the doorway of the glass enclosed ICU room, afraid to take a step inside. James lay unmoving in the bed, a sunken figure surrounded by white. She'd never been in a room where dread hung so thickly in the air. She shook her head at Nicole.

"No. Your family needs to be together right now. I'll be just down the hall if you need me."

Nicole pushed her mother's wheelchair into James' room and his eyes crinkled when he smiled at Irene. Emily stood and moved to a corner, making room for the older woman. Irene laid her head on the bed next to her son's hand as she had last time. James stroked his mother's thin hair and a few stray tears rolled from the corners of his eyes.

"Jamie, I'm so happy you're awake now," she whispered to him.

Irene patted James' hand and told him he'd be fine, he had good doctors, he just had to try to get well.

James caught Nicole's gaze and she nodded encouragingly at him, wishing she could ignore the look in her brother's exhausted, deep set eyes. A part of him had already let go. Nicole pressed the call button for Lucy and looked at Danny.

He was seeing the same change in James that she was. "I'll go get someone," he murmured and moved quickly out the door.

In his quiet, raspy voice, James told their mother, "I know you tried to protect us. I know you loved us."

A loud, aching sob burst from Irene's lungs and she covered her face with both hands, her shoulders shaking. "I did, I do, I just wasn't strong enough, brave enough--" another sob wracked her body. Nicole was quick to kneel at her side, hugging her gently, rocking her.

"Mom. Mom, it's all right, please. Stop crying, we know, we really do," she told her as the older woman uncovered her face to look at Nicole.

"But then, why?" Her mother's eyes were clear and she sounded perfectly lucid, logical. "When you brought me here the other day, I saw him, but he's dead. I know he's dead because I saw your father kill him, but he was here! Why are you lying to me?" She stared at Nicole, waiting for an answer.

Nicole's mouth opened and then closed again. She had no words, no reply for this. She looked at James, whose eyes were drooping a bit.

Lucy's voice came over the PA system in the room. "Hello, what can I help you with?"

As Nicole told the nurse James needed help, Irene turned to him, demanding, "You saw him, too, didn't you Jamie? He was right here in your room, but he couldn't have been!" James didn't even seem to rally at the nonsensical question; his eyes looked glazed to Nicole.

Nicole glanced in fear at her brother and quickly pressed the call button again, shouting the nurse's name. Something was not right. She darted to the doorway, casting over her shoulder to Irene, "Mother, calm down. Who do you think you saw?"

She looked at Nicole as if she were an idiot. "Daniel's father," she said, oblivious to her other son giving up his fight only inches away. "I saw Daniel's father, and I know you did too."

From the hallway, where she was met by Danny, Lucy and three others racing toward the room, Nicole looked back at her brother. James' eyes were closed and the heart monitor above the bed was beeping crazily.

The group of medical staff swarmed the room, one of them pushing a red crash cart.

CHAPTER NINETEEN

The day of James' funeral dawned sunny and warm. Nicole woke too early, well before 6:00 a.m., and was still sitting on the balcony off their bedroom when she heard the front door close and Laura's hushed voice talking on her cell phone just below her. Nicole tucked her feet up underneath her robe and closed her eyes, trying not to eavesdrop, tired but not sleepy. Laura was obviously talking to Charlie. She allowed herself to try to imagine her own unborn child, hand lightly resting on her belly. This only made her throat close with grief for James.

She tried to see him in her mind's eye the way he was, before. But before what? It was so hard for her to recall a time when her brother wasn't plagued by the chaos that was their life. The only image in her mind was the most recent one. She would find a way to replace it with better ones.

Nicole left her sunny balcony and found Laura doing dishes, a new pot of coffee brewing, and the scent of something cinnamony and delicious coming from the oven.

"Don't you ever just sit down and relax?"

Laura jumped a little and turned off the water. "Not much," she smiled. "How are you feeling?"

Nicole shrugged. "Better, I think." Her eyes were red and puffy from two days of crying jags, but they looked a bit brighter this morning.

She sat at the counter, staring past Laura. "I wish I could undo it all. He was too young. He struggled for too long. He still had his whole life to live. But I keep remembering how he looked the last time he was here," she met Laura's eyes. "He's free now. He never has to feel that way again."

Laura nodded silently and hugged her, setting down the coffee cups she'd been holding. "You're right."

"They arrested the guy that shot him. Hugo--a friend of ours among enemies--gave them a tip, I think. The guy still had the gun. The bullets matched the ones they took out of James." She took a sip of the steaming coffee. "He never really got to be a kid, you know?"

"I know," Laura agreed. "Neither did you."

"I know. But I think it was different for James. When our father left, he felt like he was supposed to step up and, I don't know, support us, I guess. He was barely even a teenager." Nicole realized it felt good to talk about him. It somehow made it a tiny bit easier, missing him.

"He worked all these odd jobs in junior high and high school, trying to help out. He'd get up at 5:00 a.m. every day to deliver papers, and he bussed tables most nights after school. We did okay for a little while. Aunt Emily said that's how she pictured us, pulling ourselves up by our bootstraps and living a better life. I don't know what happened."

"Yes, you do," Laura said. "None of you were adults, equipped to deal with all of that. James got burned out and decided to try being a normal teenager. You took on the entire responsibility of raising your brothers when your mom got sick. You and James made some bad choices under a lot of stress. Daniel had a breakdown. You got raped." She knew she sounded harsh and she didn't mean to. She reached out and squeezed Nicole's hand. "You did the best you could under terrible circumstances."

Nicole smiled wryly. "That's what she said, remember? My mom said she did the best she could. I guess she did. She tried." She looked at Laura. "Aunt Emily says our mom tried to run away once, but she gave in to his threats. And she fought to get us back that time protective services took us away."

"There are probably a hundred things she wishes she could go back and do differently, Nic. It can't have been easy."

"Somehow I just always figured James would get it straightened out. He was so smart, such a good person underneath it all." Nicole pressed the heel of her hand to her temple, holding up her throbbing head. "Wanna know something?"

Laura nodded, lightly resting a hand on Nicole's arm.

"Sometimes I think it would be easier to be high," she whispered. She rested a hand on the flat belly that betrayed no trace of the baby within. "Nothing hurt then. Nothing mattered. This is so much harder." She met Laura's eyes. "I've gotten so good at locking all of this away, you know? Safe. Pain-free. But I can't anymore."

Laura sat, still, waiting. She knew this was important, and Nicole must come to it on her own.

"It wouldn't be right, wouldn't be fair to James. We spent our whole lives running away. It's time to face what we've been running from. If I don't--if I can't--then losing James means nothing. It could have been me. He gave me this. I have to make it mean something." She sucked in a deep breath, searching Laura's eyes for understanding. "I can't block anything out anymore. It doesn't work."

Laura bit her lip and squeezed Nicole's arm, tears rolling down her own cheeks now.

"It's the only way I can keep him with me. My brother," a pained smile broke through her tears. "He's free. And I'll never be the same again. And that's a good thing," she nodded.

Laura thought Nicole had never looked so beautiful as at that moment. Hair pulled back messily, tear streaked face, bright green eyes alive with the realization that her brother was not broken anymore. James was at peace. Nicole would give her child the life she and her brothers never had.

Laura stood and closed the space between them, kissing her friend's forehead. "You're going to be an amazing mother, Nicole."

Nicole broke down into a new round of tears and rested her head on Laura's shoulder. That was all she wanted. She hoped it was true.

After a while, Nicole sat back, wiping the tears away once and for all. At least for now. She pulled a folded piece of paper from the pocket of her robe. "I finished my eulogy," she handed it to Laura. "Would you read it and make sure it sounds okay?" She straightened up and drifted over to the stove, peeking inside at the cream cheese coffee cake her friend was making.

"Go ahead and take that out, it should be done by now. You need some breakfast before we head to the church," Laura told her.

Irene made it through the service at the funeral home, the eulogy given by Nicole, and an impromptu one from Hugo that warmed Nicole's heart, giving her a modicum of comfort at her brother's funeral. The big, menacing man had known a side of her brother that Nicole hadn't seen in so long, a fun-loving, joking side. It made Nicole feel good that even in his dark, desperate existence, James had moments of happiness.

It was at the cemetery that things fell apart. Perhaps it was the sight of Daniel standing over the casket with the small group who'd come to the grave site to say goodbye. Nicole knew now that Danny must look an awful lot like his real father, and maybe more so with the beard, which added years to his face. She was glad he'd gotten rid of it. Nicole knew that her mother had had an affair years ago; she knew it went on when Danny was a baby, and Dr. Sanchez at the hospital, with his HLA-typing results, had confirmed that it had been going on before Danny was ever born.

In the limousine on the way to the cemetery, Nicole tried to prepare her mother for what would happen. The funeral home had been surprisingly crowded, and her mother sat woodenly in her wheelchair with very little reaction to any of the subdued activity going on around her. Nicole explained that they would say goodbye to James here, and the minister would read a passage from the bible before the casket was lowered into the ground. Irene simply nodded. Then Nicole gently told her mother that she'd be sitting with her and Harry and Daniel. She held Irene's hand and asked her, "Do you remember seeing Daniel at the hospital?"

Irene turned and made eye contact with Nicole. "He wasn't there."

"Mom, Daniel will be there today. He's your son," she said, rummaging in her purse for the picture she had of him from last Christmas at their house.

"I know he's my son!" Irene snapped, frowning at Nicole. "Of course Daniel's my son!"

Nicole pulled out the small photograph and squeezed her mother's hand. "Mom, I think Danny looks a lot like someone else to you. I want to show you his picture so you won't be surprised, okay?"

Irene sighed and rolled her eyes. Nicole silently handed her the picture of Danny in a red and tan sweater in front of the fireplace, an easy smile on his face.

Irene, an unreadable expression on her face, stared at the image for the amount of time it took them to travel the remaining three miles to the cemetery. When they pulled onto the roundabout that was closest to

James' gravesite, Irene silently handed the picture back to Nicole, her eyes looking through her daughter to a past Nicole barely remembered.

"He's grown into such a handsome boy," she said quietly. "I wish…."

Irene didn't finish the thought, and Nicole leaned forward, squeezing her mother's hand. "You wish what, Mom?"

The limo driver chose that moment to open the door, and Irene sat back abruptly, gathering her purse and lace handkerchief into her lap. Nicole groaned inwardly and exited the car to help her mother into the wheelchair.

The minister had finished his final words, and Daniel and Nicole each dropped a handful of dirt into the hole that would swallow their brother, before Irene snapped. Only a small gathering of people had come to the cemetery, and Nicole caught movement out of the corner of her eye. Her mother was standing, the wheelchair abandoned behind her, as she took a few shaky steps toward the two standing over the grave. Her boney spine was hunched like the stem of a wilting flower. She'd made it nearly to the edge of the gaping rectangular hole before Daniel and Nicole flanked her, supporting her arms.

"Mom--"

She turned away from Nicole and held onto Daniel's forearms with both hands, looking up into his face. "I'm so sorry, Robert," she told him, her voice quavering with unshed tears. "We needed more time. I wish we had more time. I never wanted it to end like this. We were supposed to be together, in a little house on the coast, the five of us. I didn't know he'd follow me, how could I know? Danny never even got to know you, and you would have been such a good father, to Nicki and James too. And now, look--" She gestured wildly at the casket deep in the grave. "People are dying all around me again, and it's not fair," her voice broke and Daniel hugged her, her thin shoulders shaking with sobs.

Danny's eyes met Nicole's over the old woman's head, now full of knowledge, an untold story they each knew pieces of. Irene had been planning to leave their father, to run away with this man and start over. For a moment Nicole's heart ached for her poor lost mother. She had loved the wrong man and then possibly the right one, she'd seen a chance at a better life, and then lost everything: the man who'd really loved her, her home, her mind, and now her oldest son. They remained in a tight knot at the gravesite, Harry with an arm protectively around Nicole, Nicole gently patting Irene's back, Daniel holding her and slowly swaying back and forth, until the minister cleared his throat and Nicole became aware of the rustle of people shifting uncomfortably in the small group behind them.

Glad it was a small crowd, she gingerly took Irene's right arm while Danny held the other, and they eased her back into the wheelchair that Laura had retrieved. Irene now seemed deflated, her eyes cast at the ground, her body limp and pliant. Nicole stood with Danny and their mother as people slowly began to leave, murmuring quiet words of consolation to them on the way.

When they were gone, she crouched down in front of the wheelchair, determined to make some sense of her mother's confusion.

Irene raised her eyes to Nicole's. I'd better make each question count, she thought, not knowing how much more her mother had in her. She saw Laura out of the corner of her eye. Her amazing friend had pulled a slip of paper from her purse and was furiously making notes. A wave of gratitude washed over Nicole as she realized she was suddenly one huge step closer to finding resolution to the chaos ruling her history.

"Mom, what happened to Robert?"

Irene blinked. "We were going to leave. He had a little place in South Carolina. He could get a job there. You kids would love it there. But John," Irene grimaced and looked away. "John wrecked it. Like he always does."

"How did he wreck it?" Nicole wanted the answer but wasn't sure she was ready to hear it. She glanced up at Danny standing silently next to Irene, and could see the nerve-wracking anticipation written in his features as well.

"Why, he killed him, of course. It's my fault. I should have known. He destroys everything, your father does. And nobody knows. Nobody cares. He's evil, your father." Her eyes seemed to focus on Nicole now for the first time since the scene over the grave. "I could've stopped it all, I never should have talked to Robert, should have kept to myself," she rested her head on her hand, clearly exhausted. "Can I go home now, please?"

Nicole could feel her heart racing in her chest. "Yes, Mom, we'll go. Right now." She stood. "But, Mom, what was Robert's last name?"

Irene looked up at her blankly.

"His last name, Mom. Danny's father, his real father."

Irene shook her head. "No. No no no. I promised John he was the real father. I had to make him believe it. And poor Robert, now he's swallowed up forever in the deep dark sea," she said, and laughed, a disturbing sound that changed to a soft, whining cry after a few moments.

Nicole looked questioningly at her brother, who inclined his head to the open grave nearby, and shrugged. She must still be confusing the two deaths, Nicole thought.

"Why didn't you go to the police, mom? Did you ever tell anyone?"

"The police officers don't care. They take away my children, and then they give them back. They come and they go, they don't see a thing. And the one that does, it's his funeral," she said, laughing again, and Nicole fought a wave of disgust for this woman who'd kept so many secrets that even she herself didn't seem to know what was real anymore.

***

Nicole climbed the winding staircase into the attic with equal parts anticipation and trepidation. She knew her journals were stored up here somewhere. She found them easily after moving a few containers of old linens out of the way. Her entire collection of belongings she'd brought with her when she married Harry was held in two medium-sized cardboard boxes marked Nicole Murdock. She'd emptied her clothing, shoes and toiletries from one when she moved in, and now the other one stood under the attic window, untouched since then. Nicole pulled up a small stool and sat, hands clasped, not ready yet to open it.

James' funeral was yesterday. He'd been gone four days now. In the past two years, she'd only seen him a handful of times, each time farther down in the pit of his own self-destruction. She knew that she was lucky to have escaped the same fate, and that Danny, though he'd have to be vigilant with his medication program, was going to be fine eventually. She just couldn't shake off this melancholy that had seemed to settle in her chest the day James died. Laura had reminded her that her wounds were fresh. She'd said the sadness never really leaves, but that it somehow would get a little easier over time. She would someday feel normal again. Nicole thought maybe she'd feel almost normal. She couldn't imagine ever shedding the sense of emptiness, a void in her soul where her brother belonged. She needed normalcy again, especially for the baby. She wanted to feel happy about the baby. But right now, she was wading through each day in a shroud of sadness and loss. She looked at this Nicole Murdock box from her former life. Maybe she could fill the time until normal doing something she hoped would help her heal.

As she unfolded the dusty flaps of the box, she heard her mother's voice in her head again, that day at the hospital: 'Daniel's father; I saw him, but it couldn't have been him,' she'd said. 'I know it couldn't have been him, because your father killed him.' And then at the funeral yesterday, it was as if Irene's mind had finally broken open and all the years of hidden truths and layers of deception had come spilling out. Laura was working on making sense of it all. Nicole hoped to add a few missing pieces to the puzzle.

Laura was making good headway fitting together the scraps of information they had. Even after her late flight home yesterday, she'd called Nicole this morning to tell her that Emily was true to her word. She had personally driven her stack of postcards from John Murdock the three hours to Orsonville, handing Laura the little bundle of clues to the man's last seventeen years and thanking her for her help.

Nicole rummaged through the remnants of her past, pulling out two yellowed spiral notebooks, the covers decorated with pink and purple flowery designs. She turned the brittle pages of the first, the one marked "#8," catching glimpses in her handwritten thoughts of her teenaged life, a crush on a boy named Rick, a failed math test she'd hidden from her parents. She stopped at the last few pages, flipping back to find the beginning of the entry.

August 18: "Today was the greatest day ever," her bubbly, curly handwriting began. "Laura's sister Jenny said she'll take us to the concert this weekend. I can't believe we really get to go. Mom doesn't know yet that we have tickets, but I'll tell her that we won them, that they were free.... She's got to let us go. Jenny's almost nineteen, and she'll be with us the whole time, so we'll be safe, it's not like it's a big deal. I'm going to wait 'till after Dad is asleep tonight and then talk to Mom. I can't wait!"

August 19: "We can go we can go we can go!! Mom says we can go as soon as she gets home from working at the church Saturday afternoon, and that should be in plenty of time, I just have to watch Jamie and Danny 'till then. I can't believe I'm going to my first concert!"

August 22: "I hate her. I hate her so much I wish she was dead." Here Nicole's writing had gotten less curly and rounded, more slanted and angry. "She's the worst excuse for a mom ever. I don't know why she even wanted to have kids, if she can't take care of them, and she doesn't even care about them. She knew I had to leave for the concert by 6:00, she promised—PROMISED—that she would be home in time. Jenny and Laura even waited all the way until almost 7:00 to leave. She walks in at 8:30, like it's no big deal. She even forgot that I had plans! I never get to do anything! She didn't even tell me why she was so late, she just walked in all happy and smiley. Even when I yelled at her, all she said was, 'Oh, Nicki, it's okay, don't worry, things are going to change for us, blah blah blah.' I yelled, 'Where were you? How come you couldn't get home in time for me to go, I never ask you for stuff like this, this was special!' And she just had some stupid excuse, like, 'I had something very important to take care of, something that will help all of us. Someday you'll understand.' What a total cop-out. As long as I'm always here to babysit, that's what counts, right? I hate both of them."

September 1: "Something's going on. I don't know what, but Mom has been gone more and more lately, she says it's the church, but yesterday I caught her in a total lie. She said she had to go out after dinner to work on the church rummage sale with Mrs. Bourdain, but then today at school I talked to Brenda, and she said her mom and the other ladies finished up with that stuff like, a week ago. So where's she going? Dad is so out of it all the time, he doesn't even know she's gone. I keep the boys quiet playing in their room or outside, he drinks 'till he passes out after dinner, and she's usually home by the time he wakes up to go to bed. So today I decided. I'm going to follow her. If she expects me to take care of everything here all the time, I want to know why. Tonight when she leaves, 'cause I know she'll come up with some excuse to go out, I'm going to have Laura keep an eye on the boys while they play outside and I'll take Dad's car and see where she goes. I already have my permit, and I'm a better driver than the old drunk anyway, so fuck him."

That was the last entry. Nicole hadn't recalled being so incredibly angry during her teen years. Her memory seemed to have blurred that time of her life, so that when she did have to think back, she didn't usually think about how she had reacted to all of it. She dropped the journal on the floor and looked at the other one in her lap, labeled "#9." With a sinking feeling she remembered some of what was coming, she took a shaky breath and opened it.

September 2: "Well, now I know. I guess I should have figured it out sooner. I can't believe she'd do this. I can't believe she'd take a chance that Dad might find out. I feel like I don't even know her. Dad's been on the warpath the last couple days, so Mom hung around acting like a good wife until tonight. He's mad about something going on at work or whatever, but tonight he was all nice and joking around at dinner, and then finished his usual gallon of whiskey and passed out in front of TV again. Mom left right after, big surprise. Some crap about needing to go grocery shopping, like we don't have a freezer full of food. It was easy to get out, Laura sat outside with the boys and fed them popsicles and I jumped in Dad's car and stayed as far as I could behind her. She only went to the McDonald's right in town, and parked. But then this other car pulled up next to her, the guy got out, a tall guy with dark blond hair and a beard, and went over to my mom's car. She got out and hugged him! They stood there for a minute and talked, then got in his car and took off. She just left her car there. I wanted to follow them, but I was scared Dad would wake up. I didn't want him to yell at Laura for me being gone, or take it out on Jamie and Danny instead. I don't know what to do. Do I talk to her, ask her to tell me what's going on? I need to talk to someone, I need to tell Laura, but … how can I? Look at her family! Wasn't mine screwed up enough already? I can't tell her this, what will she think of me? I don't know what to do."

The next entry was days later, around two weeks before Nicole's father had ferreted the family away in the middle of the night.

September 9: "I haven't been able to follow Mom again. It's driving me crazy. And now I'm thinking maybe it's not what I thought. Maybe the guy is a counselor or a cop or something. Maybe she's trying to find a way to get us help. I keep thinking about what she said the day she made me miss the concert, that she was doing something important that will help us. I don't think she would actually cheat on Dad, I think I was just jumping to conclusions. But now that I know that she's trying to get help, I really need to talk to her about it ... I need to find a way."

September 20: "I really messed up, I think I got Mom in huge trouble with Dad, and I don't think I can fix things. That guy came to our house yesterday. It was weird, it was in the afternoon, like right before Dad usually gets home from work, and he seemed like he was in a really big hurry. He didn't even wait for me to get Mom, she was upstairs with Danny. He just gave me an envelope to give her, and he said thank you and left. It was sealed. Oh geez, did I want to open it! I didn't, I took it up to her, and she wouldn't open it, she just tucked it into her pocket. So I asked her, 'who's the guy?' She said, 'what do you mean?' I said, 'it's the same guy I saw you with in McDonald's parking lot.' Mom's face went totally white and she was quiet for a long time. She picked up Danny and started walking down the stairs. I followed her, and I'm so stupid, I knew Dad was going to be home any minute, but I just opened my big mouth and kept bugging her about it. 'Why won't you tell me who he is? Is he going to help us? What are you planning?' And I came around the corner into the living room and Dad was standing there, his keys still in his hand, and his face was all red. Mom turned her head and looked back at me, put Danny down, and said, 'take him out to play please, Nicole.' That's it. She went into the kitchen, he went upstairs, and that was two hours ago, and he's gone, probably at the bar, and I don't even want to be here later when he gets back home again."

September 21: "They've been fighting and fighting ... worse than usual, way worse, and the kind of scary thing is Dad's been leaving us alone, just going after Mom. I heard them talking, she explained to him that the guy who came by the house is just some financial advisor guy from her work, dropping off papers for her to fill out for some bank stuff or something. She even showed Dad some papers, but I don't think he believed her. She hasn't gone anywhere in the evenings in four days, and he hasn't passed out in his chair, either. It's really tense all the time. I can't believe I'm saying this, but I hope things go back to normal soon, this is just giving me the worst stomach ache all the time."

The last entry was only a few lines long, and sloppy. That night came back to her the instant she read the words, spinning through her mind as if on a movie reel.

September 23: "Dad didn't go to work today. He got mad at Danny for crying and slammed him into the wall behind the couch. Danny's eyes rolled back in his head and he stopped moving. I thought he was dead. Mom came in after and didn't say a word, just picked him up and went upstairs. If I knew a way to kill my father, I would."

That day was rainy and cold, dark clouds hanging low in the autumn sky for hours. She didn't know why her father hadn't gone to work, only that there was a nervous silence in the house, some kind of temporary truce between her parents. James had gone to school as usual, as had she, and when she arrived home at 2:30, the climate in the house was just as chilly and tense. Danny was fussy, wouldn't nap, wouldn't eat, and was following their mother around whining while her father sat in his easy chair and stared at the blank TV screen. This simple thing alone she recalled taking as a bad sign. The TV was never off when John Murdock was home. It happened so fast there was no way she could have stopped it, she knew that now. He was up and out of his chair, across the room, with Danny dangling in the air by the back of his shirt like an errant dog caught by the scruff before Nicole even registered what was going on.

"Enough!" he'd roared, his booming voice gaining the three year old's full attention, Danny's eyes wide and locked onto the big man's furious glare. The flick of his wrist, Nicole remembered, reminded her of someone shooing away a fly, careless and quick, and the small boy sailed the eight or ten feet into the wall with a sickening thud, gently bouncing down onto the couch below, eyes closed, body perfectly still.

CHAPTER TWENTY

A thousand miles away in the County Sheriff's Office, Laura flipped through pages of police reports from seventeen years ago, waiting for the name Robert to leap out at her. Irene Murdock had said that her husband killed Daniel's father, Robert. Even without a last name, it couldn't be that difficult to isolate the case that had led to the family's disappearance. Laura was still exhausted from her brief, busy trip to Texas. She'd appeared at work this morning to find Emily Murdock waiting patiently in the lobby for her, stack of postcards tied with a piece of twine sitting in her large lap. The woman must have gotten up before dawn to drive the postcards to this side of the state this early.

Emily claimed not to know the man whom Irene was planning to run away with. She admitted that she had tried to help her sister in law get away from her volatile brother a year or two before they'd all gone missing, but that things went badly. John Murdock found out and threatened everything he could to make her stay: that he'd hurt the kids, hunt her down and kill her, kill himself. Irene had believed him and stayed. Laura couldn't help wondering how differently things might have turned out if she hadn't.

The postcards sat, for the moment, neglected on her desktop, still tied with twine. Emily Murdock said there were a fair variety of different locales over the last fourteen years, and she dreaded the prospect of attempting to narrow down a concrete location. However, it was something, a small step in the right direction, at least. She now knew in what country the man resided. Mexico had already been her first guess, given its proximity to Texas, but now she had confirmation.

Her gaze caught the name Robert before her fingers could stop flipping pages. She backed up, wishing again that these files were computerized. Robert Forsythe was the name in the report in front of her. He was currently wanted for killing a police officer the same night Nicole's family fled Orsonville. Officer Black had been gunned down during a routine traffic stop in Williamsberg. It was the same file Laura set aside initially, thinking that there was probably no connection but including it just in case. A pang of disappointment hit her as she realized this couldn't be Irene's Robert. She quickly rifled through and found the pages on the bar fight, perusing the names in the file … no Robert or Bob anywhere in there. She went back to the hit and run that had happened that same night. There were no names at all in that file except for the brother of the victim. His name was Gary. No Robert.

Laura heaved a huge sigh and groaned. She'd have to go back through all of the files again. The first time around, there really hadn't been anything that would have supported a connection to Murdock except the few files she'd set aside. She'd knocked Connor off the list. The bar fight didn't fit either. There was just no way a man like John Murdock would have uprooted his family and gone into hiding over a fight, even one where someone lost an eye. She didn't buy it. The hit and run was a dead end. Which left the officer shooting.

How this could be connected to Murdock's disappearance, she couldn't fathom. But, she thought, trying to rally, that didn't mean there was no connection. She flipped open the file and began reading.

Officer Black had just completed his second year with the Williamsberg Police Department. He was what anyone would consider "green," still learning the ropes, especially since a town like Williamsberg didn't typically see a lot of action. An exciting night on the books might involve a couple domestic disputes, an unruly teen gathering needing to be broken up in the local park, a few questionable traffic stops in which the officer would have to issue a Breathalyzer test and act accordingly. The protocol for such stops was routine and simple, and Laura was sure Officer Black had been through his share. But his final traffic stop hadn't been a case of someone from the bar in town having a few too many.

Black had radioed in the make, model and plate number of the car, registered to a Robert Forsythe, and the reason for the stop: broken taillight. Black pulled Forsythe over on Shiawassee Road, a long dirt road that ran east to west from one side of the town to the other, but fairly far north, a good six miles or so from the center of town. Shiawassee didn't typically have much traffic, as it was much easier to travel down a mile and head the same direction on the paved surface of Burkhart Road. Laura flipped through the file to see where Forsythe lived, and then wondered what sort of trouble he could have been getting up to past midnight, heading in the opposite direction of his house.

When dispatch had been unable to get a response from Officer Black after twenty minutes, a second car was sent out to the site, where Black was found in a pool of his own blood, already dead from two gunshot wounds to the chest. The officer's gun, a Glock 9 mm, was missing, and the bullets pulled from his chest during the autopsy would be police issued 9 millimeter. Robert Forsythe had apparently fled the scene. An APB was activated, with a description of the sedan he was driving, the plate number, and, once they were able to get it, a description of the man. Forsythe's house was watched, the main road in and out of town was blocked, and Williamsberg called in the county boys to assist in blocking off the many back roads and dirt roads adjacent to Shiawassee where Forsythe could have escaped.

The effort yielded paltry results. When the man had not been captured within the first two hours, the call had gone out to the Michigan State Police, as well as the bordering states, Indiana, Ohio and Illinois. No trace was ever found of the man or his silver Ford sedan. In fact, after that evening, his house had remained vacant and all of his belongings abandoned, for a year or so before it was sold at auction. There was no family, both parents deceased, no siblings. Other than a couple friends in town, there was really no one to even watch for signs of contact in case the man surfaced again.

Laura perused the file further, wanting to know what would provoke a bank clerk to shoot and kill a police officer, a feat not only heinous but difficult as well. How had he managed to shoot Black with his own gun? Protocol for any traffic stop dictated that an officer must approach the vehicle with hand on weapon, ready to draw. She wondered if, it being a small town, Black had known his killer. Maybe Forsythe had engaged him in some light banter to distract him, especially since the stop was only for a taillight out. He could have caught Black off guard ... she frowned at the pages in front of her, wishing the area patrol cars had been equipped with cameras back then. The technology was still new and the expense unjustified for a small town police department, Laura guessed. Where was the motive? What had triggered Forsythe?

This file told her virtually nothing about the man, she decided, and that was frustrating. The only snippet of insight into his personality came from an interview with his closest neighbor, and that wasn't actually geographically close. Forsythe's house rested on twenty acres of heavily wooded land, the nearest house almost a quarter mile away on its own piece of land. The couple interviewed in the report described Forsythe as a quiet man who kept to himself. They'd only really spoken to him a handful of times in the years he'd lived there. The woman added that she'd thought he was a decent person, he'd always plowed their drive when it snowed, and that she'd felt a bit sorry for him, as he didn't really seem to have anyone—no wife, no family.

How could Laura begin to formulate a theory, and then figure out where John Murdock possibly fit in, without knowing a thing about Forsythe other than he was generous with his plow and led a quiet life? What would make a mild-mannered bank clerk come unhinged to the point that he would kill? And how could all of this even involve Murdock? She needed a connection, a tangible link in the chain between the crime and the man, if it existed at all.

Her thoughts returned to the scene of the crime again. Officer Black must have stumbled onto Forsythe doing something illegal ... or suspicious … but what? She supposed there could have been a second party in the car with him. What if Murdock had been there too? That could be her link. Laura stood abruptly, her chair sliding back on its rollers and gently hitting the wall. Glancing at the clock, she saw it was a long time until her normal lunch hour. She had work piled up, real work, waiting for her. But she'd made a promise to Nicole. It wouldn't hurt anyone if she took an early lunch break, she thought.

She didn't have a concrete idea in her head just yet of what she thought she'd find, only that she knew there was more to the story than was outlined in the report. She wanted to talk to the current occupants of Forsythe's house. Maybe she'd stop in and see if the same neighbors still lived next door, too. Between the two, she hoped to find a thread to follow to Murdock.

Thirty minutes later, Laura stared at the bullet in Stacy Holloway's hand. She was still standing in the doorway. She'd rung the doorbell, hoping whoever lived there now might know something of the owner seventeen years ago. Instead, the woman who answered the door excitedly told her to stand right there while she took off into the kitchen, returning with the bullet. Laura looked from the bullet back to Stacy, this time not seeing the current occupant of Robert Forsythe's old house, but a new piece to the puzzle.

"I'm so rude, please come in," Stacy said.

"Would you please show me exactly where you found this?" Laura pulled a small evidence bag from her pocket for the woman to drop the bullet into and followed her from the small foyer into a large living room where a baby played happily in his swing.

"That's Colton, my grandson." The woman moved to the roll-top desk sitting against the wall and, with a grunt, shoved it over a couple feet. She crouched down to point out the very small hole in the floor, right against the molding. The desk had rested in front of it.

"We found it while rearranging furniture years ago. At first we just thought there was a flaw in the wood, but it was too big. I shined a flashlight in, and there was the bullet, just sitting there not even a half inch in. Got it out pretty easily." She shrugged. "We figured it was probably from kids messing around in here when the house stood empty for a few months, before we got it. The man before us left, he must have gotten transferred for work or something, and the bank couldn't sell it right away. We got a good deal on it."

Laura said nothing, kneeling down for a closer look. She flipped back the corner of a large green throw rug, noting an obvious dark mahogany tone to a portion of the old oak floorboards underneath. She wondered if this woman had ever noticed the probable blood stain ingrained in the wooden farmhouse floor. She stood and looked intently at Stacy Holloway. "Would you mind if I gathered some information? I might need to take a few small slivers of wood here," she ran her fingertips across the floor.

Stacy's excitement was written in her features. "I don't mind at all. Please, go ahead."

Laura exited out the front door and placed a quick call to her sister. She updated her on the Holloway house and her own thoughts, leaving a brief message on Jenny's voicemail. She was back in the house with a small back case in hand, and bent immediately to the task. She set a numbered card down between the bullet hole and the dark mark on the floor and snapped a few pictures of the entire area. She used a small notepad and made a rough sketch, including measurements she recorded using a tape measure from her case.

Next, she took the rod she'd brought in from her car, inserted the end of it into the bullet hole, stood up straight and deliberately took two steps backwards, head down and eyes on the hole. She jotted down more notes, slid the notepad back into her pocket, and took a few more photos.

Pulling a fine, sharp scalpel from her case to take a sample from the floorboards, she spoke to Stacy. "How long have you lived here?"

She couldn't believe her luck when the woman answered, "Oh, forever. Must be over fifteen years or so. My daughter--Colton's mom--was in first grade, she would've been eight, and she's twenty-four now. So, yeah, we've been here about sixteen years."

"And you said it was vacant before that? You don't know what happened to the man who owned it before you?"

"I can't really remember what our real estate agent said. For some reason, the bank was selling it at auction. I think I just assumed he moved suddenly for work or whatnot. I'm sorry I can't remember. I don't think our agent knew much about it, either."

Fat chance, Laura thought, given the exhaustive manhunt for the previous owner, but she didn't see any reason to get into that with Mrs. Holloway. She finished labeling her evidence and packed up her case neatly. "You've never noticed anything else unusual in the house, nothing else that struck you as odd, damage to any of the walls?"

Stacy shook her head. Laura was so grateful for what she knew had to be a break in the case, she felt compelled to offer a little explanation. "That bullet may have actually hit someone before it entered the wood. We'll calculate the exact angle of entry into the wood," she gestured toward the hole in the floor along the molding, "and that helps determine where the shot was fired from, depending on the height of the shooter. We'll also analyze the bullet and see if we get a match in the system. And that," she gestured to the floor where the rug was folded back, "may be blood. If it is, we can DNA test it to try to learn whose it was." She waited for questions or confusion from the woman. She was still new enough at this herself to appreciate the coolness of the science.

"That is really fascinating," Stacy shook her head. "You know, we've been here so long I think we never really questioned that spot in the wood. It's an old house. When we found that bullet, my husband made a bet with me that someone got killed here. I told him he was crazy. Will you let us know what you find out?"

"That'll depend on what we find. Your husband might be right," she said, "or it could also just be kids messing around when the house was standing empty. But I'm working on a case that this could be important to. We may be in touch if we need to look at anything else. I appreciate your cooperation." She handed Stacy her card with Detective Jenny Leone's contact number written on the back before she left.

She came to a stop on the shoulder about a mile from the Forsythe house. She pulled a U-turn and headed back the way she'd come, this time turning left onto Shiawassee Road instead of right to return to the house. She quickly flipped through the file on the passenger seat, finding the crossroad nearest the point where Officer Black was killed. She needed to put together a timeline of that night. It took her less than five minutes to reach the spot, 500 feet or so before Vernon Road. The road was deeply rutted and bumpy from the snow they'd already had. She carefully pulled off the road again, half expecting to see the ghosts of Black and Forsythe still wandering around the scene, and a third person, too, she was sure of it now. Murdock was there, but not in the capacity she'd originally suspected. She couldn't deny she was a bit out of her depth, she was an Evidence Tech, not a detective, and she'd have to wait to talk to Jenny, but the theory swirling around in her head was beginning to make a whole lot of sense to her.

She checked her notes once more, finding the name of the bank where Forsythe had worked: National First in Orsonville, a small satellite branch housed in the same building as the local grocery store, pharmacy and video rental joint. Laura nodded to herself. Irene had met him in the bank.

Laura would check into which bank the Murdock family had used all those years ago, but she was betting it was National First. Irene had developed a rapport with the nice bank teller Robert Forsythe, and eventually it had turned into something more. He fit the description, based on Irene's reaction to Danny. Laura and Nicole agreed that the product of Nicole's mother's affair was Daniel. After the words from the doctor about the HLA typing results, and Irene's own admission, there was no doubt in her mind. Where things went from there, and how they deteriorated into a series of life-altering events, Laura could guess. She hoped she could back those guesses up with proof.

She knew Robert was planning to take Irene and the children away, down to South Carolina. The delivery of the envelope that Nicole told her about led her to believe there'd been airline tickets or bus tickets, a concrete plan. Nicole had told Laura over the phone last night about the rediscovery of two of her journals, and about the extreme change in Murdock's mood and actions just days before their disappearance. She knew it was splitting hairs, as he'd never shown a distaste for violence, but the scene she described the afternoon before the family vanished was a definite escalation. And it was no coincidence that the target of Murdock's rage that day had been little Daniel. He'd known. Whether he'd seen with his own eyes or just put the pieces together, Laura didn't know, but John

Murdock knew his wife had been with another man, probably for quite a while. And he acted on that knowledge.

Laura was struck suddenly with a zing, a light-bulb moment. The classic rock music playing through the car speakers faded and Irene's words at the funeral came back to her. "Swallowed up forever in the deep dark sea," she'd said. Robert was swallowed up in the deep dark sea. And right on the heels of that, the needling sensation that there was something else. She dug around in her purse and found the folded paper she'd been furiously scribbling notes on at graveside.

"The police officers don't see a thing," she'd written. She'd been jotting down the words so fast her writing was barely legible. But she made out the next line: "and the one who does, it's his funeral." Ramblings of a crazy old woman with Swiss cheese for a brain? Laura didn't think so anymore.

Laura looked up at the long, winding dirt road. She punched in coordinates on her GPS and a map of the area popped onto the screen. Shiawassee Road crawled most of the entire thirty-seven mile span from the east side of the county to the west. Forsythe's house sat just off a side road, two miles from where she was parked. She tapped the zoom on the screen twice and brought this portion of the county in for a closer look. An old gravel pit-turned-fishing hole and a small lake were in the vicinity, both accessible from short side roads jutting off this way and that over the next three miles or so. Then a straight shot down the paved Carter Road to get back to Grand River Avenue, leading right into Orsonville, right toward Murdock's old house. Between Forsythe's house and theirs, there wasn't much else in the landscape that grabbed her attention, at least nothing big enough to lose a car in.

As plausible as it seemed to Laura, it wasn't enough. It definitely wasn't enough to justify the expense of lake dragging equipment, vehicles and manpower, even if she could get Jenny to back her up--she had no doubt her sister would connect the dots the same way she had. On top of that, if something didn't happen soon, they'd be waiting until spring and hoping for an early thaw. Right now was their last chance, coming up on December. Michigan winters always had a few false starts before things got really serious. They had maybe one or two weeks left of fall before the temperatures settled down in the teens and stayed there for the duration. She needed something concrete: a car at the bottom of a lake; a confession from a man who'd vanished years ago into thin air.

Laura swallowed the aggravation that danced at the edge of her thoughts, concentrating instead on getting the evidence back to the lab. Then there was the waiting. Waiting for analysis of the bullet to come back, waiting for the blood in the floor to tell her a story. Until then, she could speculate all she wanted, it was just exactly that: speculation. She picked up her phone to fill Nicole in on where the day had taken her. She had a feeling she'd be seeing her old friend much sooner than they'd planned when Laura left Texas two days ago.

CHAPTER TWENTY-ONE

Laura's house was messier than Jenny had ever seen it. Usually her sister was a nit-picky housekeeper, but there was a suitcase still by the door, half the contents strewn into the living room. Dishes were stacked in the sink and on the counter. Charlie's video games, various game systems and controllers lay scattered over the floor in front of the TV. Jenny carefully stepped around the articles of clothing and a few toiletries on her way through to the kitchen, where she knew Laura would be at this time of day, getting dinner ready. She'd sounded excited and stressed and rushed all at once when she called Jenny earlier that day and asked her to stop by as soon as she could.

"If I didn't know better, I'd think you've been robbed and ransacked," she joked, grabbing a Coke from the fridge and sitting at the kitchen table.

Laura spun around to greet her sister. “I just need a few extra hours in the day. The house is a mess, my kid is a slob, and I’m so behind on laundry I had to choose whether to wear boy undies to work today or go commando.” Her hair was pulled back into a wild blond knot, several strands floating loose around her face and neck.

Jenny couldn’t help laughing. “So, how are the boy undies? Nice and comfy?”

Laura looked at her sister. “Like I’m gonna fit into my skinny teenage son’s shorts. I’ve got a load in the dryer,” she wiggled and pulled down on one side of her pants.

“Where is my fashionable nephew, anyway?”

“He’s with Dad at the basketball court. He got Detroit Pistons tickets for tomorrow night, he’s so excited!”

“How cool! Is Dad taking him?”

“Nope, I am. With Adam,” she added, keeping her eyes on the green pepper she was chopping.

“Really?” Jenny couldn’t keep the surprise out of her voice. “Are you bending your rule? I thought you had to have no less than forty-three dates before introducing a new boyfriend to Charlie.”

Laura rolled her eyes at her sister. “Quit making fun of me. I never put a number on it. And it’s not like I have a whole stream of new boyfriends coming and going. I just said I needed to know things were serious before getting Charlie involved, that’s all.”

“Mmm hmmm,” Jenny smiled.

"So maybe things are serious, okay?" She felt her heart speed up as she spoke the words, a rush of fear and excitement. She shrugged and threw her hands up. "Shut up, will you? It's not a big deal."

"Oh, no, not at all," Jenny nodded.

"Now you're just being condescending." Laura emptied the cutting board into the frying pan full of chicken. "Okay, just say whatever you're going to say, tell me why this is all a bad idea, that I'm rebounding, rushing."

Jenny shrugged. "Nope, not gonna say that. I think you're being smart about your love life this time around. Just … be careful. I don't want you to get hurt."

Laura looked at Jenny. "Yeah," she said after a moment. "Me neither."

"Listen," she said, eager to get off the terrifying topic of Adam, "I need to fill you in on what I found out about Nicole's dad, or what I think I found out. I was hoping you might know someone in Texas, someone who could go interview Irene officially."

She stopped Jenny before she could protest. "I know she's sick and her memory is full of holes. But Nicole says she's on some new medicine that's helping a little, and the information that poured out of her during the funeral was just spot on accurate, given the right context. I really need to know what her account is of the night they disappeared."

Jenny agreed to work on it. Laura was certain this time there would be a more fruitful outcome to her sister's investigation.

The phone rang just after her sister left. Nicole had gotten Laura's excited message about finding the bullet and informed her that she'd be flying in sometime in the next few days. Laura's heart leapt at how little time she had to try to pull together some concrete result. She was close, she could feel it. She knew Nicole would want to be here when they broke the case. She cautioned her not to get her hopes up, asked if she wouldn't rather wait until the preliminary forensics reports were in. She was quickly reminded how impossible it was to talk her intrepid friend out of anything she was determined to do. Laura was glad that at least one of them had the means to flit back and forth across the country at will. She was tapped after her last impromptu trip.

Adam seemed to be the topic of the day. Before hanging up, Nicole said, "Besides all that, hon, I really need to meet your Airport Hottie. You get all giggly and blushy every time you mention him. Set that up for while I'm in town, would you?"

Laura chuckled. "All right, but you guys have to stop with the nickname. Between you and my sister, you're going to slip one day and call him that to his face. I'll try to plan something for next week. I just saw him last night."

"You've already seen him? But you just got home last night."

She told Nicole about Adam's sudden presence on her front porch late last night, leaving out the details. They'd been talking on the phone, and she knew there was something different in his voice. He'd called her every day while she was in Texas. Even though they hadn't spent a lot of time together before she left, it was different somehow knowing they were hundreds of miles apart. She knew he missed her, and she didn't know how she'd live through the next two or three days without seeing him, waiting for the weekend to come. She was curled up on the couch under a blanket, already in her nightie and old pink fuzzy robe, phone to her ear, ignoring all of the neglected housework and laundry needing attention before she had to go back to work the next day.

"I need to see you," he said, and her cheeks filled with heat at his deep voice, the soft caress of those simple words.

"I know. I miss you too," she said quietly. They'd already been talking for a while, had covered the details of her trip home, his past few days at the clinic, and neither wanted to hang up just yet, though it was past midnight. She watched the glow from headlights creep across her living room ceiling and glanced reflexively out the front window. His car was in her driveway.

Laura jumped up and unlocked the door, throwing it open to find him already climbing her porch steps. He wore his heavy Carhart coat against the chill, hands in the pockets, chin tucked down just a bit as he gave her the sexiest half-smile she'd ever seen. She quite literally threw herself at him, laughing as he got his hands out of his pockets and wrapped his arms around her, squeezing her so tight she could feel his body heat through the thick coat. His hand came up into her hair and she pressed her face to his neck, inhaling the scent of him, eyes closed. She thought her crazy heart would jump right out of her chest.

When she'd regained a bit of her calm, she started to pull back and tipped her head up to look at him. His arms didn't loosen. He returned her gaze with blue eyes so dark they appeared almost black, brows furrowed a bit. The intensity of his stare gave her a small stab of fright … how had things gotten to this point so fast?

"Adam?" She didn't finish the sentence, she didn't have the words. She wanted to know he was all right.

"I missed you, Laura." His hand came up to cup her jaw, but the passionate kiss she expected, craved, was short and uncertain. His arms went back around her and he rested his cheek lightly on her forehead as he hugged her again.

Laura found an opening in his coat and pulled the zipper down, sliding her arms inside and around him. She rubbed his back slowly, feeling some new emotion in him, more than the familiar heat she was used to whenever they were close like this. He was there with her, she couldn't deny that inside his strong embrace, but he was holding something back. It had been so long since she'd cared so much what a man was thinking. She didn't want to push him, but she hadn't seen him like this before. She settled for simply relaxing into him, conforming her body to his as she continued to lightly stroke his back.

He pulled back slightly, hands on her arms. "You must be freezing. Can we go in and talk, just for a minute?"

She stood with him in her foyer, his arms loosely around her waist, her hands floating between his chest and firm stomach. She had a very difficult time keeping her hands off of him when he was close.

"Are you okay, Adam?"

He smiled at her. "I am now. I just--" his voice was quiet and he shook his head, cutting his eyes away from her for a moment. "I just missed you … I didn't realize until you were gone," he stopped, frowning.

"What?" Her voice came out a whisper. She did not need Charlie waking up just now. She tugged at his shirt.

He dropped his voice lower to match hers. "God, I hope I'm not screwing things up here, but--I can't believe what you do to me." He attempted another smile but it failed. "I guess I didn't realize until you were gone how much I love you. Sorry," he paused, not sounding sorry. "I know it's too soon."

The air left her lungs in a whoosh—she hadn't known she'd been holding her breath until that moment. She reached up and held his face in her hands, finally kissing him the way she'd imagined kissing him the entire time she'd been in Texas. It was a good kiss, slow, warm, wet, her tongue finding his, tasting his delicious mouth; it was a promise of things to come.

Adam's arms tightened around her, his hands finding their way inside her bathrobe, pressing into the small of her back, and then roaming lower, melding her into him. He escalated the intensity effortlessly, and she heard a little moan escape her throat as one leg came up and around him and he groaned and picked her up, backing her up against the wall in the foyer. She gasped and rocked her hips into him, trembling hands now under his shirt in the back, her fingers sliding under his belted jeans, feeling the warmth of his skin. Laura arched her back and wished there were no clothing between them. Adam held her easily, not loosening his grip for a moment. He bent his head to her neck, kissing and licking lower. He pulled down the flimsy nightgown and found her breast with his mouth.

"Oh!" Laura was overcome with a rush of tingling heat as she tangled her fingers in his hair, grinding her hips against him, his hand sliding under her thigh and pushing aside the thin fabric. She felt his fingers grip the underside of her bare thigh and all she wanted was for him to be inside her.

"Adam," she breathed, a whisper. She slid a hand around to his hot belly, under his belt, and felt the silky hardness of him. Her eyes fluttered closed, and she knew she was ready, insecurities evaporated.

From the back of the house, Laura heard a door snap softly shut. In an instant, she was jolted firmly back to her reality. Charlie must have gotten up to use the bathroom. She wondered if he'd heard them. She cringed at the idea that he might have seen them. The foyer was shielded by a half wall, and the living room and hallway beyond remained dark and still. Laura thought she'd have heard him if Charlie decided to come out here.

Adam released his grip on her, breathing hard, allowing her to straighten her clothing. He cast a glance toward the hallway through the living room, then back at her. "Shit, I'm sorry."

Now she looked back up at him, surprised. "I'm sorry!" She shook her head, taking a shaky breath, and pulled him back into her by his belt, planting a kiss on his neck. "I'm sorry," she whispered. "I can't. Not like this."

Laura might have been snapped back to reality but Adam was still a few moments behind. She lightly ran a hand across the front of his jeans, feeling the hard bulge through the fabric. She rolled her eyes and groaned in frustration.

He kissed her again and she had a fleeting thought of sneaking him into her bedroom. Or going outside to his car … surrounded by her sleeping neighbors. Crazy thoughts. No. She knew this would have to wait, much as she wanted him right this second.

"I know," he murmured against her mouth, as though she'd spoken. "It's okay. I can wait."

She looked at him and smiled. "Man, I don't know how you can say that." Her hand still rested over his zipper. She couldn't bring herself to move it.

He kissed her again, more lightly now. He took her hand and pulled her arm around his waist. "We have all the time in the world."

She laughed, couldn't help it. "Yeah, I'm not waiting that long."

He matched her smile. "Well, good, 'cause I don't think I can let you."

Laura shook her head, stunned at how fast she'd lost control with Adam, after all the years of her self-enforced single-mom rules. She hugged him, this amazing, irresistible man who somehow wanted only her. Her heart was still racing.

"I love you, Adam," she whispered into his ear. That he could come to her house, see her in her ratty old bathrobe and nightgown, tired as she was, and do this to her … she laughed softly, kissing his ear.

He kissed her temple and she relaxed now into his embrace, the tension between them calming.

"Who are you?" she asked him. "I don't do things like this. Make out with a guy in my foyer at midnight while my son sleeps."

"You do now." He grinned at her. "And I'm glad you do."

She flushed a hot red and tucked her head into his neck. "God, Adam."

"Laura." His voice was a low murmur. "I don't know if you noticed, but I'd say this is getting serious." She smiled into his neck. She could stay here in his arms all night.

But she couldn't … she finally drew back and looked at him. "We have to go to bed."

He grinned, one eyebrow cocked. "Okay. Now?" He was killing her.

Laura walked him out to his car, her hand in his. She was gripped with an overwhelming sadness that he was leaving.

He'd left his car running this whole time, and when he opened the door, a tiny black and brown puppy curled on a bundle of blankets in a box on the passenger seat lifted its head to look at her. The little mouth stretched into a big yawn followed by a whimper before the puppy put its head back down on its paws.

"Oh, he is the cutest little thing!" She reached out and Adam placed the puppy gently in her arms. He was no bigger than a small cat, and his fur was silky soft with puppy down. He twisted his body around to climb up Laura and sniff, then lick, her face.

"This is Snickers." Adam scratched the puppy behind the ears, prompting a whole new set of wiggles and squirms. "His owners found homes for all of his litter-mates, but he was returned because of a rare bone condition … the owners actually brought him in to be put down." The corners of Adam's mouth turned down with distaste as he told Laura this. "There's no way I could do it. All he needs is a pill once a day. Big deal."

Laura's eyebrows went up. "So you got yourself a dog, huh?"

Adam laughed. "Are you kidding? Imagine my house if I kept every unwanted pet that came into the clinic! No, we'll board him for a while and try to find a home for him, someone who won't mind the medical issue. I just felt too sorry for him to leave him there his first night." The puppy whined between them as he was squeezed in their goodbye hug.

Laura ran back through the frosty night air to the warmth of her house and watched Adam's taillights fade. She passed the mirror in the entry way and momentarily paused to shake her head at the goofy grin plastered on her face.

When he called her from home nearly an hour later to say goodnight, she invited him to the Pistons game with her and Charlie. She expected to wake up the next morning and regret the snap decision, but she didn't. Now she just hoped Charlie liked him.

CHAPTER TWENTY-TWO

The Iosco County Forensics Tech glanced up at Laura again over his computer monitor. "Don't you have something you're supposed to be doing? For our active case files? Standing here watching me won't make the system work any faster."

Laura suppressed a grin at the annoyance in his tone. "I'm off the clock today, remember? Got nothing to do. At all. Except wait."

"Okay," he sat up a bit straighter and scrubbed his hand over his close-cropped waves. Chad Scott looked no older than twenty, but she knew he'd been here at least four or five years. He was dealing with the bullet taken from Forsythe's house and the hardwood floor sample, which Laura was certain would come back positive for blood.

"We can't do a blood wash on the bullet," he told her. "Too many years have passed, and who knows how many people have handled it. But

I can tell you that it's from a Smith and Wesson .38 caliber. And here's the clincher," he paused for effect, making Laura want to strangle him.

"Oh, come on!" she growled at him, peering around him at the screen.

"The markings on the bullet are consistent with the patterns found on the .38 rounds from the Texas convenience store shooting, meaning--"

Laura cut him off. "Meaning that since Murdock was the known gunman at that scene, he used the same gun four years earlier to kill Robert Forsythe in his own home!"

"No," Scott said, "meaning that somebody used that gun to shoot someone at the Forsythe/now Holloway residence. You can't prove it was Murdock or that Forsythe is dead."

"Watch me," she grinned confidently. "I can connect Murdock to Forsythe through the affair with Irene--"

"A witness with Alzheimer's," Scott interrupted.

"--and once we do the lake drag," she continued as if he hadn't spoken, "we'll have a car registered to Forsythe with a body in it, disappearing the same night Murdock went on the run."

Scott regarded her with a cool poker face, playing devil's advocate. "How can you prove Forsythe didn't kill Officer Black and just ditch his own car in the lake?"

"I can't yet. But I will, once Lieutenant approves the lake and gravel pit survey, providing we can find what we need in the next couple days before the temperature drops again." She paused, bending to peer at the computer screen. "And it looks like that is blood in the floorboards, coming back greater than two years old." She knew DNA would take a while, but it was something. "I think Forsythe bled onto the floor before Murdock could move him. Which holds with Irene Murdock's story. I bet this gets us the lake drag."

Laura enjoyed the smooth surge of adrenalin she always felt when she knew she'd made a solid connection in a case. Until this moment, she hadn't been sure. In spite of how Irene's story made all the pieces fit, it wouldn't get a conviction. Without evidence, it was just a good story. She was certain they'd find the rest of what they needed underwater. She went to call her sister.

Three hours later, she stood along the sloped shore of the old gravel pit she'd actually gone swimming in as a teenager. It was only a quarter-mile off Shiawassee Road, but lay nestled behind a cluster of homes some delusional developer had plunked down way out here in the sticks, a good twenty or thirty minutes from any freeway access. Many of the homes sported for-sale signs and overgrown yards. The small suburb's common areas hadn't been tended in years, making it difficult at first to even locate the quarry.

Trees dotted the perimeter, mostly bare of leaves in the late autumn chill. A few stragglers still clung to the branches. Dry leaves littered the ground, reds, oranges and yellows rustling lightly atop the dead ones beneath.

Just after the lake survey company got the boat into the water, Laura watched a black Town Car roll up. She smiled as Nicole got out and directed the driver to set her bags over by Laura's car.

She picked her way over to Laura in four-inch heels, shaking a dark red leaf off one shoe. Pregnancy had done nothing to her friend's fashion sense. "You weren't kidding when you said you were out in the middle of nowhere! Am I in time? Did you find anything yet?"

Laura hugged her and laughed. "We've barely started. And you are gonna freeze your buns off, I told you to go to the house and I'd meet you there." She took off her own gloves and scarf and handed them to Nicole.

"I couldn't. I can't stand this prickly anticipation. Even after what I heard of the interview Mother gave that detective, I still have so many questions. I need to be here. What exactly is it that you're hoping to find?"

"Let's go sit in my car, I can explain the theory we're working with."

They sat warming up and watching the towboat troll slowly from one side of the quarry to the other. Laura could see one of the crew on deck operating the remote for the ROV that made its way unseen below the surface of the murky water. The maximum depth listed in the records was 65 feet. The small underwater vehicle doing their searching for them was equipped with a side-scan sonar device that provided images of anything standing out from the bottom surface. Optimistic as she tried to be that any minute the operator would shout out that they had something, Laura's money was on the small lake rather than the gravel pit. Murdock had covered his tracks so well, his plan so nearly flawless, she doubted he'd have taken a chance on some swimmer accidentally discovering the car he'd dumped. For that matter, she knew Murdock had been a hunter and fisherman, and she was sure his first thoughts would have gone to the small lake he'd most likely fished in that was only miles from his wife's lover's home. The county was peppered with lakes, and most good fishermen knew of them all.

"Got something!"

Laura jumped and she jerked the two-way radio to her mouth to answer. Before she could speak, the crewman's voice came through to her again: "Never mind, it's registering as some type of craft like a canoe or kayak."

She set the radio down poured two cups of hot chocolate from the thermos she'd brought. Nicole wrapped her hands around hers and shivered.

"I don't miss Michigan at all on days like this."

"Yeah, this sucks. It's gotta be colder than 40 degrees," Laura grumbled, watching her breath turn into puffs of smoke in the air.

"Thirty-seven, actually," Nicole replied.

"I wonder how much longer this will take. We need to get over to the lake. I want to do it today."

"What makes you think we'll need to?"

She shrugged. She didn't want to voice her hunch, her gut-feeling, until she was sure she was right. "Don't worry, we've got them 'till tomorrow night," she gestured toward the Cedar Rapids Underwater Search and Rescue truck, trailer and crane parked behind them.

She wished she'd insisted they do the lake first. She had meant to spend this time coming up with ways to find Murdock. With the approval on the lake survey, her Lieutenant had gone federal with the recent developments and they'd already been in touch with border patrol and Mexican Law Enforcement. The emphasis focused on the small village of Mixistlan, where the most recent postcards had come from. So far they had nothing. She imagined an army of law enforcement wandering around Mexico looking for a man who'd been invisible for the last seventeen years. Besides, now that the forensic evidence had hit the national database, she knew the FBI would become very interested in the bullet from the Forsythe house matching the one from the Texas convenience store shooting Daniel had witnessed, with possible connections to an unsolved police officer slaying. She had a feeling the federal guys might just take the problem of finding Murdock right off her plate.

She turned and sat sideways in her seat, facing Nicole. "I'm not sure exactly how much you heard in that interview the other day," she began.

Nicole nodded. "The detective they sent asked me to leave the room about halfway through. My mother kept looking over at me and stopping. I know my presence was screwing up her concentration. I stood outside the door trying to listen … I caught some of it. But I'd really love to know what you know. Could you tell me from the beginning?"

"Of course." Laura took her friend's hand and began.

Irene had no idea they'd been followed. She and Forsythe had left her car in town and driven to his house, way out in the boonies. Murdock quietly entered the house, surprising them. They'd been in the living room, Irene said, discussing the logistics of the plan to leave John Murdock and flee to the Outer Banks with the kids. Irene remembered him so clearly standing there, in her lover's home, out of context, because of the pink towel. He stood in the foyer, pink bath towel in one hand and Smith and Wesson in the other. Irene tried to reason with him. She attempted to grab hold of his arm, the one with the gun, and he gave her a good enough shove to knock her onto the floor. He rushed Forsythe then, easily taking him down. Murdock was, after all, a jack-of-all-trades in construction, while Forsythe spent his days behind a bank counter.

Irene watched helplessly as Murdock pinned Robert Forsythe and proceeded to beat the life out of him. She got up and tried at one point to pull him off, and Murdock backhanded her in the head so hard she hit the floor again. Murdock wrapped the barrel of the gun in the towel and stood over Forsythe then and shot him in the head. Ballistics supported the gunshot from no more than six or eight feet away.

"Your mother says she thinks she lost consciousness at this point, because the next thing she remembers--and the telling remains the same whether it's the detective sitting with her or my sister asking her over the phone days later--is Murdock reentering the house, this time with a big tarp." Laura paused, gauging Nicole's reaction thus far.

"I'm fine," she told Laura quietly. "You forget that I lived with him over half my life. Go on."

Laura went on. Irene begged Murdock to stop, to check if Forsythe was still alive, and he shut her up by kicking her hard in the stomach. He rolled Forsythe up in the tarp, might have picked up his shell casing, but never thought to retrieve the bullet. Maybe he assumed it was still in Forsythe's skull. He heaved the body up over his shoulder, left again, and came back a third time with more towels to clean up the blood. He pulled a rug and some piece of furniture over the area. When Forsythe's house was later searched to get a line on his whereabouts, Laura pointed out to Nicole, they weren't treating it as a crime scene. They wouldn't have been looking for blood.

From there, Murdock got Irene on her feet, put her in his truck and told her to follow him down Shiawassee Road. He took Forsythe's car. He spent the whole time he was cleaning up the blood threatening Irene that he would go home and cut Daniel's throat if she didn't do as he said.

Nicole nodded at this. "She knew he was serious, after what he'd just done to Daniel earlier that day--" She glanced at Laura, who still didn't know the whole story, "he slammed my baby brother against a wall so hard he passed out." Nicole's tone was matter-of-fact. The only thing she felt in this moment was pure anger, the desire to finally make her father pay for his crimes.

Laura stared at her, swallowing a lump of nausea. She didn't want to see Danny like that, in her mind's eye, sweet, tow-headed little boy. Nobody deserved that.

Nicole sighed. "So you think you my father dumped Forsythe's car with the body in it somewhere around here? What about the officer that was shot? What the hell happened?"

Laura nodded at Scott. "Irene didn't see it. She saw Murdock get pulled over driving Forsythe's car, and she passed the cruiser and the car and went a distance down the road to wait. She didn't know what else to do, she said she thought about trying to beat him home and run with the kids, but she was too afraid of him. She says she heard the gunshots, and then Murdock caught up with her and led her to what she calls a pond. Officer Black pulled Murdock over for a burned out tail-light. We know that much since he radioed it in--no video cameras yet in patrol cars back then. Best I can figure, Murdock smooth talked the officer long enough to get his guard down, then surprised him, took his Glock and shot him with it, point blank. They pulled police-issue 9mm shells out of Black, but never recovered the gun.

"When they got to this pond, body of water, whatever, Murdock put the car in neutral and rolled it in. Irene never saw Forsythe's body, doesn't know if it was in the back seat or trunk but I'm betting it will be in that car when we find it. I'm hoping we'll get really lucky and find the Glock, too, since we know Murdock later used the Smith and Wesson in the convenience store shooting."

She looked up to see the ROV surfacing and the towboat slowly heading into shore. Her radio crackled and she heard, "we got nothing, let's pack up and head over to the second location."

"Roger that, good deal, we can at least get started."

In the car on the way to the lake, her phone buzzed and she saw she'd missed a call from Adam. Her mouth was a desert as she listened to the voicemail, dropping the phone back into the console without saying a word.

Nicole nudged her after a few minutes. "Are you even listening to me? Laura, what if they don't find anything?" She stopped, catching her friend's expression. "Hey, what is it? Is Charlie okay?"

Laura shook her head, then nodded. "Yes. Yes, he's fine, it's not Charlie. It was Adam. He wants to see me tonight. To talk."

"Honey, what is wrong with you? That could mean anything! You told me things were going fantastic."

"I thought they were. But I'm obviously no expert on relationships. I can just tell, I can hear it in his voice. Here, listen," she began to pull her phone back out.

Nicole covered her hand. "No. I am not entertaining this, catering to your low self-esteem. You're bonkers, no offense. The guy sounds crazy about you. He and Charlie got along great. So he wants to talk, how can you make that into something bad?"

Laura sighed, focusing her attention now on the towboat slowly launching into the lake. "It's not just my imagination. He's different since I got back. He says all these wonderful things, but he seems so hesitant sometimes, like he's about to say something and then he doesn't. Now he wants to see me tonight, alone, so we can talk. That's what he said, he said he needs to talk to me ALONE."

Nicole could see the last word in capital letters as sure as if her friend had spelled it out that way. "All right, just quit freaking out. It doesn't sound bad, it sounds personal. You have to admit you're a tad deficient in the confidence department, I think you're reading way too much negativity into this whole thing. Maybe he wants to ask you to go steady or something."

She cringed at Laura's outraged response, knowing she should have bitten her tongue. Some things never changed; Laura had no sense of humor when she was stressed, not as a teenager and definitely not now.

"You're not helping! Is that supposed to be funny? Nic, we've been on eight dates so far. He likes my son. He's nice, smart, successful, unbelievably hot, and now the other shoe is going to drop, I'm telling you. This is it. He's tired of waiting for me to put out, or he's found someone who's not tied down by kids and insecurities, or--"

Nicole interrupted her. "What do you mean he's tired of waiting for you to put out? Are you sixteen? Did you lose the key to your chastity belt? What on earth are you waiting for?"

"I don't know!" She shrugged helplessly. "Nothing! I want to, but, I don't know, I just get scared, and what if I'm rebounding from Steve? Do you know how long it's been since I did this? How soon is too soon?"

Nicole laughed. "Darlin', you missed the 'too soon' bus a while ago."

"Ugh! That's what it is then! I knew it. I was going to sleep with him, too, it's been so hard not to, you can't imagine…." She thought of that night in her foyer, heat instantly turning her cheeks pink. She'd seen him since then, but between work and everything else, it had been impossible. "I thought it would happen on our next date, and now it's too late," she finished, her voice breaking.

Nicole had to get her friend to calm down. She'd never seen Laura so ruffled. "Honey. Hold on. Has he said anything? Pushed you?"

"No. I mean … yes, but no, not really."

"Okay. The guy you've described to me would not dump you because of this. I can see him getting impatient, but I can't see him throwing in the towel without some warning, can you?"

Laura was quiet for a moment. "No."

"No. And so what if you're rebounding? It's not like you're still pining for the one who got away, you broke up with him."

"I know, but--this happened so fast," she said uncertainly.

"No, it didn't. Not really. It happened over the course of weeks and weeks, if you count back from the time you first met Adam--see, I used his real name--and couldn't stop thinking about him. And how does the timing mean anything anyway? The two of you had instant chemistry, and you know he's a good guy."

"Yeah...."

"Right, so where's your argument now, smarty pants? Settle down, stop using your imagination to embellish what is probably a very normal step in your relationship, and forget about it until tonight, okay?"

"Okay." She was quiet again. "Jeez, what would I do without you?"

"Well, for one thing, you wouldn't be able to spend the whole night with your boyfriend, you slut. Why don't you pack an overnight bag, just in case? Charlie and I will be fine, I promise."

"I am not spending the night with him, Nicole! What would Charlie think?!"

"Charlie will think you're staying in a hotel for the night because of an early forensics conference way over in Battle Creek, how's that?

And if you change your mind about staying at Adam's, just sneak in quietly, say your work thing got cancelled. No big deal."

Laura laughed. "Okay, that's a little scary. I hope you never use your powers for evil, quick-draw. How do you think of this stuff so fast?"

Now she and Nicole stood on the shore of the small fishing lake watching the towboat repeat the same routine. Laura finally gave in and glanced at her watch.

"Damn. It's already 5:00. It'll be dark soon, we're gonna have to shut down for the day."

"We'll find the car tomorrow," Nicole said confidently. "You've gotten us this far, I trust your instincts. You know it's in there."

"Yes, but without it, no jury in the world is going to believe this story, not coming from your mother, and that's assuming we even find the bastard wherever he's hiding out."

Nicole's blood went cold at that. They had to find him. It was what she'd wanted since they started this. But she couldn't imagine facing him. She said as much to Laura, voiced her idiotic ambivalent worries.

"We will find him," Laura back peddled. "And you will be just fine. You're the strongest person I know. We do have some evidence, no matter what, and we'll find the rest. What we took from Forsythe's house tells part of the story; your mother's account was specific and detailed. The pink bath towel he brought into Forsythe's house with him shows premeditation, that and the tarp in his truck bed make it second-degree-murder at least. We'll get him."

"I hope you're right," Nicole answered. She didn't want anything left to chance. Not if they were going to such lengths to find the monster masquerading as her father and drag him out into the light of day.

CHAPTER TWENTY-THREE

Laura threw the black skirt onto her bed and ripped off the matching top for the third time, blond hair flying with static electricity. She caught sight of herself in her dresser mirror, a tousled, scared mess.

"Fuck it!" she exclaimed, grabbing her worn, faded, holey-knee blue jeans from her closet.

"What, Mom?" Charlie called from the living room.

"Nothing, sorry." This was why she'd avoided dating for so long before Steve. She hated feeling like this. Whatever Adam wanted to talk to her about tonight, it sounded serious, he sounded nervous, and he hadn't been quite himself the last few times she'd seen him.

The Pistons game had gone great, couldn't have been better. Adam and Charlie hit it off so well that she was completely left out of their conversation at many times during the evening. Basketball stats, teams and coaches progressed to camping and fishing, and so on. Charlie eventually worked his way around to asking Adam about his job as a veterinarian and she had to give her boy credit, he got Adam to list every reason in the book why it was good for kids to have a pet. Adam and Charlie both gave her a few meaningful glances and she'd looked pointedly back at her son; she'd promised to take him again to look for a dog and hadn't had the time lately.

When she asked Charlie what he thought of Adam later that night, he gave her a short but certain, "He's cool. You traded up, Mom. When's he coming over again?"

Now she wanted to kick herself for jumping the gun and introducing Charlie to him. She pulled on a baby blue tank top followed by a soft old flannel. This was her comfy outfit, her cozy, grungy, I-don't-give-a-shit uniform. Adam would be over at 8:00 to pick her up. She had time to kill. They were out of juice, and the thought of an ice cold beer popped into her head, making the decision for her to run into town and grab a few things, get out of the house, maybe get away from her thoughts.

She walked through the living room and smiled at Charlie on the phone, must be with that girl from school, she thought, noticing how he stopped talking the moment she appeared. She motioned to the door, picking up her car keys and shrugging on her coat.

"Do you need anything from the store?"

"A Coke? And gum please?"

"Got it. I'll be right back."

He waited until she was on the way out the door before resuming his conversation, "yeah, I know, I love that band. I've been saving to see them in concert … maybe we could go together."

Laura smiled as she drove the mile into town, glad to be distracted by thoughts of her son's first crush. She was walking out of the little mom and pop grocery store, six-pack of beer in one hand, bag of gum, juice and soda in the other, when she saw Steve. He was right across from her on Second Street, shoveling patches of slushy snow out of the driveway of a tan bungalow. He lived with his mother down at the other end of Second Street. She wondered if he was clearing the driveway for some neighbor. She stood and stared for so long that of course he stopped, feeling eyes on him, and looked up to meet her gaze. His face lit up.

He crossed the street and tentatively approached her. She couldn't help smiling at him. No matter what else, he wasn't a bad person, and they'd been together for two years. He came close and gave her a light hug and she thought of the last time she'd seen him. He'd looked so unkempt and sad and forlorn. She thought now that he looked good, his scruff was only a day's worth, and she picked up a hint of the same soap he'd always used.

"How are you?" She glanced over his shoulder to the house he'd come from.

"I'm great! Well, I'm okay," he amended. "I just rented that," he nodded to the bungalow. "Figured it's about time I have my own place."

Laura knew her eyes must be wide. "Wow! Well, good for you. How'd your mom take it?" An image flashed in her head: Steve's mother bustling about in his new house, taking care of the laundry, making him casseroles. Stop it, she chided herself.

"Oh, you know," he shoved his hands in his pockets. "She'll get used to it. I'm still right down the street, in case she needs help with something. Anyway, I just … I've been meaning to call you, Laura. I wanted you to know that I'm really trying. I'm working on things, taking big steps," he gave her a little smile.

She smiled back at him. "I'm proud of you, Steve. This will be good for you."

"It could be good for us," he said.

Laura was quiet. She was surprised to find that she actually was proud of him. She felt odd, though, expecting a surge of mixed emotions … after all, wasn't this exactly what she'd wanted? For him to show some initiative, some independence? She felt a lump of sadness in her throat as she realized that pride and happiness for his accomplishments were the only things she felt now. She wondered if she'd ever really loved him at all, or if he was simply safe and convenient, just as she was for him.

She met his eyes and knew that he saw the sadness there. He misread it.

"Babe, I know you said we're done, but it doesn't have to be that way." He put his hand on her arm and gave it a little squeeze. "Things could be like they were. They could be better."

Laura didn't want to hurt him, but she couldn't make the feelings come. Even his hand on her arm, his nice words, the pleading look, did nothing. All she could think was, 'I hope he gets over us fast. I hope he finds someone.' How could she say that to him? She couldn't. But she didn't want to hurt him.

"Steve," she took his hand in hers, "I am so happy for you. I know you getting your own place is going to be a great thing. I just want you to be happy, I really do. But not with me," she squeezed his hand. "I'm sorry. I know that we aren't meant to be together. I hope maybe one day we might be friends … I hope you can call me up one day and tell me about some amazing woman you've met, and maybe you'll even invite me to your wedding." She smiled at him sadly. "I'm so sorry."

He tipped his head a bit and looked down, shrugging. "I hope you find happiness, too, Laura."

She leaned in and hugged him. As he let go of her, she stepped back and looked at him. Her sadness, her pride in his accomplishment, was now joined by a funny feeling of hope, anticipation for him; she knew he'd be okay. He seemed to be standing on his own two feet better than she'd ever seen him when they were together.

As she walked away, she felt as if some heavy weight had been lifted from her shoulders. She'd finally made a decision just for herself, without trying to please anyone else, and it felt good. She knew things were probably over with Adam. He said he needed to tell her something, and it sounded serious. And not happy serious, from the way he'd seemed to her lately. The dread that caused was crushing. But she knew she did not belong with Steve. She'd much rather be alone than be with someone she didn't love.

She put the beer in the refrigerator, cracked one open, and sat at her kitchen table. The house was quiet except for Charlie playing a video game in the next room; Nicole was taking a nap. She knew she should be getting ready for Adam to pick her up. She looked down at her old tank top and jeans, the faded oversized flannel shirt that was so thin from age and washings it was nearly transparent in spots. She made a snap decision, grabbing her phone and hitting Adam's name in her contact list.

Relieved when his voicemail picked up, she left a brief message: "Hi Adam, listen, small change in plans, I wondered if I could just meet you tonight instead … how about at that coffee house we went to last week. I'll meet you there at 8:00. See you then."

It was definitely an abrupt sign-off, compared to their recent conversations and messages. The unpleasant thought had occurred to her that if he was breaking up with her, or dropping some horrible bombshell on her, she'd be stuck relying on him for a ride back home afterward. She'd feel so much better going into this if she had her own escape route. Man, she thought, I'm just batting a thousand today. First she'd shot down hopeful Steve, now she was preparing for the worst with Adam.

Following her trend of snap decisions this afternoon, the idea struck her that she was not going to make this easy for Adam. He'd been too perfect, drawn her in too irresistibly for her to let him off the hook without regrets. She was not going to leave him with a final image of her in ripped up jeans and a baggy old flannel. He'd already seen that side of her at the basketball game. She left the beer unfinished on the table and headed for her room.

When Nicole stirred from the couch and sat up just as Laura was leaving, she whistled in awe. “Damn, girl, you look like you just stepped outta one of those hot perfume ads! I didn’t even know you knew how to do all this,” she waved her hand up and down Laura’s frame with a chuckle.

Laura blushed self-consciously but she knew, for once, that Nicole was right. She’d dressed simply in the little black skirt she had on earlier, a clingy-in-the-right-spots black top that highlighted her assets and left a bit of her shoulders bare, minimal jewelry. She’d swept her hair up in the back, letting big pieces fall loose around her face. A generous application of black smudgy eyeliner and some pale pink lipstick finished things off nicely.

Nicole hugged her on her way out, whispering, “Knock ‘em dead, kid.”

Laura smiled back at her, actually much less nervous now than she’d been. She could handle whatever happened. She’d been fine before Adam. She’d be fine after him. If she repeated that enough in her head, eventually she’d believe it.

She arrived early, choosing to stand near her car and wait for him. He pulled up next to her, jumped out and was in front of her, in her space, all six feet two inches of him. She took in his black wavy hair, his smiling blue eyes, his warm spicy scent … and then his hand at the back of her neck and his mouth covering hers and a deep, quiet sound escaping his throat, almost like a low hum, as her body rebelled and responded, molded into him and she kissed him back, and she knew she would not be fine.

When it was over she took a short, shaky gasp of air and put her hand on his chest, meeting his eyes, feeling the intensity radiating between them. He covered her hand on his chest and frowned at her.

"God you're gorgeous," he growled. "I know you're mad, upset, worried, whatever. I never meant to alarm you, Laura. I could hear it in your voice. I'm sorry."

She pushed a bit with her hand and got a little space between them. "What's going on, Adam? I would prefer to talk here. I don't want to go sit down in some stupid restaurant and pretend everything is fine. I want to know what's going on. I could hear it in *your* voice," she told him. "What do you need to talk to me about?"

He sighed. "I had planned to wait a little longer to tell you about this, but … I don't think I should. I didn't mean for you to worry, it's just something you should know."

She tried to arrange her expression into something a bit more composed, but knew she probably wasn't having much success. She remained silent and let him continue.

"Look, maybe this is too soon to bring this up, but the way I feel about you … I guess I don't think it is too soon. I need you to know, up front, so you're going in with all the information…."

He wasn't doing very well spitting it out, which was amplifying her anxiety. She stamped her feet in the cold air and gave him a wide-eyed impatient look. Whatever it was, he was just making it worse.

"Okay!" he responded to her unspoken nudge. "All right. You know I was married. My ex-wife wanted children. *We* wanted children.

After trying for a long time, too long, we started looking into why it wasn't happening. Turns out it was me. I'm why."

She took this in, looking at the worry lines just barely visible in his forehead. This news was having the opposite effect on her than he'd anticipated. If he was talking to her about babies, about children or not being able to have children, then … she smiled a bit … then that meant he really was committed to this thing they had, he really did see it going somewhere. A little thrill ran up her spine at the thought of a future with Adam. Ten minutes ago she'd been resigning herself to the idea that that would never happen.

He was searching her face, looking for clues to her reaction. When she was silent, he continued, more urgently now. "We found this out after years, you see. I don't think it ever occurred to either of us that it just wouldn't happen at all. Kimberly was more persistent than I about pursuing other options. We eventually tried in vitro from a donor. It didn't take, and we were out of money. Our only option, in my mind, was adoption. I got us on all the right waiting lists, we started saving, making plans again, talking about the nursery, and then one day she just woke up and decided she couldn't do it. She'd wanted a baby for so long, her own baby, she said, that she couldn't settle for adoption." Laura heard the thinly concealed bitterness in the word "settle."

He went on, "She couldn't deprive herself of the experience. We fought. I reasoned that she'd love the adopted child just as much as if she'd given birth to it, and that's where the argument remained. She disagreed. She felt that she wouldn't," he paused.

Laura saw now what had happened. Adam was adopted. If this had been their stalemate, how could Adam go on? His ex-wife really believed that she would never feel about an adopted child as strongly as she would her own. Adam truly believed she would, and why wouldn't he? His own parents and family sounded nothing short of wonderful. She was certain they'd showered as much love on him as they had his subsequent brothers and sisters.

"She said she knew she'd always regret not having a child of her own if she stayed with me. She wouldn't consider adoption. I couldn't change her mind. After I while, I stopped wanting to." He shrugged. "I signed the divorce papers the day she served me with them. I don't miss her, and I'm not sorry. But I don't want you to go any further without knowing what you're getting into, Laura. You're young. You've probably thought of having more children. If there was any way…."

He finally stopped, put his hands in his pockets and looked at her, clearly in agony. "Would you please just say something?"

Her mind was racing. He'd forced her to think beyond what she'd allowed herself thus far. What if they stayed together? What if they got married? How would she feel, knowing she'd never have another baby grow inside her? Charlie had been so long ago, when she was practically a kid. Until a few weeks ago, the thought of more children had never crossed her mind at all. Being with Adam had made her think crazy, far-fetched wishes, not even thoughts or plans, just wild ideas. Sharing her life with him, and maybe getting to raise a child with him, their adopted child, sounded wonderful.

She snaked her hands into his coat pockets and found his, squeezing them. “Adam, I don’t care. I love you for telling me this now, for worrying and being honest with me. But I don’t care. The thought of us being together long enough to make a decision about adopting a baby--if that happens, I would absolutely love to raise a child with you, you’ll be the most amazing dad and it just makes me--” she broke off, surprised when tears welled up in her eyes. She tried to blink them back and went on. “I can’t imagine anything better,” she whispered. “It doesn’t matter how it happens.”

She watched his throat as he swallowed hard, processing her response. He was quiet for a long moment.

“Thank you, Laura. I wasn’t sure how this would go … are you positive you feel that way? Maybe you need more time to think about it.” His voice was very low, thick with emotion.

She smiled and shook her head, letting go of his hands to hug him. “I’m positive.”

She felt him take a deep breath in and let it out, and his whole body seemed to relax.

“Come on,” he stepped back abruptly. “Can we please go now? I actually did have plans for us. I’ll drive.”

They got a table at the same Italian restaurant they’d gone to on their first date. With it being middle of the week they got the best spot, right in front of the fireplace, perfect for the chill in the air. The weather was fluctuating from just below freezing to just above it, leaving no real snow on the ground but definitely making it feel as if there were. The thought instantly brought with it the nerve-wracking worry of finding the evidence they needed before everything froze for the season. She hoped they would find the car and it would yield what they were looking for before the freeze came.

The waitress cleared their dinner plates and said she'd return with two fresh glasses of wine. Laura looked into the fire, her fingers lightly touching Adam's on the table. She could stay like this forever, so cozy and content and happy with him … neither of them had spoken in the last few minutes. She met his eyes and found him watching her. His gaze made her feel as if she were wrapped in his arms rather than across the table, barely touching him. The waitress reappeared with their wine.

Laura stared at the sparkling diamond ring dangling from a red satin ribbon around the base of her wine glass. She felt the color drain from her face as she dragged her eyes away from the ring to look at Adam. He wore a huge smile.

Then he was next to her, on one knee, turning her chair to face him. He took both her hands in his. "Laura, will you marry me?"

As quickly as the blood had left her head, it returned full force, her cheeks flushed a hot red. She smiled, then laughed and nearly tipped him over as she leaned forward out of her chair to hug him, whispering "yes, yes, Adam, yes!"

He caught her and kissed her, both of them stopping to laugh as their smiles interfered with the kissing. She sat back down in her chair and looked around self-consciously. All eyes in the restaurant were on them as Adam pulled the ribbon and slid the ring off and onto her finger. The people near them who'd seen what was happening clapped enthusiastically. Laura blushed fiercely but didn't care.

Adam leaned in and said quietly, "Let's get out of here, huh?"

She felt like she was literally walking on air to the car. The cold air didn't bother her, she didn't even notice it. She watched the puffs of smoke in the air as they talked and laughed, she watched his eyes smile whenever his mouth did, and she watched how he watched her constantly. She thought she could do a flip if someone had asked her to. He opened the car door for her and she climbed into the Mountaineer but remained facing sideways, her stocking clad legs against him as she grabbed the collar of his coat and pulled him down for a real kiss. She wrapped one leg loosely around his hip and he leaned into her, an arm braced along the door.

They were both breathing hard when she let him go. He stood smiling at her, his seductive half smile, his eyes heavy lidded, a deep iridescent blue. The freckles over his nose stood out against his pale skin in the cold air. She put her lips close to his ear. "Let's have a sleepover."

The drive to his house was much too long. She slipped her arms around his waist as he unlocked the front door, and she had his belt buckle undone before she'd even stepped inside. He turned to face her and pulled her into him, bending to kiss her in private now, no tentative politeness but all longing and need. She raised her arms as he stripped off her shirt, and he backed into his bedroom, holding her around the waist.

Laura slid a hand under the waistband of his pants and pushed the fabric down as he led her to the bed. She boldly caressed him, loving the hard, silky feel of him under her fingers. She pulled him down on top of her, his mouth covering her breasts through her lacy black bra, and then without it as he released the clasp and got rid of it. His tongue worked magic and she arched her back under him, finally urging him back to her lips, unable to get enough of him. His hand slid up her thigh under the skirt and she kicked her panties off, pressing against the hot hardness of him.

Adam braced on strong arms over her and Laura drew him in with her legs around his hips. She felt his hand cup her bottom and then the welcome, hard length of him filled her, making her cry out. He paused and bent his head to her breast, then came back up to her mouth. She felt Adam move inside her, and she kissed him urgently, hands sliding up his muscular shoulders as she moved her hips in rhythm to his. He groaned, one hand stroking her side and resting on her thigh, forcing her to slow a bit. Her eyes fluttered open and she met his. She wanted to swim in the passion there, wanted nothing but him. Nothing in her life had ever felt this good. Ever. She wrapped her legs around him, gradually moving faster, unable to stop.

Adam's muscles tightened as he thrust into her, and she watched as his dark lashes fanned out on his skin when his eyes closed and his brow crinkled, shuddering with sensation. He pushed her over the edge and she sucked in a sharp gulp of air, a quiet little shriek leaving her lips and her fingers dug into his back as ecstasy overtook her body and mind. He didn't stop, and Laura leaned into the starbursts behind her eyelids, the tingling fire that crept from her thighs, between her legs, over her belly and breasts and up to the top of her head. She rode the waves of what he'd elicited in her, at last relaxing against him, one limp arm around him as he finally slowed.

After a while, he rolled onto his side next to her, keeping her close. She waited for her breathing to return to normal, looking at him through heavy lidded eyes.

He lightly stroked her hair with his fingertips. "Wow," his low voice rumbled near her ear, and she thought she would just stay here with him, like this, until forever.

"Wow to you." She looked up at him, feeling like a wet noodle. She didn't want to sleep. She didn't want to miss a thing. She'd only close her eyes for a minute.

When she opened them again, she had a sense it was much later. Adam lay on his back, one arm folded behind his head, and she thought he was sleeping, he looked so peaceful. Laura silently let her gaze cover his well-muscled arms, his chest, the enticing line of hair that crept from his navel down under the sheets. I'd like to lick that line, she thought, smiling to herself. She would get to. Laura gingerly reached up and stroked the black cowlick at his temple, and he turned toward her, awake, drowsy. "Hey."

She smiled. "Hey."

"I have some ideas…." he said.

She laughed. He must be able to read her mind. "What, no recovery time?"

Now he had to laugh. "No, ideas about us. We are engaged, you know."

"Ah, yes, you are right. Ideas. Like?"

"I don't think Charlie should have to move and change schools. He's a freshman; he has friends, basketball, extracurricular stuff."

Laura couldn't help being reminded of Steve's lack of regard for Charlie, failure to include her son in any of their long-term plans. "You're right."

"So, what if I just moved in with you after the wedding? Charlie could stay right where he is, plus your family's close by--mine is all over the place so it won't matter. My clinic is only a half hour away. If we need more room, we can always add on. I'll get a good price for this place. We'll have a nice chunk to put in the bank." As an afterthought he added, "of course, we could always look for something bigger in the same school district. I don't want your family to think I'm a free-loader."

She laughed at him. "Oh my God, Adam, you have no idea," she said between giggles. "You really have this all planned out, don't you? And largely based on how it'll all affect my kid? Unbelievable." She fanned the blankets up and straddled him, hugging him and breathing in his scent, raking her fingers into his silky black hair.

His strong arms were around her and he ran his hands up her back to her shoulders. "Laura," he growled, "I wasn't done." He kissed her collarbone and shoulder and his hands found their way back down. "Listen," he said, hoarsely, "There's one last thing."

She sat up a little and tilted her head, looking at him. "Man, you're determined," she teased, bending to lick his chest.

His hands were on her waist then and his mouth covered hers. His one last thought would have to wait.

Much, much later, Laura lay curled up next to him with her arm across his chest as the first pink of dawn crept over the cornfield across the road and soft rays filtered into the room. Her eyelids were so heavy, she might actually have to sleep.

"What was your one last thing that was so important?" she murmured.

Adam's sea blue eyes closed and opened once, a slow blink, sated now, as he watched her. He covered her arm with his and pulled her closer against him. "I'd like Charlie to take Snickers, if he wants him. That puppy from my clinic. I think they'll be good for each other."

CHAPTER TWENTY-FOUR

Laura stood silently watching the dripping, once-silver Ford Granada as it crawled up the ramp onto the county flatbed to be taken into evidence. A preliminary search had revealed the body of Robert Forsythe, wrapped in the tattered remains of a tarp, rotted beyond recognition. The man's wallet, which dissolved into a puddle of black slime when Laura carefully fished it out of the car's trunk that had become Forsythe's coffin, still held the man's driver's license. His name was barely legible through the muck and deterioration, but it was there.

The car had been resting at the bottom of Silver Lake for nearly eighteen years. The poor man had been blamed for the murder of a police officer, while all the while he was lying dead in the trunk of his own car at the bottom of a lake. Laura was thankful now that the man had no family, but it was one more thing to add to the growing list of reasons she had for hoping Murdock could be found. Anyone Forsythe had known had assumed the man was a murderer this whole time, when his real crime had only been to try to help a desperate woman.

The on-site search they'd done had not revealed any other evidence that would help them. No Glock 9mm handgun. What were the odds Murdock had kept both those guns all these years: both the police issue Glock as well as his own Smith and Wesson he'd used to kill Forsythe and the victim at the Texas convenience store shooting? The man would have to be either a complete idiot, or unbelievably arrogant and egotistical. Well, she thought, there was some evidence to that effect, at least. Maybe they'd be lucky. If they found him.

Laura nodded to her sister as the vehicles started pulling away from the lake, she and Nicole in one car, Jenny heading back to the Sheriff's Office in another, following the wet car on the flatbed tow truck and leaving the lake survey company to pack up their equipment.

"Let me know if you find anything," she called.

Jenny nodded back. "Right away."

Nicole was pensive and quiet on the ride home. Laura was sure the day's events were taking a toll on her. "Are you okay?"

Nicole nodded, more to herself than Laura. "I guess. Yeah. I just feel so bad for that man, Danny's father. I mean--"

She didn't finish and Laura frowned at her, waiting.

Nicole sighed. "I know what my father was. Is. But that--seeing that car, and that poor man who lost his life, seeing that--it's just very concrete. You know?"

Laura nodded. "Kind of in-your-face evidence of who he was, right?"

"Yeah," Nicole said softly. "He was a monster. He ruined so many lives, and never looked back."

Laura reached over and squeezed her friend's hand. "You're doing that for him. This is almost over, Nicole. You're cleaning up everything he destroyed."

Nicole shrugged. "Not all of it," and Laura knew she meant James.

When Laura's phone rang late the next night, she grabbed it off her nightstand after the first ring.

"You got the Glock?" she said into the phone, waiting for her sister's reply.

"No. But they got Murdock." Jenny's tone was laced with satisfaction.

Laura padded on bare feet into the bathroom and shut the door so as not to wake the sleeping house. She sat on the edge of the tub and rubbed her eyes, giving her cheek a couple light smacks.

"What? They got Murdock? Are you kidding me?"

"Nope. Lieutenant got notification from the FBI about twenty minutes ago that they got him. They found him in a little shack in Mixistlan, living with a common-law wife, sitting on a ton of Mexican blow and a nice collection of firearms."

Laura exhaled forcefully, now wide awake. "Wow. I mean, just--wow. I have to tell Nicole. I guess I didn't really think they'd be able to find him. And dealing guns and coke? Nice!" She paused for a moment.

"But…." Jenny said, waiting.

"But, won't that hurt us trying to get him extradited? Mexican government's got their own issues with him."

"No, we get him. The U.S. has an extradition treaty with Mexico. We've got three dead bodies, one of them a cop. All they've got is some drug and firearm charges."

"Okay," Laura nodded to herself, "good. And the firearms … damn," she breathed, "do you think maybe the Glock and the .38 are in there somewhere?" Her voice went up hopefully. She knew it was a long shot, especially if he'd been selling guns … anyone with half a brain would've unloaded those guns at the first chance.

"You know, from what we know about the guy, I wouldn't put it past him to keep the guns as a … souvenir, you know, memorabilia. We'll find out soon."

***

The small witness room of the Callahan County, Texas, courthouse was stuffy and crowded the day the trial began. Seated across the table from the county prosecutor and his aide were the remaining members of the Murdock family: Irene flanked by Nicole, Harry and Danny. Danny had come in this morning clean shaven, an attempt to help set things straight in his mother's mind a bit, since he seemed to bear such a resemblance to his real father, especially wearing his beard. Nicole's hand rested on her mother's, her other hand on her growing belly.

She still could hardly believe she was six months pregnant. She'd called Laura on the way home from her ultrasound a few weeks ago, unable to contain her excitement.

"It's a girl!!" She couldn't help shouting it into the phone. She smiled at Laura's little shriek on the other end, all the way up north in Michigan but sounding like she was right in the next room.

"Nic, I'm so excited for you! A baby girl!"

They'd discussed baby names briefly, then before hanging up, Nicole asked if she could fly Laura in for the trial. At least for the beginning.

"I haven't seen my dad yet. I haven't seen him since I was nineteen, right before he took off. I'd feel a lot better if you could be here with me."

Laura shouldn't have been surprised to hear the nervous, shaky tone to Nicole's voice, but she was. The woman had weathered so much, remained so strong, somehow Laura always reverted back to her adolescent view of her lifelong friend: fearless. Sometimes she forgot to look beyond the outward bravado Nicole exuded to the scared, beaten little girl underneath. She was still there.

"Of course I'll come," she said, and she and Adam had arrived yesterday. Laura had debated whether to bring her fiancée, but Nicole urged her to.

“I’ve only met him once. Don’t you think your matron of honor should have a better idea of whom you’re marrying? Please bring him, if he doesn’t mind.”

Now Nicole’s eyes went to the door that led out of the witness room, knowing Laura would be waiting on the other side, sitting on the bench against the wall with Adam, waiting to enter the courtroom with her. Her attention was pulled back to matters at hand when she heard her name.

“Isn’t that right, Nicole?” the prosecutor was waiting for her response to some question she hadn’t heard.

“I’m sorry,” she cleared her throat, wiping her sweaty hands on the expensive black silk of her pants. “Please repeat that, sir, I apologize.” She felt Harry squeeze her shoulder.

Duane Davids, a prosecuting attorney Harry had assured Nicole was one of the good guys, smiled reassuringly at her. “It’s all right. This is all preliminary, before we go in front of the judge today. I was explaining to your mother that all she has to do is tell the people in there,” he gestured toward the door, and the courtroom beyond, “just what she told the detectives about her husband; what constituted normal behavior for him, and what happened the night your family left Michigan.”

Harry spoke up. “The charges in Michigan for the slain police officer and for Mr. Forsythe,” he glanced at Daniel, “won’t be considered admissible here, but we do need to establish your father’s personality, it goes toward showing how he would have come to kill Andrew Clayton at the convenience store four years later in front of Irene and Daniel. The defense will try to block some of the information, but I believe we'll get our point across. Your mom should not hold back when she's questioned. We need to show that this shooting was not aberrant behavior for your father."

Nicole nodded, leaning into her mother and reminding her quietly, "Remember when the detectives talked to you about how Dad killed Robert, Mom?"

Irene gave her an odd look. "Of course I remember!" Her mother was always relatively sharp in the early part of the day, and had been more lucid in general these past months. Nicole wasn't sure if it was due to the doctors continuing to adjust her medications, or if it was simply that now there was nothing left to hide. In either case, her mother appeared to be having no trouble following what the prosecutor was saying.

Irene would be the first witness called to the stand after opening statements. Daniel would be next, to tell the story of how he'd watched his dad shoot and kill a customer named Andrew Clayton, who'd had the bad luck of being in the wrong place at the wrong time when Murdock had attempted to rob the store with his kid in the car.

It had been explained to Nicole that they were in Texas, rather than Michigan, not because of the nature of the crime Murdock had committed here, but because Texas had the death penalty for capital murder, and that was what the prosecutor was going for. Capital murder trials were divided into two parts. If, during the trial-phase, Murdock was found guilty by the jury, the punishment-phase would commence, in which the jury would determine if he would be sentenced to death. He would only be extradited to Michigan and tried for the double murder there if he escaped receiving the death penalty sentence here in Texas. It did make sense to Nicole once Harry and the prosecutor went over it all with her and Danny. Harry had assured her that the evidence would speak for itself in the Texas case. They had Daniel's memory, security tape footage from the convenience store, and they had the gun.

The Smith and Wesson .38 caliber handgun used to kill Andrew Clayton was the same gun used to kill Robert Forsythe, the same gun registered to John Murdock years ago when he first purchased it. The .38 and the police issue Glock 9mm that had been used to kill the officer were both found in the little shack Murdock had called home, not mixed in with the stockpile of over thirty other guns in a compartment under the floorboards, but kept separate, wrapped almost lovingly in several pieces of Mexican wool inside a box under Murdock's bed.

Nicole felt immensely relieved to know that even if her father was not sentenced to death, he would never again live a life of freedom. Even without the death penalty, the time he'd have to serve for this murder, plus the two very concrete murder cases in Michigan, guaranteed John Murdock would die in prison. One way or another. Nicole hoped that being comforted by that thought didn't make her a horrible person.

The prosecutor and his aide stood to head into the courtroom. It was time. Nicole started to stand and realized she was glued to her seat. A deafening whooshing sound filled her ears, loud and fast, and the room began to spin as she felt the blood drain from her face, the energy rushing out of her as if from an open wound. She closed her eyes slowly, the sound ringing in her ears, and felt Harry's arms around her. There was another sound, Danny's voice, very faint, and finally the surging whoosh inside her ears and her brain started to quiet. Her breathing slowed, her eyes opened, and the sound was gone. She was in Harry's lap, on the floor. Danny's face loomed over her.

Harry smoothed the hair back from her face. "You passed out. How are you feeling?"

The prosecutor's aide appeared and wordlessly handed Danny a cold washcloth, which he gently applied to Nicole's forehead.

Nicole sat up a little and blinked, giving her head a small shake. "Well, shoot! What the hell?"

Now a plump older woman entered and bent to give Nicole a glass of orange juice. "Here you go, dear, you'd better drink up and take care of that little one there," she smiled at Nicole's small round basketball of a belly. She waited for Nicole to drink, standing with hands on her hips.

Nicole laughed nervously, turning her head to look at Harry. He gave her a small, wan smile but she read the worry in his eyes. He stroked one hand up and down her bare arm. "Are you all right, sweetheart?"

"I'm fine," she said, a bit too loudly. "I'm fine, really," she told the assembled group around her. "I just got too hot, and I forgot to eat breakfast this morning. My bad." She smiled sheepishly, trying not to think of the real reason she'd taken an abrupt nap on the witness room floor. She began to stand, and Danny took her arm, Harry bracing her with his hands on her hips as he stood with her.

"Oh, my goodness, people! Just go on now, I'm fine. See?" She took a long swallow of the orange juice. "Thank you," she said to the plump woman, who nodded at the still half-full glass and looked at Nicole.

She sighed and finished the juice. "There. Thank you," she said again, handing the glass back. "That was very nice of you. I am fine. Are we ready?" She looked around at Danny and Irene.

Danny turned and wheeled Irene out in her wheelchair, followed by the aide and the juice-bringing woman. Harry moved toward the door, motioning a worried looking Laura into the small room before shutting it, leaving just the three of them in the room.

"Sit down," he told Nicole.

Nicole obediently sat, feeling better now that the orange juice was hitting her system. She knew better than to argue with Harry with that tone to his voice.

"What's going on? Is it the baby?" His voice was filled with concern.

Nicole shrugged. Laura sat next to her, watching the interchange. "I don't know. I feel better now. I just…."

He waited but no words came to her. She ran a shaky hand through her long red curls.

"I know." Laura took her hand and held it between hers. "Nicole, you'll be absolutely fine. I promise you. He can't hurt you anymore. He's old, and broken, and he's on trial for murder. He's finished. He won't ever hurt you again."

Understanding washed over Harry's features and Laura saw his adam's apple move up and down in his throat, his jaw clenched. He was so busy handling things from the legal angle, the husband angle had escaped him.

Laura leaned in and hugged Nicole, patting her back. She didn't say another word, but she already felt calmer, her hands had stopped shaking.

"I know you're right," she said into Laura's shoulder. Her eyes met Harry's and she smiled at him, a real smile, a confident Nicole smile. "You're right," she repeated.

Laura let go of her and they stood.

"I can't believe I let that son of a bitch get to me. Again. Let's go out there. I will be *fine*," she emphasized, convincing herself. She was done letting her father beat her.

Harry slid his arm around her waist and kissed the top of her head. "You can do this," he told her quietly. "You've been waiting your whole life to do this."

The trial took only three days. Jury deliberation took less than a day. The verdict came back at 1:00 pm and the judge directed the foreman to stand to read it: guilty of capital murder. The judge had instructed the jury before they were sequestered that their second duty, if they should find John Murdock guilty beyond a reasonable doubt of capital murder, would be to decide punishment. The jury foreman cleared his throat for this and stole a glance at Murdock, then looked only at the judge.

"We the jury found this crime to be particularly malicious and heinous. We unanimously agree that the punishment is death."

Nicole was allowed into the little holding room to see her father before he was taken from the courthouse that day. Laura and Adam waited in the vestibule. She left Harry outside the door, in spite of his protests. She looked her husband in the eyes before going in, wordlessly telling him this was something she had to do. Danny was with her.

Danny put his arm out, stopping her before she opened the door to see their father. Nicole looked at him in surprise. "Don't you want to see him?"

Danny shrugged. "I do. I need to. But you need to know something, Nicole." He paused, weighing his words. He glanced down the long hallway where Irene sat in her wheelchair with Laura and Adam. Nicole followed his gaze to their hunched over mother. She'd weathered the trial better than either of them had expected. But she was still the same woman who'd endured and allowed all of the damaging events of their childhood, an empty shell of terrible memories and failure to act.

Nicole looked into Danny's eyes, certain she knew what he was thinking. She didn't. Not exactly.

"That man in there is not our father," Danny said. "I know he's not mine, but he's not yours anymore either. He's not a parent. He doesn't deserve that title."

Nicole nodded at her remaining brother silently, sadly. "I know," she whispered.

"You've been a better parent to me than I could ever have asked for, Nicole," and he bent and kissed her cheek. "I hope you know that."

Nicole's eyes filled with a rush tears that she hadn't needed to shed throughout the entire trial. Nothing in the last four days impacted her like Danny's words. She drew in several deep breaths and nodded, looking down at the floor, trying not to cry, and finally giving up and looking at her brother. She hugged him tightly. He had no way of knowing how much his words meant to her, how she needed to hear that she had done a good job. It told her that she could be a good mother, that she would do a good job with her daughter. Her throat closed and she rested her head on her brother's chest, hugging him.

He said nothing, only hugged her back.

When she could speak, she pulled back from him, a little embarrassed now. "Thank you," she whispered.

She took his hand and opened the door.

Murdock was seated at a table, wrist and ankle shackles back in place since leaving the courtroom. Two very large guards stood behind him.

Nicole's fearlessness evaporated. She hung back a bit by the door. Seeing him on the other side of the courtroom was entirely different than seeing him here, feet away from her. Her little brother walked right in and stood in front of the man, looking down at him. Danny was silent. Nicole took in the yellow, sallow cast to her father's skin. Age and hard living had taken their toll on him. His fat belly dwarfed the rest of him, his skinny arms and legs and neck. Deep, shadowed wrinkles creased his face and made hollows under his eyes. For a split second she was reminded, against her will, of James.

But his eyes were not the same. Not the same as James. His small, mean eyes looked out at her, then at Danny, then back at her, and saw nothing. His expression did not change. She saw no remorse, no sadness, no regret, not for the lives he'd wrecked and not for his own life. Not like James at all. Her brother was a better man in his short life than her father had ever been, she thought.

She looked at Danny, standing there in front of him. Danny, such a big man in every sense of the word; so smart, so strong, so healthy finally. Danny, who was lucky enough not to be this man's child. Her little brother's face was drawn into a mask of disgust. He had nothing to say to the man. He silently shook his head, looked at Nicole, glanced back at Murdock once more and went to the door.

"Let's go," he said to her. "He's already dead."

The guard moved to let Daniel out, and Nicole stopped him. "I'm not coming yet. You go."

He looked at her questioningly. "Are you sure?"

She nodded, looking at Murdock.

The door closed and she took the few steps to stand in front of the table, facing her father. She had thought about this day for so long. She'd rehearsed all the things she wanted to say to him. All the different ways to make him understand what he'd done to her, how he'd decimated their family. Danny was right, she realized. This man was not her father any longer. The father she had such limited memories of, the nice father that she'd started life with, the one who'd taken her to ballet class and the park and said sweet things to her, that father was gone. He was gone a long time ago. And this man in front of her … her brother was right. This man was already dead.

But he hadn't been, a few short months ago when he'd been caught like a cockroach in his little shithole, hiding out all these years. He'd still been doing business. Selling drugs. Guns. Probably beating his common-law wife. So this man in front of her was maybe not quite dead. Not yet.

She caught his eyes on her round belly, the tiny, new, vulnerable, unborn little girl inside her, and she snapped. She put her hands on the table and leaned down, leaned into his space, and she could smell his stench, she was breathing his foul air. Like something rotting from the inside out. She leaned closer to him, her face hot and her eyes on fire. She could see the ugly pores on his red nose and in the folds of his yellow skin. The guards took a few steps in, standing inches behind Murdock now.

"Ma'am," one of them said, a warning.

She ignored him. She looked into Murdock's bloodshot eyes and knew her own face was painted in the same portrait of revulsion Daniel's had been.

"You can't hurt me," she whispered to him. "You will not, you will never hurt me again," her voice was louder now, strong. "Do you hear me? I know what you are. I know what you've done. I remember everything. And I know you will spend the rest of your days suffering. Your life is over. You are over. You reap what you sow," she told him.

"You tried to break me, break all of us, but you didn't. James' blood is on your hands." Her breath caught here, and she had to stop. Tears threatened behind her eyes and she swallowed hard, furious, determined not to let him see her cry. He didn't deserve her tears. She would cry for James later. Away from the poisonous air around this man. "Think about James, your little boy, with his blue eyes just like yours, his laugh, his fears, his amazing spirit." A tear spilled over and Nicole angrily swiped it away. "Think about your dead son while you're waiting to be put down like a goddamn dog. Think about the wreckage you've caused. And think about me and Danny. Think about the grand-daughter you will never ever meet. You didn't win. We did."

She straightened up, her heart racing. She went to the door and stopped to look back at him. Nicole was stunned to see tears running down his face. His hands struggled to come up but were stopped by the shackles. He settled for ducking his head down and sobbing silently. She fought through her anger, the toxic anger that she could at last let go of. She wanted nothing of this man, no legacy of rage and bitterness. She found a trace of pity for this animal who was once her father. She stood watching him another moment, then turned her back and walked out the door without looking back.

CHAPTER TWENTY-FIVE

Laura and Adam's wedding day was a perfect 75 degrees, sunny, breezy, the scent of lilacs in the air. Laura beamed at Adam, standing with the minister in the new gazebo from his parents, as she made her way toward him through an archway of pale lavender clematis flowers. Tom Miller turned and kissed his daughter's cheek before stepping aside and shaking Adam's hand in both of his.

Charlie stood tall next to Adam, with Adam's three brothers alongside him in the gazebo. Laura knew without looking that her parents would be in tears already as her dad joined her mom in the very small group of guests seated in chairs in her backyard. There was an arrangement of dining tables and a catered buffet off behind the guests, and Nicole had surprised her by having an elaborate dance floor set up, complete with soft white twinkle lights around it and a very good band, currently playing a rendition of Pachelbel's Canon in D. Nicole caught

Laura's eye and winked at her, smiling, as she took the pink rose bouquet from her to free her hands. Laura turned to face Adam.

She saw his grin start at the corners of his eyes and spread out over his face like sunshine as he squeezed her hands in his. She couldn't imagine ever feeling less than captivated with him. Her life until this moment had been quite a ride, Laura wouldn't trade a second of it. Everything that came before had brought her to Adam.

Dancing with him, their first dance as husband and wife, she leaned up a little to whisper to him and he lowered his head to hers, kissing her neck while she tried to remember what she wanted to say. His warm hand was at the small of her back, the other folded securely around hers as he guided her in a small circle on the dance floor. He'd warned her he was not a good dancer, but he needn't have; she wouldn't have noticed.

She put her lips close to his ear, let her hand come up off his shoulder and wove her fingers lightly into the silky black hair above his collar.

"Adam," she whispered, "we are always going to be this happy." She knew it was sappy and sentimental, but she also knew it was true.

He chuckled lightly, a low rumble in his chest. He looked down at her, tipping his head to one side and giving her that slightly lopsided grin.

"I know," he said, and kissed her.

While Adam was deep in conversation with Jenny's husband, she took a break to sit and have a drink and covertly watch Charlie chatting with his new girlfriend. He'd been so excited, he even let Laura help him choose a dashing tuxedo rather than going with standard suits like the rest of the wedding party. She thought it was fitting, too, since Adam had convinced him to be his best man. Adam's brothers were beyond nice. They instantly got along with her family and included Charlie in their sibling antics right from their arrival.

Now, watching her son, she thought this day couldn't get any better. He'd said something to make his girlfriend laugh and she had her hand on his forearm, completely absorbed. He glanced in her direction. Uh oh, she'd been caught.

He smiled at her and Shannon looked up as well. "Mom, Shannon and I are going inside to check on Snickers, okay?"

She nodded, "Sure." Adam had not officially moved in yet, but Snickers had, just as soon as the puppy was healthy enough to leave the clinic a couple months ago. She'd never seen her son as thrilled as he was the day Adam brought the puppy home to him. Snickers slept with him, followed him everywhere, and generally lazed around acting sad and pouty each day when Charlie was at school. She watched the two teenagers enter the house, passing Nicole on her way outside with a pink bundle in her arms.

Laura jumped up to go grab the baby from Nicole and nearly tripped on her wedding gown. It wasn't overly long or full but the swishy layers to the skirt tangled up her feet. Nicole giggled at her as Laura righted herself.

"Hey darlin, I don't let drunkards hold my baby, so just back off now," she joked.

Laura offered her pinky for Jaime to wrap her tiny fingers around. Nicole had smiled up at her friend from her hospital bed in Labor and Delivery, her voice breaking as she introduced Laura to her new baby daughter: Jaime Catherine Peterson. Laura thought it was perfect.

She shook her head now, appraising Nicole's already slim figure.

"Oh, you disgust me. Are you eating at all?" The baby had been born less than two months ago and Nicole already looked as if she'd never been pregnant. Laura suspected that she would probably gain baby weight just adopting a child. Her heart jumped a bit at the thought … she and Adam had discussed it frequently in the recent months. They would bring the idea up to Charlie after the wedding.

"Give her to me, it's my turn," Laura said, taking the tiny baby girl carefully from her. "Go dance with your husband, where is he?"

Nicole looked around, saying, "I've actually been trying to find your sister, I never got to properly thank her for her part in helping find my father--" she interrupted herself. "There they both are, come with me," she said, leading Laura across the yard.

Harry and Jenny were engrossed in a serious debate when they approached. Harry was saying, "Well, you have to take into consideration what precedent's been set before determining cause, and then--"

Nicole squeezed his arm as she sidled up next to him, smiling at Jenny. "Sounds absolutely riveting, really, I'm sorry to interrupt." She rolled her eyes at Harry. "Do you really have to talk shop *everywhere*?"

Jenny laughed. "It's my fault. I was asking him about a case I'm working on."

Nicole nodded. “Jenny, I just wanted to thank you for all you did for my family. Without you and Laura, nothing would’ve been settled.”

Jenny shrugged. “I don’t know about that. It’s not like he ever got tried in this state for anything he did, no matter what we discovered.”

“I know. But you two found my father. You made him responsible for what he’s done.” She spoke to both Laura and Jenny. “You did my brother Daniel a great service, more than you know, figuring out who his father was and clearing his name. That police officer’s family can be at peace now, knowing that the man who carelessly took his life has been caught. And you finally answered for us what atrocious thing my father did that night we fled town. It explained so much. We needed to understand, at last, what really happened, no matter how awful.”

Laura was impressed with Nicole’s candor. She sounded healthy, open. No trace of anger, no hint of denial. Just honesty. Her friend had come to reconcile the fact that the man sitting on death row in Texas no longer held the privilege of his family’s love and concern. Everyone is capable of a mistake, of one terribly wrong or misjudged decision. John Murdock’s life had been a repetitive series of primal, malicious decisions, she thought.

Laura leaned in and hugged Nicole, Jenny following suit, the whole thing becoming a group hug until the little pink bundle squirmed, protesting, and broke up it. They separated and Laura gave baby Jaime back to her, kissing her friend on the cheek.

The night wound down, the band began their last set, and soon nearly all of the guests were gone.

Laura offered to have Harry and Nicole stay at the house that night. Nicole declined, calling her ridiculous.

"Laura, you know I love you, but this is your first night with your new husband. Your son is at your mom's. All your wedding guests have gone." She dropped her voice to a conspirators pitch, taking Laura's shoulders and gently turning her friend to look toward the yard where Adam and Harry were chatting, the sleeping baby in Harry's arms.

"Look at him. Your sweet, wonderful Airport Hottie. Girl, I think you might be a little busy tonight." She turned Laura back to face her and they burst into giggles, Laura flinging her arms around Nicole.

"Thanks for setting me straight," she said, in between snorts of laughter. She glanced back again at her new husband. "What the hell was I thinking, inviting you to stay?"

Laura stood on her front porch and watched Nicole and Harry's taillights disappear. She felt Adam's arm around her waist and looked silently up at him, suddenly struck with a realization. She and Nicole, sunbathing and dreaming; struggling and losing hope. She wished now that she could whisper into the air of their fifteenth year. Their beautiful life would arrive. Not without losses, but here it was. Tears stung her eyes. She gazed through them at Adam. His eyes were dark, and in them she could see the stars.

He bent and swept her up in his arms, wedding gown ruffling about her. Laura's arms went around his neck and she pressed her cheek to his, then drew back just enough. He kissed her and stepped inside to greet their future.

ACKNOWLEDGEMENTS

Before anything else, I must say thank you to my family. The Fall of Our Secrets would still be an idea on a few notebook pages if not for them. My husband's limitless faith in my writing and the patience and cheerleading I receive from two of the best kids ever made the completion of this novel possible. My parents raised me to believe I could accomplish anything, and to enjoy the journey along the way. This leg of the journey is exhilarating!

I owe a debt of gratitude to the amazing Fran Black of E-Lit Books. Fran saw something in my words and suddenly my life changed. Her sharp eye and dedication to her craft is breathtaking, and I am fortunate to have this talented, passionate woman in my corner. The entire team, including Jennifer Mishler, Debra J. Caruso, Candice Frederick and Charleen Famiglietti, has been invaluable in guiding me through this very involved process. I'd have been completely lost without them.

Martin Blanco's artistic and beautiful cover floored me when I saw it. He somehow was able to bring to life the concept and vision the team had for the best portrayal of this story. I never imagined such a perfect presentation for my work.

Several people were instrumental in the creation of this book. My first readers, my biased parents Joni and David, of course loved the story even in its roughest draft. I know my dad is well aware of the achievement of my dream, even though he's sadly not here with me anymore. I grew up in a home where my vibrant, creative mom composed poems and short stories between jobs as teacher, hair-dresser and fun-loving parent extraordinaire, where my dad graded high school papers in his easy chair and shared with me his love of the written word (literary classics and popular fiction alike) and music (Beethoven and Zeppelin alike), and where weekly trips to the library were both cherished and highly anticipated. This no doubt shaped my desire to be part of the world in which I am most comfortable. I was never without music as a kid doing homework, reading or writing; words and music are inseparable to me now. Thank you Dad.

The love and genuine interest from my husband and best friend Joe and our awesome kids Kayla and Joseph kept me going even when frustration caused me to try to *not* be a writer (as if!). Becoming a mom and watching my daughter and son grow shaped the storyline of The Fall of Our Secrets and Nicole's drive to know the other side of a parent child relationship. My big-hearted sister Julie Velentzas deserves thanks as well. Julie is the reason main character Laura has a sister: I could never imagine life without mine.

Wonderful friends Ann Harden Sullivan, Rocsana Oana, Kim Nelson and Sandy Simonson all had insightful thoughts to offer as they read the evolving manuscript and Lisa Glegola Standley was kind enough to use her photography skill to come up with a few nice author photos. I'm also blessed with a large ensemble of support, including Suzette Nelson, Jimmy James Doyle, F. A. Gardner and Kathleen Overton, among friends and family who believe in me and my writing passion. Thomas L. Ashton, an engaging literary fiction writer and my very first impartial reader, gave me the priceless gift of the big picture: stepping back and finding the overall theme in my work, something so tough to do this close to the story.

Paul Mark, a Detroit Police Officer assigned to the Crime Scene Unit as an Evidence Technician, provided me his expertise in the nuts and bolts of the crime aspect of this story. His input was intriguing and vital. Any technical errors are mine and mine alone. Thanks to Mike Mark for connecting us. Janna Coumoundouros of Lilacpop Studio allowed me use of her gorgeous photography as I built an online presence for my book, and introduced me to Kelly Holden Allen, who gave me my first author platform in Verite magazine. I will be forever grateful to these two talented ladies.

Finally and with great fanfare, thank you so very much, Reader, for taking an interest in this book. You are the reason I have the amazing opportunity to write acknowledgements.

CPSIA information can be obtained at www.ICGtesting.com
Printed in the USA
BVOW03s1229280714

360562BV00001B/32/P

9 780989 401173